Murder, Mather
and Mayhem

For Carol —

Tap your feet into
a Fancy mystery!

♡

Marilyn
(M.E. KEMP)

Murder, Mather and Mayhem

M.E. Kemp

To order additional copies of this book, contact:
Xlibris Corporation
1-888-795-4274
www.Xlibris.com
Orders@Xlibris.com
20337

FOR JACK, MY GEODE AND
FOR RACHEL, OUR DIAMOND . . . SHINE ON!

Characters

Hetty Henry:	A rich young widow, cousin of Abigail Mather
Increase "Creasy" Cotton:	A young Puritan minister to a poor Boston church
Cotton Mather:	26-year-old minister to Second Church of Boston, the largest church in the colonies
Abigail Mather:	Wife of Cotton Mather and Hetty's cousin
Edmund Andros:	Royal Governor of New York-New England
Edward Ruckenmaul:	Secretary of the Provinces for Andros
Deacon Lamb:	A hardy old Puritan farmer
Rachel Lamb:	The Deacon's young and lonely wife
Zillah:	Hetty's West Indies servant
Gammar Pisspot:	An old woman arrested for murder
Tom Pisspot:	A big bully in Ruckenmaul's pay; Gammar's son
Deborah Piscopot:	Gammar's lovely daughter and Tom's sister
Victim's:	
Absalom Lott:	Minister of Ipswich; leader of a tax revolt
Naboth Chieves:	Minister of Rumney Marsh; lady's man

Prologue

The smell of urine-soaked straw and overflowing chamber pot assailed his nostrils as the young minister entered the dark cell. He pulled a crisp square of linen from his pocket, coughing with delicacy as a ruse to cover his nose. Neither of his two companions seemed to notice the foul odor, both jailer and sailor oblivious to the stench. His eyes widened in the dim light; he could see the outline of a bare cot and a three-legged stool. Perhaps the witch had escaped! His heart beat so loud in his ears he thought the other two must hear the pounding.

The jailer held a lantern aloft, announcing in a hearty voice, "Come, Gammar, here's a fine gentleman come all the way from Boston to see you."

The young minister heard a crackling of straw; he followed the shift of the lantern's rays to a thin, spectral figure crouched against the wall. The thing grinned at him with black, gaping mouth. The minister's flesh quivered with goosebumps. A witch! A confessed witch!

"Come Gammar, there's a good girl." The jailer chirruped with his lips much as he would call a dog. He set the lantern upon the stool.

The skeletal figure in wretched rags crept forward, drawn to the light.

The minister stared at the withered face, her beak of a nose curving like a bird of prey to meet a pointed chin. Black eyes darted from one man to another with the rapid flick of an adder's tongue. She grinned at them through toothless gums. "Can she speak?" the minister whispered.

"Bless you, yes," the jailer chuckled. "She speaks Irish, but she can understand you in English, Sir. Ask her what you will." He beamed at the old woman. "Now, Gammar, the fine gentleman wants to ask you some questions. He won't hurt you."

"Oh no, I shan't harm her. Tell her that," the minister instructed his interpreter, the stripe-shirted sailor who stood beside him.

The mariner's body exuded fumes of rum. He spoke Gaelic in a thin, lilting cadence.

The old woman fixed glittering eyes upon the young minister.

"I have come here to pray with you," the minister began, lowering the handkerchief from his nose. "I would offer you the comfort of the Reformed religion."

The creature did not respond; she stared at him with her black adder's eyes.

"With which evil spirits are you familiar?" he asked, wishing to know the form of his enemy.

She did not answer.

"Have you made a contract with the devil?" he persisted.

The old woman remained silent, proving dumb to his questions, his exhortations, and his prayers alike.

"She won't speak to me. Why won't she speak?" He turned in bewilderment to the jailer "Didn't she confess to the constable?"

"She did," the jailer affirmed.

"And her confession was of her own free will, not under torture?" The young minister would not accept physical abuse as a means of obtaining confession, not even for such a wicked crime as *maleficium*.

"Her confession was freely given, Sir," the jailer said. "We found the evidence—poppets stuffed with goat hair, stuck with pins. Some had twisted limbs." He turned with a benevolent smile. "You even showed us how you tormented your babies, didn't you, Gammar? She calls them her babies," he added in an aside to the minister.

The old woman nodded, her black eyes glinting in the lantern light.

"Have you got your stone, Gammar?" the jailer asked. "Show the gentleman how you cast your spells, that's a good girl."

The old woman took a narrow, smooth gray stone from her pocket. She put two hooked fingers into her mouth, drooled upon them, and stroked the stone with spittle-wet fingers.

"Enough!" The young minister cried out, dashing the stone from the aged hands. "No more of these hellish demonstrations! Oh what a direful thing is it to fall into the hands of devils!"

The old woman cackled.

"You have seen the Man in Black. Confess!" The minister shook his finger before the wrinkled face.

A high, rapid screech of words in Gaelic came from the creature's withered gums.

The sailor translated: "Yes. He is in this room."

The minister drew back, glancing into the dim shadows. The interpreter stood beside him; the jailer leaned against the wall. Only the three men occupied the room. (Of course, spirits can be invisible when they like, he thought.)

"Don't serve him," the minister begged with clasped hands. "Let us pray together against the power of the devil!"

The old woman whined in a high, wild voice that raised the hairs upon the minister's bewigged neck.

"Her spirits curse all the ministers of New England, who are nothing more than the slaves of Satan," translated the sailor.

"How so?" The minister's shoulders twitched with an involuntary shudder.

And the witch taunted him, her black eyes glittering like coals. "The ministers are grown so high and mighty only that Satan might laugh at their fall."

"Then is it Satan's design to overthrow the Kingdom of Christ here in New England?" the minister pressed, awed at the scope of the Fallen Archangel's plan.

The old woman prophesied; dire threats that one would hang for his impudence and another choke on his words . . . .

The troubled young minister rode a skittish mare home to Boston. He stood on the forefront of battle with Evil, the like of which no mortal man had ever faced. Who was there to counsel him in this war against Satan? With Increase Mather in London, there was no wise parent to advise him, no solemn shield of pious integrity to protect him . . . . He was only twenty-six years old! What if he should fail to save this New England Kingdom of Christ? What if he should fail? What if he should fail?

The mare beat out this tattoo with her hooves all the way home to Boston.

The young minister felt a quick moment of cheer at the sight of his comely young wife, who stood upon the doorstep to greet him, her pretty arms outstretched. In her hand was a message just come for him. With a sigh at the thought of forsaking her dimpling promise—duty, ah duty—he broke open the seal to read the letter's contents.

The sheet fluttered to the ground from the palsied hands of young Cotton Mather. The minister, face waxen as the letter's seal, cried out in agony. "Father . . . why have you forsaken me?"

Chapter One

It was a very unsettled time, you understand, what with Governor Andros' spies skulking in the streets and the sheriff ready to arrest Uncle Increase Mather the moment he stepped foot out of doors. Well, what could I do but answer the summons of my cousin Abigail Mather? Abigail's husband Cotton fell into a bout of nerves. Nerves plagued the man so he plagued Abigail, the poor woman.

Abigail Mather is my best friend as well as cousin. She is sweet natured, loyal, cheerful and very efficient in running her household, but she does have a blind spot when it comes to her husband. I suppose this to be a natural, womanly trait. I've never had it myself and I've been married twice.

We'd succeeded in removing my uncle under the sheriff's nose. It was my idea to disguise him in woman's wig and cloak and quite boldly walk past the unsuspecting sheriff as I held the arm of my elderly, aristocratic grandmother. I delivered her/him safely to Uncle Philip's boat, which rowed him out to the waiting ship, which whisked him off to London.

One problem solved. The larger problem of false taxation, government corruption and illegal imprisonment of our citizens I was not yet prepared to undertake.

It was amusing to witness the effort Cousin Cotton made to fill his father's large boots. He thrust back his shoulders, straightened his spine and marched to his duties as minister to Boston's largest, wealthiest congregation. He really did try. It was the old witch who did for him; the one they arrested for the murder of his colleague in Rumney Marsh. I admit the news unsettled me as well; I knew them both, the old woman and the murdered minister. I have a farm in Rumney Marsh—my late husband's legacy. Had I known about the interview I would have insisted upon traveling with him, but Cousin Cotton tells me nothing.

As it happened, he returned that evening with the astounding news that Satan had succeeded in murdering four of his ministerial adversaries in this New England Kingdom of Christ and that he, Cotton Mather, was designated as the next victim. Whereupon he took to his bed, refusing to leave it except to cast himself in the dust with great gusts of weeping. Abigail was frightened out of what wit she has. Abby is the dearest, sweetest of souls, but the life of the mind she leaves to her husband, who certainly knows all there is to know.

There was, Abigail declared through her own tears, only one man who could calm Mister Mather when these fits took him. She sent for him. I opened the door at his pounding. A tall, lanky fellow with a long face stood there. Before I could ask his business he pushed past me.

"Abigail!"

"Creasy!"

The black-visaged scarecrow opened his arms and Abigail flew down the hall into them.

I had the presence of mind to close the door lest all of Boston witness this unseemly display.

Abigail's face flushed rosily, teardrops trembling upon her soft lids, her rosebud mouth quivering. Abby is one of those women who can cry without becoming a red-eyed hag.

"My God," the scarecrow croaked, "what's wrong?"

"Oh Creasy . . . ." Abigail wept into the shoulder of a shabby, bottle green coat.

The crow made soothing sounds, his arms wrapped around her waist with a grip an octopus would envy.

I cleared my throat three times, with force. So this is Increase Cotton, nephew of Increase Mather. I could see a likeness in the thin nose, the long mouth, but little else. Increase Cotton ministers to a poor parish in the South End. He is four years younger than his cousin Cotton and three years older than Abby, who is nineteen. I am younger than Cotton Mather.

"What is it, my dear girl?" he crooned, ignoring my presence.

Abby lifted her head, brown curls fetchingly loose from her white cap. A pearl of a tear slid down the curve of her rosy cheek. The sly dark eyes above her watched its course with the thirst of a desert lizard. I half expected a forked tongue to flick the pearl away.

Abigail plucked at some loose threads on the bottle green coat. "He is ill . . . he suffers! He raves and weeps upon the floor! I could not think but to send for you, Creasy, I did not know what else to do." Abigail swallowed a sob, bravely looking up into the sly face.

"Shush, my dear," he crooned, "you were right to send for me."

"Oh, Creasy, I am such a goose!" She forced a tremulous smile. "I've been so worried, and he will not let me send for a physician. He says 'tis not a bodily ill that consumes him."

"Ah . . . ." The fellow gave a thoughtful sigh. "Is that all?" He loosened his arms about my cousin, no doubt conscious of my presence and their inappropriate stance. "It's a bout with his nerves. Your husband is as skittish as a colt hearing the howl of a wolf." He shook her dainty shoulders and smiled down at her. "Leave him to me. I know how to deal with his vapors. You go brew us some tea. Aunt Maria used to make him an infusion with borage leaves when he acted up like this. Mind you add some borage to the pot," he commanded.

Abigail disengaged herself from him and would have sped off down the hall, had I not blocked her way with an outstretched arm.

"Oh," she recalled her manners, "Cousin Creasy, this is Cousin Hetty. Had you two not met? I just assumed . . . ." Abigail waved a shapely hand at me and hurried off.

"Some cakes, too," Mister Cotton called, ignoring the introduction. "Something sweet to go with the tea. He'll perk up. You'll see."

"How do you do?" I reached out my hand, which he grasped but promptly forgot, his eyes upon the figure flying down the hallway.

"Mister Cotton!" I snatched back my hand. "I'm afraid things are in a pretty pickle at the moment. Cousin Mather has taken to his bed, convinced he is about to be murdered. There has been another minister died in Ipswich—Absalom Lott of the tax revolt, you must know him. Although his death appears to be a suicide. I'm afraid that coming on top of Mister Chieves' murder, it has quite unhinged Cousin Mather . . . ."

"Hmmmm?" Two thin black brows scowled at me. He'd not heard a word of my explanation.

"Mister Cotton, I am Mehitable Henry, a cousin of Abigail." I began again, shouting in his face.

He jumped. "My God, woman—I'm not deaf!"

"Are you not, Sir?" I lisped with a sweet smile. "Forgive me my error. A natural mistake, since I presume your close hold upon my cousin was so that you could hear her words."

The crow had the grace to turn a fiery red. He turned and made for the staircase, taking the steps two at a time with his long legs. I followed, hampered by my skirts. I would not miss this interview for the booty of a Spanish galleon. (My first husband, Jack, had captured such a prize.)

At the open doorway to the bedchamber, Increase Cotton paused. So close did I follow I nearly bumped into him. Inside the room a man knelt upon the floor in feverish prayer. Fine, full lips moved in a stream of self~condemnation. I caught the words:

"Unworthy . . . vile . . . weak . . . horrifical failure . . . ." The handsome face of Cotton Mather was ghost-pale, dark eyes large and liquid, cheeks tear-stained. The countenance was noble, even in distress. The Mather family believed that The Lord had selected this one child and poured all His gifts upon him, as an example of what Mankind might achieve. If one didn't know better, this was the image of a Saint. I knew better.

From his unconcerned manner, Increase Cotton knew better also. He rapped upon the doorframe with his large knuckles and sauntered in, not waiting for an invitation. "Go on with your prayers," he said, "I'll wait."

Cotton Mather raised tear-clouded eyes. "Who is it? Who speaks to this unworthy soul?" The pious voice cracked.

"It's me. Creasy."

I stood behind, unobserved, convinced that Cousin Mather would speak more freely were I not known to be present. He thought me an interfering female.

"Ah, Cousin!" Mather squeaked, raising a pitiful countenance. "You see before you a lump of despised clay! I must be about my prayers . . . I fear your wait shall be a long one. There is another and better world for us, Cousin Creasy, where we shall speak with the tongues of angels . . . ."

"So there is, Cousin, yet I fear I am not ready to speak with angels." Increase Cotton leaned against the bedpost.

I much admired his casual manner; people usually toadied to the Mather heir.

"Come, come—this excess of grief smacks of vanity. What would your father say?"

That, I knew, was the right tone. Cotton Mather idolized his father. Certainly Uncle Increase Mather was worthy of the highest respect, but his son took everything to extremes.

"Ah, that paragon of parents!" the woeful voice cried. "Shall I never behold his dear face in this world?"

"You shall," Increase Cotton insisted. "He's had great success in his mission, I have come to tell you." Increase Cotton, who was named for his famous uncle, reached down and grasped his cousin's elbow, lifting him firmly to his feet. "Let me help you to your bed. You're frightening your wife with these melancholy humors of yours, and you must not do that. Indeed, you must not frighten Abigail."

Cotton Mather tottered feebly beneath his cousin's hand. He was led to his bed, laid down upon it and covered with blankets as if he were a child.

I was quite impressed. I should never have had such patience.

"You've heard from my father?" Mather whispered, raising eyes as pitiful as a spaniel pup.

Increase poked the covers beneath the down mattress in short jabs. The covers were tucked in tight enough to hold a lunatic. "I have," he answered. "Uncle Increase has had an audience with the King and been most kindly received. Now, I have sent Abigail for a pot of tea, and when she brings it, I shall tell you my news. And you shall tell me your troubles, Cousin, for it's clear something has upset you besides your father's flight to England, of course."

'Of course,' I agreed in silence. Cotton Mather without his father was helpless as an abandoned fawn. Like a fawn, his eyes were wide and frightened.

He plucked at the coverlet with long, handsome fingers. "Creasy," he paused, staring at the white-lime ceiling overhead, "I think I am being poisoned."

Chapter Two

Creasy Cotton set the tea tray upon his cousin's bed, pouring hot golden liquid into two china cups. He divided the cakes upon the plates. I had stationed myself in a hard chair by the window, out of Cousin Mather's sight. Neither man noticed me, all to the good.

"There now," Creasy spoke in soothing tones, as if his cousin's nervosa melancholia had deepened into madness. "See? Abigail has brought us some borage tea, like Aunt Maria used to make for us when we were ill." To encourage the sick man Creasy took the first sips, smacking his lips in enjoyment. He'd taken the tea tray from Abigail's soft hands and sent her away; me he could not budge. I'd merely put a cautioning finger to my lips.

Cotton Mather drank his tea meek as a child; he nibbled upon the cakes. The color returned to his cheeks; the fear in the fawn eyes diminished. Creasy placed a large molasses cookie upon Mather's plate as a reward.

I could not understand such patience with the man!

"Come, come, Cousin—what is this about poison? Can you think for a moment that Abigail would be capable of such a heinous act?"

"My dear heart? Oh, never!" Mather glanced with wistful longing at the bedchamber door. Creasy had closed it tight.

"Or your servants, Sir?" Creasy persisted. "Can you think your maids guilty of such wicked folly?" He threw a lightening glance in my corner.

'Twas then I realized the oaf thought I was a paid companion

19

or a maidservant in the household. Just because I had dressed for dusting in my plain old dark frock

"No . . . not my servants." Mather's eyes were wide and intent.

"What is this foolishness, then?" Creasy Cotton scolded. He did sound like his uncle. "Whom do you accuse of poisoning?"

"The Papists," Cotton whispered.

"Papists!" Creasy croaked in derision. "Why, do you think Jesuit priests stroll freely about our streets, poisoning our food and wine?"

"What of Nabal Clapp? Did he not die after drinking wine?" Mather pointed out, voice trembling.

"Clapp died of apoplexy," Creasy soothed.

(I had heard that Nabal Clapp, the minister in Charlestown, dropped down dead at an ordination dinner. Mister Clapp was well known as a vociferous critic of everything ungodly, from maypoles to the corrupt government of Edmund Andros.)

"What of Mister Brock, the minister at Redding? Or Naboth Chieves or Absalom Lott of Ipswich? Creasy, we are in great danger, we ministers! We are all in danger!" Mather leaned forward, nearly tumbling the tea tray, which Creasy caught.

"Hear me out," Mather pleaded.

Creasy Cotton removed the tray to the safety of the bedside stand. He sat upon the edge of the high bed. "I will listen if you do not overexcite yourself. Uncle Increase asked me to look out for you—he was afraid your health would suffer from overwork. It seems that's what has happened."

"Oh, excellent parent," Mather groaned. Tears glistened in his eyes. "Shall I ever see his face in this world?"

"You shall, of course you shall," Creasy reassured in a hearty voice. "Uncle Increase writes that he will return with a new charter, think of that! He's had an audience with King James himself. If there is any man who can persuade the King of the injustices done us here in New England, it is your father."

(The laws of our colony had been revoked by the dastardly Royal Governor, Edmund Andros. We had to pay twice over for land we'd owned for fifty years. As a ship owner—the legacy of my first husband—I knew all too well the double levies and bribes we were forced to pay to unload our cargo. I found myself sitting upon the edge of my seat, ready to cheer aloud.)

Increase Cotton went on in a stirring voice.

"Can you doubt that with the ear of the King we shall regain our rights—the rights of all Englishmen?"

A tear rolled down the handsome cheek of Cotton Mather, whether for our lost liberties, his father's success in London or in self-pity, I could not say.

"I pray to see his face, that of my earthly father . . . ."

"Be easy, Cousin, so you shall. Tell me what troubles you." Increase settled himself upon the bed, patting the shapely fingers of the invalid.

"There have been four ministers died within the past few months . . ." Cotton began.

Increase continued to pat the pale hand upon the bedcovers. "I know of this. A great loss to all. That is I knew of the first three, and have only just learned of the death of Absalom Lott of Ipswich."

So, I thought, he had absorbed some of my words!

"This was all prophesied," Cotton Mather groaned. "Witchcraft! No, let me speak," he said as Increase made a move to calm him.

"Samuel Willard took council with me upon learning of the dreadful death of Naboth Chieves in Rumney Marsh. I journeyed there at his request, both to preside over the funeral and to question the old woman arrested . . . . So many godly men have died," Mather moaned. "First there was Mister Brock in Redding; a hearty, hale man of sixty-two years . . . . Then there followed Nabal Clapp, then Naboth Chieves who was only two years before me at Harvard. They found the old woman dancing about the fallen body of the minister. I went to see her—she had the black eyes of an adder!" Mather shuddered visibly. "I spoke to her through an interpreter. The woman speaks in Gaelic, but she did understand me. Irish, Papist and a witch . . . oh, she confessed to it," Mather brushed away his cousin's hand, who sought to restrain him.

"I asked her why she harmed a good man of God—she said her spirits would have it so."

Mather related his encounter with the old woman in the Rumney Marsh jail. "And the place stank!" He wrinkled a Roman nose at the memory.

"You make too much of this," Creasy advised, "the ravings of an ignorant old woman, frightened out of what little wits she has by her arrest."

Sitting quietly in my corner I thought this a clever assessment. I knew Gammar Pisspot, the woman concerned, if not by social acquaintance. She was a harmless old bird, somewhat eccentric.

"Nay . . . hear me out. She went on with a horrible demon cackle that one minister had suffered his fall and one other would hang for his deeds, and one of the Mathers of Boston would be poisoned by his own words . . . . When I offered to pray for her she came at me like a Fury, and cursed me and said her Prince would protect her. She called upon Satan in my presence!" Mather raised a feverish head, which his cousin gently pressed back upon the pillow.

"I thought as you did, Creasy. I came away and rode back to Boston. A letter awaited me from the Selectmen in Ipswich. Young Absalom Lott was found a suicide, hanging from an oak tree, and would I please come advise them whether he might be buried in church ground . . . . 0, I cannot go on! I cannot fight this alone! I woke in the night scarce able to breathe, with a pain in my bowels like a knife slicing into me! I am poisoned, Creasy, poisoned, I tell you!" Sweat broke out in shiny drops upon the high forehead.

I shivered in spite of myself, feeling pity for the man. Still, I kept my silence.

"Calm yourself, Cousin Cotton," Increase commanded. "Think of all who depend upon you."

"I am ill . . . I will fail them!" came the moan.

"You are not alone in this, Cousin, nor shall you fail, unless it be in your health. That is your concern, Cousin, for Abigail and for your absent father. You must recruit your strength—keep to your bed, Cousin, and I will see to the rest. I will go to Ipswich in your place, and see what must be done. I shall also go to Rumney Marsh"

"You believe we are in danger, then." Mather sniffed.

"Oh yes, I believe there is some danger, but not to you, Cousin, so long as you keep to your bed."

"You will be careful for your own self, Creasy? I would not have you harmed in my stead . . . ."

"Don't worry about me, Cousin Cotton."

"There are devils, Creasy . . . ." Mather whispered.

"Yes, there are devils, but I don't believe these devils come in black robes." Increase Cotton's eyes were grim as coal.

I glided to the door and slipped out, unnoticed. My head swarmed with plans; someone was murdering the ministers of Massachusetts Bay and the situation concerned every good citizen. I must return to my farm at once.

Chapter Three

Increase Cotton, pastor of the Summer Street Church, set out on horseback for the Ipswich ferry. Despite his somber errand, his mouth curved in a generous smile. Thin black brows winged over an angular face and curious brown eyes sought out every sign of gentle Spring's return.

A pale golden dawn swirling with soft breezes promised a fine day for travel. The fluted call of a robin greeted him and over his sleek dark head, bud-swollen tree limbs hung in a canopy of wine colored lace. Beneath his long legs, the mare swayed and raised her brown bobbed tail as if she were a filly in pasture. How could one's heart not rejoice on such a day as this? Creasy clicked his tongue, brushed the mare's flanks with boots of English leather and swung into an easy trot.

Near Rumney Marsh he followed a long, five-rail fence; a herd of cattle browsed in the meadow beyond. The fence ran to a two story, cedar-shaked farmhouse. A wooden stable and several wooden coops housed a variety of stock; chickens and geese pecked for bugs on the rain-softened ground. Men in smocks bustled about the yard. Above the roof shingles smoke puffed from a great brick chimney. The smell of baking bread escaped an open door and wafted across the road, tantalizing his aristocratic nose. He took a deep breath, making a mental vow to stop at this prosperous farm upon his return.

The land was rich in Rumney Marsh; he knew of several Boston merchants who kept farms here. When his business in Ipswich was completed he must return here to question the old woman accused of murdering the Rumney Marsh minister; that done, he would stop at this farm and beg a crust of bread.

The salty odor of the marsh grew in his nostrils as he continued his journey. Blackbirds flashed stripes of scarlet as they flitted among the tall roadside grasses. A gull soared with raucous cries across the blue sky. Feeling the effects of the ride, Creasy reined in by a small grove of pines and jumped off the mare to relieve himself. In the cover of the waist high reeds he adjusted his smallclothes, aiming a steady stream at a bright circlet of lime-colored new grass. A sigh of contentment escaped from his lips.

The loud whinny startled him. He twisted his neck in time to glimpse the brown bobbed tail of the mare whisk up like the flag of a deer and disappear from sight in a clatter of hooves. There was no time to cry out as the roadside grasses quivered in violent passage. A horrid snarl rent the morning air.

Glimpsing a tawny hide, Creasy panicked. "Lions!"

He bolted for the nearest tree. The pine, hardly more than a shrub, received him within its thin branches with prickly intolerance. He clawed his way to the top, clinging vulture-like to the trunk. The pine tilted, quivering beneath his weight.

Underneath him quaking rushes fell before the onslaught of the marauding beast. Its terrible shrieks pierced his gut. The wild creature charged through the reeds, stopping at the trunk of the tree to peer up at him with red gimlet eyes. The beast sniffed the air, loose gobs of slimy slather slobbering upon the ground from its bristling jaws, an evil grin exposing yellowed fangs.

"Hell-creature! Satan's minion! Go away," Creasy shouted.

He clung to the pine, his hands sticky with sap. Small cones sharp as nettles slashed into his fingers, pine needles rent his clothes. He hung on in grim prayer,

The beast backed a step and circled the tree, figuring how best to reach its quarry. All the while it rasped and slathered and snorted.

Sweat beaded Creasy's forehead as the creature planted itself squarely beneath him, swinging its great slobbering snout from side to side. This was no mortal animal but a cloven-hoofed Satan come to carry him away to the horrid fires of damnation! And here was he, hanging betwixt Heaven and earth, trapped by the Infernal Fiend who ordered his legion of unholy imps to torment him! Black flies swarmed around him, stinging his eyes, filling his ears, crowding the thin caverns of his nostrils until he felt he must choke. Nor could he defend himself from the fiendish legions, lest he pitch from his perch and fall beneath the hooves of this frightful creature.

The beast raised its massive jaws in a grin, eyeing him through red beady rims as if to charm him like a snake charms the bird from the bush.

"Damn you," Creasy cursed, "damn, damn, damn!" Give in he never would. Clasping hard with both knees and one hand, he freed his right hand and began to pelt the beast with the small, sharp cones of the pine.

Satan laughed at him, a silvery peal of Circe-like music that raised the hairs upon the back of his neck. Oh, that such sweet sound could issue from the hairy, yellow-toothed jaws beneath him! Icy water flowed through his veins, his limbs went numb at the horror.

"Get thee hence," he screamed, the pitch of his voice rising with each desperate word.

Satan mocked him with silvery sound.

Creasy peered down through watery lids and discovered his mistake. There in the rushes he beheld a tattered crone, doubled over, holding her ragged sides in mirth.

"Hi," he called out in warning, "there's a wild beast here!"

The crone straightened, blotting her bleary eyes with a corner of her stained apron. Settling a battered crowned hat upon her old head, she marched straight at the ferocious beast and flicked its broad hide with a willow switch.

"Get home, Priscilla. Get home at once," she ordered.

The beast squealed and lumbered off through the reeds.

"You can come down now," the crone coaxed, "she won't hurt you. She's just friendly."

Two vixen eyes peered up at him. A black cloth beneath the hat was tied under a pointed chin, concealing her hair.

This was no old crone but a young swineherd in bare feet and ragged petticoats. She wore a man's doublet, which hid her slender figure. A stoneware jug was tied around her waist with a piece of rope. Little wonder he'd mistaken her age.

Creasy backed down the trunk, branches whipping his face. His eyelids were red and swollen, his coatsleeves stained with pitch, his stockings torn. They must look a pretty sight, he thought, the two of them; a rural Jack and his Joan. He planted his boots upon the ground and straightened his coat.

Eyes green as a cat's examined him. "I'm sorry I laughed, Sir, but you did make a comical sight. Priscilla is my prize sow. She's really gentle, you know, she's just curious about strangers. She didn't mean to frighten you."

Creasy's back stiffened.

"I wasn't frightened," he objected, "I was merely taken unawares."

"Well, I wouldn't blame you if you were," the swineherd said. "She's an enormous beast and she's due to farrow soon."

Creasy swatted at a cloud of black flies. 'Saucy jade,' he thought.

"You frightened away my horse," he complained aloud. He frowned down at his hands, turning the palms to reveal smudges of black sticky pitch. Creasy inspected the rents and sticky patches upon his coatsleeves and stuck out a lanky leg to observe the damage done to his stockings.

"What a picture I shall present to the Selectmen of Ipswich! I have important business there!"

"Sir, I can mend those clothes for you, and you may wash up at the farm. I'll send a man for your animal—that will be the brown mare I saw running down the road. She'll not have gone far." The maid had the impudence to grab his hand and pull him through the reeds.

"Impertinence," Creasy grumbled all the way back to the neat farmhouse he'd passed by the five-rail fence. "Swine run amok . . . best stockings torn . . . late for the Selectmen . . . ."

But the ragged maid kept a firm grip upon his hand and he

had to stride to keep up with her dirty little feet which danced over the ground like a spring zephyr.

In the yard a gawky young farmhand stopped to stare at them. Creasy felt his face crimson in mortification.

"You, 'Lijah, go down ferry-ward and look for a brown bobtail that got away from this gentleman." The swineherd ordered the young man off in a voice as imperious as Caesar. "Tell Bob Stubb he's a gentleman to ferry. Go quick, I say." She stamped her little foot upon the ground. Two geese waddled away in fright; a flock of chickens dispersed with squawks. The young man ran.

"You see?" She turned with a cheery smile. "You shan't miss your ferry."

She dragged him though the door of a dark ell. Baskets were piled against the walls; Creasy heard faint noises as small creatures scurried into hiding.

"That's just the rats," she said, pushing him through a second door as she spoke.

Creasy stumbled into a kitchen and was thrust on through to a latched stairwell. The swineherd reached around him and opened the door, waving him up a narrow staircase that he discovered led into a small bedchamber. He ducked his head to enter the room. The chamber was spartan in furnishings but neat and clean. A green and black checked wool blanket covered a narrow bed and a stand with a basin stood next to the bed.

"Take off your clothes," the young woman ordered.

Creasy turned and gaped at her, his mouth open.

Laughter as merry as sleighbells filled the little room.

"I shan't peek, I promise you." Still giggling, the swineherd bounced down the stairwell. "I'll send you up a robe," she called back. "Put your things to be mended on the bed."

It was with a feeling of relief that he heard the door slam and the latch fall into place.

There being no other means of escape from the room, he resolved to make the best of the situation. A tiny window in the eaves gave some light; he squatted on his heels for a look. The yard spread below him where the chickens and geese had resumed their peckings and scratchings. By the corner of the stable his nemesis, the pig Priscilla, wallowed in the dirt. She did not appear nearly so formidable as she flopped lazily from side to side.

A young black woman raised a bucket from the well, placed it upon her head and walked with quiet dignity across the yard, out of his sight. Creasy sighed. Turning, he unbuttoned his coat and shrugged himself out of it, dropping it upon the bed.

He stood clad in his shirt and boots, the bed between him and the door. Soft footsteps announced the appearance of the servant as she climbed the steps and entered the room. She carried a pitcher of water, a loose-sleeved robe of tea color folded over her arm. Her dark eyes were kept modestly lowered as she set the pitcher in the wash basin. She set out a soft cloth upon the stand. That done, the robe was placed upon the bed and his stained clothing collected in capable brown hands. The servant departed with as quiet a grace as she had come.

Creasy exhaled a deep breath. The house kept at least one modest servant, he thought, donning the robe and tying its silk sash about his waist. The robe was handsome, light and comfortable, but it was meant for a short, stout figure. His boots stuck out below the hem.

Creasy went to the wash basin, lifted the pitcher and poured water into the round bowl. Without bothering with the cloth, he sunk his long fingers into the cool liquid and splashed it on his face, easing the bites and stings of the infernal flies. He picked up the cloth to blot his eyes and a bar of soap fell out. He picked it up and sniffed it, wrinkling his nose at the smell of spoiled fat. Still, the soap did the job as he scrubbed his hands and his face. Black specks discolored the sudsy basin, patches of pitch peeled away; the stinging flesh only meant healing, he reminded himself. Refreshed, he sat down upon the bed.

Voices drifted up from the kitchen. He must thank the mistress of the house for her hospitality. He would not mention the saucy swineheard. Servants were hard to find.

Chapter Four

"Come in, Sir, come in," I called to the young minister, even as I inspected the stockings I'd mended for him. "Zillah has set out some bread and butter for you."

The man glanced from me to Zillah sponging off his coat near the hearth, then to the table which held a loaf of crusty bread, a crock of butter and a pitcher of cider. I could see the yearning in his eyes as he regarded the bread. Well, men were in a better mood when fed and this particular man had been very put out by my finding him in such a humiliating position. I could even sympathize with him for it as he lingered in the doorway.

"Please seat yourself, Sir. We do not stand upon formality here," I said. "Zillah is cleaning your coat, it will be good as new. She's mended a tear in the sleeve, so you need not worry how you appear to the Selectmen. Zillah is a skilled seamstress, much better than I am at the needle but I've done my best with these." I extended the stockings for him to see.

He looked puzzled; it was then I realized he did not recognize me. He had no idea of my identity! And I'd even put on a clean apron and cap, so my attire was no excuse.

"Is the lady of the house at home?" he asked, his tone lofty. Lifting one boot high in the air, he took a step into the kitchen, rather like a stork wading in water.

The man had a habit of mistaking me for a servant, but he'd learn sooner or later. I ignored his incivility.

"Please sit down, Sir. Take some refreshment for your journey.

I'm sorry my late husband's robe does not fit but we'll have you mended and sponged and on your way in short order."

Increase Cotton advanced, pulled out a chair and sat himself down at the table with all the solemnity of a funeral service.

I motioned to Zillah, who left the coat and set about placing a mug and plate before the gentleman. She cut thick slices of bread for him and poured a cascade of amber cider into his mug.

"Thank you," the man nodded at Zillah then turned to me. "I am beholden to you for your hospitality, Mistress . . . Mistress . . . ?" He leant forward, his brows raised in inquiry.

I set my needle and thread in the stockings with care. "I thought you did not recognize me, Sir." I smiled amiably. "I am Mehitable Henry, We met two days ago at the Mathers. Did Abigail send you to me? I told her that she might."

The poor man's face turned a fiery red. I felt quite sorry for him. First I'd caught him in such an undignified situation up a tree, then he'd forgotten who I was! Twice humiliated, twice as cranky, I surmised with some foresight.

"Mrs. Henry—of course! Forgive me, Madame. Abigail, that is Mrs. Mather, did give me your address, but I did not realize . . . . I'd thought to stop and renew our acquaintance upon my return from Ipswich," he said.

I wondered what he'd really thought of me but it was best to be polite.

"Yes," I agreed, "we'll have a great deal to discuss then. Go ahead," I motioned to the food, "please help yourself."

Increase Cotton occupied himself for some time buttering and eating the bread. I took note of his hearty appetite. I don't trust a man who doesn't like his food. In no time he had polished off the loaf. Zillah brought him a plate of sliced cold beef and a chunk of cheese. She refilled his mug.

Finally he leaned back in his chair, regarding me with a peculiar expression.

"I'm sorry I did not recognize you at once, Mrs. Henry. I should have, but the circumstances were so unusual . . . ."

I waved away his apology. "You could not know what a sweet nature poor Priscilla possesses."

"The animal did not show me her sweet nature." He frowned, his thin black brows in a wedge. "She came at me like a ravenous beast. It seemed wise to put some distance between us, that's all."

"I am sorry she frightened you, Mister Cotton." I spoke in as soothing a voice as I could muster. There was no use reminding the man of his cowardice, after all. "Tell me of your mission here and how I may help you to it."

"Madame, no doubt you are concerned for the safety of Mister Mather. I can assure you, you need not worry for him."

I could tell by his patronizing tone he did not anticipate my assistance.

"I am concerned for Cousin Mather's safety, yes," I said, "but we'll both know more about that danger when you've spoken to the Selectmen and I've spoken to my neighbors in Rumney Marsh. We shall compare findings when you return."

"Findings, Madame?"

"Yes, Sir. I'd like to know whether the suicide of Absalom Lott is connected to the death of Naboth Chieves. Chieves was minister to our congregation here in Rumney Marsh," I reminded him. "I knew the man quite well, and I was somewhat acquainted with Mister Lott. I don't believe the old woman could possibly have murdered a strong man like Naboth Chieves. The man was in his prime! I want to know how he died. Then there are the other two . . . ." I stopped to inspect my darning. I could find no fault with the weaving.

"Spare yourself, Mrs. Henry. I shall undertake to answer your questions in time. And excellent questions they are," he added, reaching out for the stockings. "You may leave your concerns with me."

"Oh, may I?" I was amused by his assumption that I would sit back and let such dire happenings disrupt my community without doing my best to resolve them. What would either of my late husbands do? Why, my Jack would have leapt in with both boots. My wise magistrate Hezekiah would deliver justice on behalf of the victims, ensuring the safety of the Commonwealth. Could I do any the less?

I relinquished the stockings, but not to him. I handed them to Zillah, who took them away with the clean coat and the mended linen. The woman was a jewel.

"I had best be on my way. The ferry . . . ." Creasy Cotton rose to his feet.

"The ferry will wait for you, Sir."

The man looked askance, but the ferryman was in my pay.

"You'll find your clothing laid out upon the bed, Sir. As soon as you are dressed I will show you the way. We'll stable your bobtail for you, if you wish. I doubt you'll need her in Ipswich." I rose from my seat and waved to the stairwell.

Increase Cotton was not pleased at my insistence I walk with him to the ferry, but wisely, he did not argue. I let him brood a bit before I questioned him. The day was pleasant, blackbirds flitted about the reeds with their cheerful chrrr's, flashing red and yellow stripes upon ebony wings.

"Did you know your colleague from Rumney Marsh?" I asked, breaking the silence between us.

"I met him once at a church council." His tone was curt.

"Ah . . ." I hazarded, "Was that the council that suspended him from the Ipswich church? I believe the charge was for intemperate words spoken in an ale house."

"Yes.

"Did you vote for suspension?" I was curious.

"I did not!"

"The man was outspoken, a trait not to everyone's liking," I observed. "Cousin Mather also served upon the committee." With the mention of that name I unlocked a key to the man's mouth.

"Cousin Cotton voted to suspend Chieves from his duties, not I. We had an argument upon it at the time. I saw Chieves' comments as an attempt at wit—perhaps somewhat bawdy, but wit of a kind. Of course my cousin is devoid of wit. He has as much humor in him as a barnacle."

The man blushed. "You must forgive me. I know the fair sex admire my cousin to distraction, but I've known him since we were children. He spent summers in Plymouth with us. I'm afraid my disagreements with him are a perverse childhood habit."

"You don't think him a genius?" I asked, hiding a smile. I reached out to pluck a straw from the roadside, fingering it as we walked.

"He is commonly accorded to be one," the man answered. He changed the subject. "You knew Naboth Chieves—what manner of man was he? Why would the old woman want him dead? Had he given her cause?"

I held up my hand. "I shall endeavor to answer your questions in time, Mister Cotton," I mimicked. "As for Chieves, he had a very sharp wit. I found him quite good company. Many an evening we spent with Chieves, my husband Hezekiah and I, lamenting the corruption that has arrived upon our shores . . . . Royal Governor Andros and that villain of a Secretary, Edward Ruckenmaul!" I could scarce pronounce the names without gritting my teeth.

"Scoundrel Ruckenmaul sets his revenue thugs upon us with their greedy hands out for bribes. When we refuse to pay, our ships are denied permission to unload their cargoes. Merchants who protest are thrown in jail." I forced myself to desist from my harangue, a common refrain in Boston.

My companion gave a nod of understanding, however.

"Absalom Lott, the Ipswich minister, was jailed for writing a pamphlet urging citizens not to pay these illegal taxes," he noted. "My uncle fled the country from the persecutions of the Royal Governor and his Secretary."

"*Our* uncle, if you please. I helped him escape. You see, I have a stake in this. I know the old woman, too, the one they've accused of Chieves' murder. She's a harmless old bird. I'll find out what happened. She'll speak to me, where she may not speak to a stranger." My offer was sincere.

"No!" He grabbed my arm, stopping me in the road. "Don't go near the old woman!"

"Let go of me, Sir." I was startled by his vehement reaction but I kept my composure.

He dropped my arm like a hot poker.

"Why, do you believe Cousin Mather's gibberish?" I taunted the man. "Do you think she is a witch? You'll find me not so easily frightened, Sir."

What cowards were these Mather cousins, grandsons of those brave Saints John Cotton and Richard Mather. Not for this generation to sail off to the unknown and savage wilderness! These two were afraid of one witless old woman.

My companion's color rose; the long mouth tightened into a line. "We are dealing with a heinous crime, Madame, whether or not the charge of *maleficiem* is involved or not. The man had enemies. It's not safe to meddle in these matters. I shall speak to the old woman upon my return from Ipswich. I beg you to stay away from her until I return. It's my duty, not yours," he snapped. He ran a thin hand across his head in exasperation.

"Oh, very well." I relented, with what I hoped was a good grace. I might need the man's cooperation, after all. "But I will be present when you interrogate her," I insisted. "I'll not have you frighten her. Besides, she knows me. My presence may calm her."

"We shall see." He turned upon his heel and stalked off to the ferry dock.

I waved to Bob Stubb as I watched Increase Cotton climb aboard the ferry. If Mr. Cotton thought he could keep me from that interview, what a surprise he'd receive! I'd know of his plans before he did. The Rumney Marsh jailer was indebted to me for his job.

Chapter Five

Creasy thought Bob Stubb the ferryman a queer figure, dressed as he was in a calf-skin coat, an odd green pipe clenched between his teeth. The pipe appeared to be carved from stone in the shape of a deathhead such as one sees in the graveyard. Stubb's face was as weathered as the little craft he sailed.

The ship was a two-masted, sharp-ended craft that rode the water like a duck, bobbing merrily along in a brisk bay breeze. They flew past the barren sheep pastures of Nahant, the sparkling spray, the exhilarating speed catching at Creasy's breath. He caught sight of the Marblehead beaches, white with drying cod. Creasy braced his body against the rail and breathed in the sea mists, ignoring great splashes of spray. The sun broke forth in all its glory. He luxuriated in its warmth.

Past Cape Ann the little craft hit the Atlantic swells; it bucked and bobbed like a colt in spring weather. The boat swung up and down, to right and to left, over and under the waves. Creasy's face grew as fiery as the sun; beads of sweat coursed down his cheeks; his head began to buzz. He clenched his lips tight.

With longing he thought of the little fishing villages that dotted the distant landscape; abandon ship and swim, he thought; beg a horse to carry him to Ipswich. He mastered the ignoble impulse and sat upright in stoic misery. Why, would he give Mrs. Henry another reason to laugh at him?

But his guts were churning like a kettle of fish chowder. The boat twisted and bobbled this way and that. 'Concentrate,' he demanded of himself, 'concentrate.' I musn't be like Cousin Cotton

Mather, falling to pieces as soon as a little trouble ensues. And turning it over to me . . . . Am I equal to it? But I musn't think like that, 'twill bring no justice to the task. I've said I'd help Cousin Cotton and I shall. Now . . . let me go over the past two days . . . except, perhaps, for the last two hours. He frowned, attempting to erase the picture of himself captured up a tree by a portly porker and a snickering swineherd.

A spray of salt water hit his face and rolled down his cloak. He screwed shut his eyes as droplets dripped from a soggy lock of his hair.

'Think . . . .' he commanded. 'Think of anything else.'

The vision popped into his head and he welcomed it, the dear face as vivid as if he stood still upon the doorstep of the Mather home, his cousin's wife warm in his arms. 'Abigail . . . Abigail . . . .' An odd sensation of fright and joy filled him.

The shelter of the harbor reached at last, the little craft slid smoothly through the calm waters, upriver to port. Creasy's rolling guts subsided into a steady slosh. He staggered from the boat onto the dock, ignoring the humorous glint in the ferryman's eyes as Bob Stubb pointed the bowl of his pipe to indicate the way to Sparke's ordinary.

Creasy waved off the ferryman's offer to wait for him. "I'll stay the night," he gasped.

He knew he must look as green as Stubb's pipe for a bystander stared at him as he passed. He straightened his spine and tried to walk without stumbling, even as phantom waves rolled under his feet. The ordinary stood near the ferry dock, much to Creasy's relief.

The landlord welcomed him at the door of the dark pine-planked inn, leading him first to a suitably anchored chair and reviving him soon thereafter with a soothing brandy. While Creasy sipped the golden liquid the landlord set out a basket of dark-shelled clams and a bottle of sack. This was followed by a platter of boiled fowl glistening in its own juices, resting upon a bed of sage.

"I'm sorry I've no pudding to offer you, Sir. It's just past dinner, you see," the genial host apologized. "Supper will be served at dusk." The landlord set down a mug of sparkling cider next to Creasy's plate.

Creasy beamed up at the good man.

The Ipswich Selectmen joined him in the taproom as the last rays of the sun sent feeble glimmerings through the small glass windows. A cheery fire in the large hearth brightened the room as the men trooped in. Creasy stood to greet them.

"Where's Young Mister Mather?" demanded a burly fellow.

"We was expecting Young Mister Mather," chimed in a tall man in the smocked attire of a laborer.

"I am Young Mister Cotton—same family," Creasy began, holding his hand for any and all to shake.

Receiving no corresponding movement, he lowered his hand.

"Mister Mather is ill. He keeps to his bed. He asked me to take his place with you." Creasy glanced around at the dour faces. "Samuel Willard of South Church agreed to me coming here," he added. "Mister Mather was most distressed about this, I assure you. He would have come if he were able to travel, but his doctor gave orders to stay in bed."

The burly man grunted. By his dress Creasy judged him to be a merchant. There was an air of confidence and quiet prosperity about the man.

"We was expecting Young Mister Mather," the smocked laborer repeated. "We sent to Young Mister Mather."

"Yes . . . well, he is indisposed," Creasy said. "I hope to be of some use to you with Mister Lott's difficulty . . . ."

"Difficulty," a voice called from the back. "Aye, it is difficult to breathe with a rope around your neck."

Creasy could not determine who spoke; the man hid behind the merchant.

The burly merchant turned and growled, silencing the entire group.

Creasy took an involuntary step backwards.

"Gentlemen . . . ." The landlord broke the silence. He carried a tray upon which he bore a huge pitcher of steaming brew and six ebony cups. With a flourish he set the tray upon the polished wooden table.

Five chairs scraped the floor in unison; five bodies a single thud as the selectmen plunked themselves down at the table. Creasy made haste to seat himself as the landlord lifted the pitcher, took aim, and poured, passing to each man a black cup of steaming brew.

Taking his cue from the company, Creasy lifted his cup and downed a piping hot mouthful of mushy tasting, molasses-sweetened beer. He felt his ears go red.

"Whip-belly-vengeance," the merchant growled.

"Sir?" Creasy started up from his seat, fists clenched. Protect himself he would from this surly crowd; he'd go down leaving a few broken heads, even if they got the best of him.

"Whip-belly-vengeance," the merchant repeated, raising his cup in toast.

Creasy's hands relaxed as he saw the blissful smile spread across the older man's face.

"Oh . . . . Is that what this drink is called?"

"Sparke's special," the laborer intoned, inspecting the contents of his cup with reverence.

"Indeed?" Creasy looked down into his own cup and saw soggy lumps floating there. Closing his eyes and his throat to the grainy texture of the drink he downed it with admirable control of his features.

Two pitchers later and he felt accepted as a lifelong friend of the Ipswich townsmen. He introduced his reason for being there.

"Was the deceased in an emotional state prior to the . . . the incident?" he asked. "This could have a bearing upon the question of his burial in the churchyard, there being precedent for such an exception in the case of suicide."

Blank looks were all he received in answer. He tried again.

"Was the deceased . . . was Absalom Lott of a melancholic nature?"

Emphatic denials came from all.

"What manner of man was he?" Creasy asked.

"Why, Man, don't ye know him?" the tall laborer drawled. "Warn't you in Boston when he was in jail there?"

"I know of his arrest, but I did not see him, myself. I've only met the gentleman once, at a church council, so I can't say that I know him at all. My uncle, Mister Mather, spoke of his plight frequently—and of his bravery! It is my cousin Cotton . . . Young Mister Mather, that is, who was acquainted with Mister Lott, not I."

"Yes, and ain't it Young Mister Mather was sent for?" the laborer reminded Creasy.

Ignoring the remark Creasy went on with his questioning. "Do you think his involvement in your town's tax protest had anything to do with his suicide? Might not he have become melancholic over his treatment? I am well aware that Governor Andros was particularly harsh in his sentence of your minister, with both jail time and a hefty fine."

"They drove him to it," someone mumbled.

"'Twas the Governor's dog, Edward Ruckenmaul," another man growled.

"Might's well have strung the rope around his neck," the laborer agreed.

"Maybe they did just that," spoke the fifth Selectman, who had been silent until that moment

Creasy glanced to the far end of the table. By his ruddy and weathered face and his creased brown coat he might be a seafaring man.

"Absalom Lott was a fighter. He wouldn't hang himself. He wouldn't, and you know it." The seaman addressed this challenge to the merchant.

"I know nothing of the kind," the merchant retorted, fingering his cup with knuckles that were thick and hairy. "I make no judgment until I hear from Doctor Enderby."

"That's the surgeon," the laborer explained for Creasy's benefit. "Why, did ye call in Enderby? I didn't hear of it. So, John, there's something amiss after all?" The laborer leaned across the table to question the merchant.

"I called for an autopsy," the merchant said, "that's proper procedure." His tone was defensive.

"As I understand it, Absalom Lott was fined fifty pounds." Creasy did not hesitate to interrupt the two men. "He was imprisoned for two weeks and forbidden to preach. You were all fined, but he was fined the highest amount, is that right?"

"Lott wrote the pamphlet, you see," the laborer explained. "He put it all down in words, for the world to see. He wrote as how we ought not to have to pay twice for land we owned fifty years, nor should we have to prove our claim on it."

"How Edward Ruckenmaul seizes our ships," the seaman added. "How we are being taxed against the law and how we should stand against Edward Ruckenmaul and claim our rights as New Englishmen. Ruckenmaul hated him for writing that pamphlet, you could see it in his face when we were all hauled before the Governor."

"That's a serious charge against the Secretary of the Provinces." Creasy tapped his glass with a fingernail, considering how much trouble Absalom Lott had gotten himself into with that pamphlet.

"We make no charge," the merchant said. "No one in this room makes charge against Edward Ruckenmaul in Lott's death." He spoke with authority.

"Aye, we paid heavy enough a price to the scoundrel as 'tis," the laborer drawled.

"You need not fear I shall report our conversation," Creasy said. "I have no love for the man. Twice he's tried to arrest my uncle, Increase Mather. Uncle Increase was forced to sneak out of the country like a thief in the night. Uncle Increase is safe in London now, and he has the ear of the King himself. Ruckenmaul will answer for his treatment of us, as will Royal Governor Andros, who usurps our churches!"

"Hear, hear . . . ." Glistening ebony cups were raised at these sentiments.

Creasy's anger flared at the thought of the Royal Governor's confiscation of South Church for his Anglican services, meanwhile good Mister Willard's congregation was left to stand outside in the cold and the rain, awaiting their turn to use their own building.

Creasy's animosity towards Edward Ruckenmaul, Secretary of the Provinces, was personal; Ruckenmaul attacked his own kin, the Mathers. But the Royal Governor's high-handed usurpation of the South Church slashed a spiritual nerve. Had not his grandfathers fled to this wilderness in order to worship in their chosen way? What if his own poor congregation of sailors and widows were to be locked out of their church? What if he were banned, like Lott, from giving them the little comfort and solace he offered?

"This situation is intolerable," he thundered.

"Aye . . . that's what Mister Lott preached to us, and he's dead." The laborer shrugged a lean shoulder.

"No charge," the merchant warned, his voice heavy. "We'll wait on Doctor Enderby's report, I say."

Creasy set down his cup with a loud clank. The man who provided the sloop for Increase Mather's escape on that dark night was Naboth Chieves—and he was dead, too.

"Where can I find Doctor Enderby?" he asked.

Chapter Six

A full hour had gone by before Mister Cotton answered my summons. I did not wait for his appearance before I began my breakfast at Sparke's ordinary, the sea voyage having given me a hearty appetite. Mister Sparke certainly catered to my gluttony, flourishing before me platters of beefsteak and boiled eels, pots of puddings both Indian and oatmeal, jugs of milk and cider, sides of new peas and conserves of plums and apples, with steaming hot journey cakes and warm slices of rye and Indian bread. I should have been very angry at the minister if I had not been so occupied with my food.

As it was, the man snuck up on me before I noticed he was there, looking more like a black crow than ever with his dingy black coat, small clothes, stockings and unpolished boots. His black hair was tied back with a black ribbon, his face the only pale thing about him.

"I'm sorry," he said, pulling out a chair and seating himself at the table. "I did not sleep very well last night and made up for it this morning, I'm afraid."

He accepted a wooden trencher from our host and proceeded to fill it, as more hot dishes replaced the cold ones.

"The pounding upon my door finally woke me. I had to get dressed for the funeral—well, I left my robe in the room but I shan't put that on until later. I hope I am not late? But then, I did not expect to see you here, Mistress Henry."

"I came for the funeral," I said. "My husband Mister Henry

and I admired Absalom Lott for his courageous stand against the policies of this administration. I came to pay my respects."

"Of course, of course," the minister mumbled as he filled his mouth.

He too, I noticed, had a healthy appetite.

"How can I be of service, Madame? The servant who woke me gave me your message."

"It is rather how I can help you," I said, taking his measure. "Did you find out any more about how the man died?"

Mister Cotton dropped his knife; it clattered on the table but he caught it before it tumbled to the floor. "How . . . how?"

"How the man died," I repeated. "I can see you that you did. Lott committed suicide? Nonsense The man was no coward, he fought against injustice and there is still the battle ahead with the Royal Governor and his corrupt cronies. No, Absalom Lott would never shirk his duties there."

The minister groaned aloud, his knife suspended in the air. "That's what the selectmen said."

"Tell me," I coaxed. "Tell me what they thought."

Creasy cut up a slice of beef and chewed before he answered. The story of his meeting with the selectmen came out between swallows. He paused at the point where he determined to seek out the coroner.

"Go on, what did he say to you? I know of Samuel Enderby by reputation, he is said to be a skilled surgeon."

"'Tis unfit for a lady to hear."

"Don't think of me as a lady, then."

The minister gave me a strange look but he went on at my request. "Absalom Lott died from asphyxiation, but he didn't hang himself. He was knocked unconscious and then hung and left to strangle."

"Enderby said that?" I was shocked, even though I had suspected as much. "This means murder. Did you see the body?"

"Mistress Henry!"

"Did you see the body?"

"This is not a fit subject to discuss." The minister was vehement.

"Why? You forget that it is we women who lay out the body, and we do this out of respect and caring for the departed."

"But you didn't see this particular body—it was a horrible sight! The man was little older than I am, a colleague, and treated in such a heinous manner." Creasy shivered visibly.

I could understand his reluctance to discuss the matter but I felt I must press him to tell me more so that I could help him find the killer. We were all obligated to bring the man to justice, after all, and so I argued.

"Very well, if you must." Creasy put down his eating utensils and took a long swig from his mug of cider. He banged the pewter mug upon the table.

"Enderby showed me the bruise upon the . . . the body's temple, where the man was hit with force enough to drop him. Enderby seemed to take pleasure in this, in pointing out purple streaks upon the poor victim's neck . . . in speaking to me of abrasions and secretions and cyanosis and other terms . . . . I could barely look at the places he pointed to without fainting! Oh, I admit to it. I've sat at bedside vigils in my duties as a minister but this is the first time I have seen death from violence . . . . A colleague, and only eight years older than I!" He shook his head, his misery plain to see.

"Was any weapon found near the site?" I asked. "Anything that might have been used to club the poor man?"

"Nothing. I did not know what to do, what to say at that point. Absalom Lott was hoisted up in that tree and left to strangle. What else would you care to know?"

He thrust his long chin at me, challenging me.

"Clearly it was meant to look like a suicide," I said. "Did Doctor Enderby remark upon anything else?"

Creasy scratched his head with a long finger. "There was one thing . . . . Doctor Enderby pointed out three tiny blue spots upon the man's chest that he could not account for, but he said the spots had no bearing upon the man's death, which was clearly by asphyxiation. Oh . . . . He said that Lott's periwig was still on his head when he was found, and that in his experience a man removes his periwig before he does away with himself. Of course, a periwig is a valuable object which one wishes to leave for his heir's use."

The man before me looked quite glum; I took pity upon him. "Thank you for telling me all this, Sir. I know it was difficult for you to view a colleague in such a horrendous situation." I rose from my seat. "I will leave you to prepare for your sad duties. Thank you for giving me your time." I nodded, taking my leave of the gentleman.

He leaped to his feet, knocking against the table in his haste. Increase Cotton insisted upon walking me to the door, pausing only to speak to the landlord that my breakfast should be added to his bill. I thanked him for his generosity. He offered to escort me, saying a walk would clear his brain and concentrate his thoughts for his sermon. I allowed him to accompany me to the home of a friend, where I intended to remain until the funeral. There I left him at the door, looking back before I entered to see the minister standing in the road, his thoughts all ready far from me.

Creasy's thoughts were very much with Mehitable Henry. No doubt she thought him a coward for what he'd told her, but it had been the truth. He'd hardly dared look at the corpse, at the dreadful unseeing eyes, the purple bruises upon the blue-tinged skin, the white thick lips. He had expected to have to deal with questions of suicide, not murder! He'd told Cotton Mather he would take care of everything but he was unprepared to deal with this. Now he'd confessed as much to a woman. What must she think of him? She who was so sure of herself, a woman of property and riches who dressed in rags like a swineherd. A busybody.

One thing he had not divulged; his vow. He'd forced himself to look down at the poor corpse of Absalom Lott and sworn—he

was not certain whether he'd sworn aloud but he felt he had—
"Justice will be done here. Justice must be done."

That night he could not sleep for the questions that flew about
his head like swallows over a chimney. What was the reason for
this good man's murder? Greed? Envy? Fear? What of? What
from? Hate? Love? Love was also a strong emotion, just remember
Salome and John the Baptist. Lott was a widower, and men in the
ministry attracted women—successful ones like Cotton Mather
did, anyhow. Lott had attracted strong passions, whether personal
or political. He had been jailed for his political opinions; Increase
Mather had been chased away for his. Oh, if only Uncle Increase
were here to advise him!

Creasy reflected that he was beginning to sound like Cousin
Cotton. He certainly hadn't expected Cousin Cotton's feverish
gibberings to come so close to the mark! He could not afford to
fall prey to his nerves as Cousin Cotton had, but was he capable
of probing such inhuman depths as this murderer's mind?

Well, the ministry trained him in logic and reasoning. He
knew how to ask questions. He had from youth learned to seek
out the guilty secrets of the soul and to expose them in public
confession. A poor colleague of his lay dead, brutally murdered,
awaiting burial in consecrated ground, and he must preach the
funeral sermon Another minister lay buried in Rumney Marsh,
murdered they said by witchcraft. He had much work to do. With
a sigh Creasy trudged along the sandy street.

Intent upon arranging his sermon thoughts in order, Creasy
did not notice the gentleman before him until he felt his progress
impeded by the point of a cane pressed against his chest. He
looked up to find the man before him dressed in plain fashion
with a high crowned hat that covered straw colored hair cut straight
across the forehead but hanging to the shoulder in frizzled waves.

"Art thou He?" the man demanded.

"Art I who?" Creasy asked, startled from his preoccupation.

"He, the Anti-Christ," was the mysterious rejoinder.

"I should hope not, friend," was Creasy's reply.

"Aye, Friend am I, but no friend to thee." The man lowered his cane and walked off.

Creasy was left to stare in bewilderment at the retreating figure. Questioning of his host at the ordinary brought a laconic reply as to the strange gentleman's identity.

"That would be Foxy Gabriel," said Sparke

"Is he touched, Mister Sparke? Creasy tapped his head with significance.

"Quaker," came the reply.

"Oh . . . ."

Further questioning revealed that Foxy Gabriel was so named because of his wily reasoning in theological debate. The Quaker had recently challenged Absalom Lott to a debate.

"Did Lott agree to this debate?"

"He warn't one to back off on a challenge." The landlord shrugged.

Creasy left to retrieve his black robe for the service, more questions ringing in his head. Who would want to murder a minister? What had Lott done to provoke such animosity? Why had the Quaker challenged Lott to a debate? Why had Lott agreed to such a debate? Certainly that indicated the minister was of sound mind, with no suggestion of severe melancholy. Was witchcraft involved in this murder, as it was alleged in the other death? Was the old woman in Rumney Marsh jail connected to both murders? Creasy wished he knew someone here with whom he could discuss his problems. Lott was a widower; there was no wife to question for a better understanding of the man's character, of his enemies. What was he to do now?

The latter question Creasy answered with a vow to preach the best sermon possible in honor of the late Absalom Lott.

Chapter Seven

I waited in the sloop, hoping that Increase Cotton would not linger over the cakes and ale at Sparke's ordinary. Success with a sermon often went to a minister's head. Scores of people from neighboring towns swelled the crowd at Absalom Lott's funeral, in tribute to the Ipswich minister. Mister Cotton's sermon was stirring; plain and well spoken His text was *Revelation—11: He that overcometh shall not be hurt of the Second Death.*

I particularly applauded the notion that the ministers should be the first to lead in the fight for our liberties, and that Lott had fallen in a noble struggle. Such words as these had Uncle Increase Mather preached—and almost been arrested for them. Perhaps the namesake held some of the spirit of the uncle after all.

Lounging by the tiller, Bob Stubb puffed patiently upon his green stone pipe. Clouds of smoke lingered over his head like the blow of a humpback whale.

Soon enough a lanky figure trotted down the path to the dock, leather bag in hand. As I breathed a sigh of relief, he clambered into the boat, tripping over me in my white, hooded cape.

"Excuse me," he stammered at my cry of pain." "I didn't see you there. I do apologize!"

"Do I look like a bundle of sail?" I began to scold, but his attention was diverted from me.

Upon the dock a disheveled, ashen creature loomed over us, one skinny, spectral finger pointing to the minister by my side. In a booming voice that belied its otherworldly appearance, the thing cried out:

"Repent! Repent! Woe woe—the Judge of the World has come!"

Increase Cotton quivered like a porcupine; his mouth dropped open, eyes rounded as lumps of coal.

"Don't be frightened—it's only Foxy Gabriel," I said. "Sometimes he is moved by the Spirit to don sackcloth, rend his clothing and pour ashes all over himself. That's just his way. He's a Quaker, after all, and harmless, except perhaps in a metaphysical debate," I explained.

"The man must be mad!" Increase Cotton could not take his eyes off the figure, mesmerized by the accusing finger.

At that moment Bob Stubb worked the tiller, the sails billowed, and our little craft skimmed away from the dock.

The call: *Repent!* followed us over the water.

"Some people find his antics anathema. I tell them to ignore Gabriel, as any notice sets him on," I warned. "Ministers of the Reformed Faith are a particular target of his."

"At first sight, I thought him Death upon a pale horse." Creasy shuddered.

"Sailing upon a pale sloop, more like," I noted.

Creasy watched the figure until it disappeared from our sight, then the gentleman turned to me. "Who is it? Mrs. Henry?" He lifted a corner and peered beneath my white hood.

"It is."

"Oh. I looked for you at the funeral, but I did not see you. There were many come to mourn the man. The numbers are a tribute—Lott was well respected by the community."

"A sad business," I sighed.

"You met the man—his death is a personal loss. I'm sorry." He offered his hand in condolence, a handsome gesture.

I took it briefly and turned my head away, gazing out over the water with silent thoughts. We passed the point of Plum Island, our wake splashing silvery lace behind us.

"This is very unpleasant business." Creasy broke the silence. "The news of his murder has not yet been made public."

"Word has spread through town just the same," I said.

"Nobody believes it was a suicide, anyway. Did you learn anything more in Ipswich"

Creasy stirred his long legs, spreading them across the deck. "Nothing. I had no time to ask questions. I was accosted by the Quaker on my return to Sparke's, but that was all. He was dressed in ordinary fashion, then. He must have gone home to change into his sackcloth and ashes."

Creasy screwed up his mouth at this observation.

I shook off my hood, the better to see him.

"There seems to be a connection to the death of Naboth Chieves," I said. "Chieves was struck a blow on the head; Lott was struck upon the head."

"Lott was hung and left to strangle. Chieves was struck with a heavy stone, so I was told. I see no connection," he concluded.

"Well, I think there is."

We were silent. I needed time to take in the implications of what I'd said. Two ministers were dead, both struck in the head. There was a connection, I was sure of it. The wind tugged at my hair, strands blew loose beneath my lace cap. I pulled my hood back in place.

"What about the other ministers who died?" I asked.

He knew of whom I spoke, shaking his head in the negative. "Both ministers died of natural causes, I made inquiries before I left Boston. Mister Brock died of old age and Nabal Clapp of apoplexy. If you knew Mister Clapp, you can well believe it."

I nodded. "Isn't he the one who cut down the maypoles?"

"*Maypoles with garlands.*" Creasy mimicked the outraged man of God, lowering his voice to a growl. "*The heathen Anglican!*"

I held in my mirth, thinking it unseemly at such a solemn time, but the young man's imitation was amusing. A sudden thought made me sit upright.

"What about Cousin Mather? Will they go after him?" A lump of coal seemed to stick in my throat. I searched the lean face before me.

"I don't think so. The Mathers are too well known; their

connections are too high. Cotton will keep to his bed, as I told him. No harm will come to him there."

"I pray you are right," I said.

We sat for quite a while in glum silence. Finally I aroused myself to a decision.

"There's only one thing for us to do."

"What is that, Mrs. Henry?" The gentleman inclined his head with polite attention.

"Oh, call me Hetty! If we're to work together on this, a certain amount of informality will be less taxing, don't you agree? We have to find this man before he strikes again."

"Mrs. Henry . . . ." My companion spoke in a firm voice. "I could not allow you to interfere . . . that is, I could not possibly place you in such a situation. There is danger in this, real danger."

I raised my hand to stop his protest. "You need my help. I know the people of Rumney Marsh. I have contacts—contacts far beyond Boston, I may say. Perhaps Abigail has told you of my business interests?" (I had seen for myself how close the two were!)

"Your cousin much admires your skills, Madame. Abigail . . . Mrs. Mather has told me how capably you run your late husband's mercantile affairs."

I thought I detected an element of disapproval in spite of the oozing flattery.

"There are many women in my situation, Sir," I said. "Especially those of us whose husbands sail the seas. Our men are away from home for months at a time. We often have more business sense than our mates, as my late husband Jack was the first to admit. 'I'm a simple sailor, Hetty has the brains.' That is what he used to say, Sir. Dear Abigail does not know the half of my holdings."

"But your cousin would blame me most heartily should I place you in a position of danger," the man countered. "And she would be right to do so. No, I could not place any woman in the way of danger, much less Abigail's cousin. She has enough to worry her without that," he added.

He had me there. I knew first hand of Abigail's difficulties and I could not argue with the man on that point. I should not like to add to her burden while she was attending to the Saintly requests of an invalid Cotton Mather.

Seeing my hesitation, the man gave me a kindly smile.

"There is one way in which you may be of great assistance," he said. "Tell me what you know of Mister Chieves and Mister Lott—their characters, their situations, whatever . . . ."

Just then we hit the swells off Cape Ann. My companion grasped the rail with both hands, his face tinged with a greenish pallor.

"Don't fight the waves, roll with them," I said. "Take ten deep breaths."

I'd never been seasick in my life, and I'd survived some heavy seas traveling with my Jack. As the gentleman gulped in air, I began a one-sided conversation.

"Naboth Chieves was a bachelor . . . he never married, although he was quite the gallant. I take it you do know that there was a woman behind that argument in the tavern, those intemperate words that led to a church council. He often directed his wit against the poor husband . . . I think he was one of those men who prefer the company of women. He could be a most amusing fellow, at least I found him so."

"How did your husband find him?" Mister Increase Cotton gasped out in between deep breaths.

I laughed. "He did not dare trifle with my husband. The late Mister Henry was much respected in Rumney Marsh. He was a magistrate, you know. But Chieves' political views were in accord with our own. He preached his views openly from the pulpit— the man was no coward, I'll say that for him. He much admired Uncle Increase Mather and often said so."

"My Uncle Mather is a great man," his namesake managed to gasp.

The man's color looked much improved, I noted. "Our Uncle Mather is indeed a great man," I agreed. "Anyhow, I always found Naboth Chieves to be good company. He liked drink, but always in moderation; his wit was sharp but never false; good company, as I say."

"And as a shepherd to his flock?"

I took a moment to consider this question. It was not so easy to answer. "He carried out his duties," I said, choosing my words. "I would not say he was a caring man in that sense. Now Absalom Lott . . . there was a caring man. Here, let this be the difference between the two men. Both were advocates against the injustices put upon us by this Royal Governor, Absalom Lott because of the poverty and hardship to his congregation, Naboth Chieves because these are the rights even the meanest of Englishmen enjoy. Does that make sense to you?" I asked, lest I begin to sound like a goose.

Creasy gestured me to go on. He was too busy breathing to speak. Since this was the case, I decided to address him by the diminutive, which Abigail had felt so free to use.

"Absalom Lott was a widower, with no children. His wife was the daughter of Deacon Lamb, one of the bearers today. Did you meet him? A fine old man, one of Cromwell's troopers, you know. Stout as they come. Janet was his only child. Deacon Lamb married one of her friends, as a matter of fact—his second wife. That was after Janet died and Lott became a widower." I paused to see whether Creasy had questions.

"Lott's life speaks for his character. You saw all the mourners—he will be missed. Of course we are all shocked in Rumney Marsh by the murder of our minister, but I don't think we shall feel the loss as will the people of Ipswich. Naboth Chieves did his duty, as I've said, but . . . ." I shrugged. Chieves' wit could be hurtful if its target was too dull to parry. And the man was not of a forgiving nature. Still, I could not speak ill of the man to his colleague.

"Absalom Lott wrote that pamphlet urging towns to withhold illegal taxes . . . ." I was struck by a sudden conviction. The thought I'd held in my brain, but now it was a conviction. "Doesn't it strike you?" I asked.

"What?" my companion gasped. He continued to breathe in deep drafts of air.

"Absalom Lott was jailed in Boston, Increase Mather was driven to flight, Naboth Chieves was murdered. All these men opposed the government, all of them are dead or driven away. There is no connection to Gammar Pisspot, the poor old woman."

"May she be connected in a way we do not know?" Creasy asked, managing to get out a complete sentence.

"Gammar Pisspot and the Royal Governor?" I hooted in disbelief. "Gammar Pisspot has no more acquaintance with such devious tyrants as Priscilla Pig. Forgive me, but the notion is ridiculous."

"There is talk of a plot with the French," Creasy said, his color returning to a flush. "The old woman is Papist . . . . May there not be a connection?"

"She is Irish, not French." I could not help but snap at the man, "How many black-robed priests have you seen sneaking about the streets?"

"It's not likely they'd be wearing their black robes if they intended to sneak, is it?"

"Just as likely as it would be for Gammar Pisspot to speak French."

"Just because she doesn't speak English, how do you know she doesn't speak French? It doesn't follow, you know."

All of a sudden the man had breath to argue.

"She's just an ignorant old woman, that's why. You don't even know her." I confess that I lost patience with the man's inane reasoning. Why do they argue so?

"That's true," he said, changing tactics. "That's why I ask you. Does she often throw stones at people?"

"Only at people she doesn't like." I wished I had a few stones of my own in the boat. I went on to describe her. "She is odd-witted, poor creature, and not responsible for her actions."

"She disliked the minister. Why?" he asked.

"How should I know? You prevented me from going to the jail and speaking to her," I reminded him.

"Well, what did Chieves think of the old woman?"

"What do ministers of the Reformed Faith think of Papists? You tell me."

"One may have theological differences which one defends to the death, yet one may have respect for an individual of another faith." Creasy frowned in thought "It seems to me that an old woman who's been raised in one religion offers poor hope for conversion, but is little danger to the Reformed Church in New England."

"But you just accused her of being part of a gun powder plot with the French!" I heard my voice become shrill with exasperation. Honestly, what do men use for brains?

"That was disputation," he explained, his smile smug and calm. "Women don't understand disputation."

"Not when the reasoning is as nonsensical as yours," I said, taking a deep breath, although I was not seasick. Best for my sanity that I change the subject.

"In any event, Mister Chieves saw sin and sinner as one, that is the way he was. Gammar Pisspot was a Papist within his fold; he could not abide that. But then many people could not abide the Pisspots. The entire family was avoided—but then they weren't the kind of family one invites into one's home for social intercourse. I questioned my neighbors about them. The husband suffered a stroke and died while he was beating the old woman, which he often did, they say. Perhaps that was a sign of God's justice. The old woman's son, Tom, has been in trouble with the magistrates since he was a child. There is a daughter but she lives elsewhere. They say she is the only one who can control the son." I paused but the man did not remark upon my observations so I went on.

"If Gammar threw a stone and hit the minister, why then it was by God's design," I said. "She is old and hasn't the strength to aim a fatal blow . . . but that won't help her before the magistrates."

"Surely they will take her age and feeble condition into consideration?" he asked.

"There's the charge of witchcraft," I reminded him. Such a charge is serious business, which Creasy must know better than I. There is not only the Biblical injunction against it, but witchcraft is a threat to the entire community. Neighbor turns against neighbor, old quarrels fester into ripening boils; the order our ancestors created out of a savage wilderness is torn asunder.

"The old woman has made free confession." Creasy's expression was grave; he understood the implications.

"I don't think she is a witch," I said. "I don't care that she admits to it. She's only a frightened old woman who's led a life of abuse. She would confess to anything."

"What you say may well be the way of it, but the poppets found in her possession, her prophesies . . . ."

Creasy did not need to continue. It did not bode well for the old Gammar, but I was not about to give in. I felt a shiver of excitement at the thought of the interview to come. So much depended upon my companion's opinion, since he was authorized to investigate the death. Would he believe the old woman to be a witch? Cousin Cotton Mather thought so, but Cousin Cotton's vivid imagination often led him to strange conclusions. I hoped I'd given the young minister before me another view of the situation.

As if he read my thoughts, Creasy spoke up. "I'll make up my own mind."

Although his glance seemed to challenge me, I kept my lips firmly closed. At least he was open to other explanations besides witchery for the murders of the two ministers.

He spent the remainder of the voyage offering gratitude to the Lord for a safe return to Rumney Marsh.

Chapter Eight

We retrieved our mounts at my farm and rode on to Rumney Marsh jail, a basket of provisions tied to my saddlebag. I promised to be quiet and let Creasy do the questioning. (By this time I'd dispensed with formality. Sometimes he slipped and called me Hetty.)

Be present at this interview I would. The more I considered the matter, the more I felt the old woman wrongly accused. Certainly there are witches—you can't be a sailor's wife and not know of strange, unnatural doings—but I associated witches with foreign lands. I couldn't remember the last time one had been hung in the Bay Colony. After all, I argued, if Gammar Pisspot was truly a witch, why had she led such a miserable existence? It didn't follow: if she possessed powers, wouldn't she use them for wealth and riches? Clearly she possessed no earthly goods, ergo she was not a witch. (And he thought women were incapable of disputation!)

I don't believe he was really listening, though. He kept jiggling one foot in the stirrup and humming David's *Psalm one hundred and nine; As he did cursing love.*

The jailer received us with a cordial smile, leading us to the spartan cell where the prisoner was confined. The smell was as unpleasant as Cousin Cotton Mather had said. No worse than many a ship's hold, though.

Creasy wrinkled his nose.

"She's quiet now," the jailer whispered. "Deb's with her. Deb's her daughter, you know. Deb won't put up with her witch-talk.

Deborah Piscopot is as good a Christian as you or me," he declared. "She be a church member over in Roxbury, in the late Mister Eliot's congregation. Now there was a saintly man, old Mister Eliot."

"The Roxbury church?" Creasy raised his brows. "I thought the family were Papists!"

"She be so, old Gammar Pisspot, but Deb was sent into service to a good Reform family when she were a bitty girl, and raised Reform Church, she were. No airs about Deb. Her father spent many a night in this same cell," the jailer recalled. "Deb would toddle in with his dinner in a basket nigh as big as she. Then her brother Tom got sent to jail and she would come over from Roxbury to get him out." The jailer shook his head at the thought of such devotion.

I peered through the gloom as my eyes adjusted to the dark room. Deborah Piscopot looked up at our entrance. She struck me at once as a cold young woman; dark eyes swept over our party with obvious disapproval. Her hair was hidden beneath a black hood; a cloak of gray wool covered a dark robe of good quality. I could not help but approve her modest dress. The only redeeming feature I could find in the young woman was a complexion as pink and white as a rose. So this was the old woman's daughter! I confess I'd pictured her as a blowsy sort of doxy.

Creasy bowed low to her as if she were a princess. I thought he'd bump his head upon the floor.

Deborah's response was a silent nod. She seated herself upon a stool, next to a straw-filled pallet where perched the other occupant of the cell; the one we had come to see. Gammar Pisspot, as she was commonly known, reminded me of a tiny brown bird with her stooped figure and leathery face wrinkled as a withered apple. Two bright black eyes glittered like coals amidst the wrinkled flesh above the beak of a nose. The old woman had an abundance of yellowing white hair, neatly combed and wound into a bun upon the back of her head. She wore no cap. I had to admit the daughter had done well by the old woman, considering her circumstances.

The old gammar's dress was a smock of homespun over a tattered but clean and pressed brown petticoat. Upon her tiny feet were serviceable kid slippers, two sizes too large, over loose green worsted stockings. At least someone cared for the old woman.

"Here's another gentleman come to see you, Gammar," the jailer announced in a cheery voice. "And it's Mrs. Henry with a basket for you You remember Mrs. Henry. She's brought you some bread and nice headcheese. Say thankee to the fine lady."

The old woman did not look up; she fingered a string of amber beads in her withered, tobacco-colored fingers.

"This gentleman's come all the way from Boston to see you, just like the other gentleman." The jailer pointed to my companion.

The old woman did not move her head; she mumbled over her beads.

"She understands," the jailer reassured Creasy. "You shan't have any trouble with her, Sir, so long as Deb's here. She'll behave herself with Deb here. You're a good girl, ain't you, Gammar Pisspot? Yes, she's a good girl she is. She won't give the gentleman any of her witchery, no, she won't."

Creasy turned to speak to the daughter "Good morning . . . . I should like to speak to your mother, if I may. If you'll be so kind as to interpret for me. I am here at the request of Mister Mather, of Second Church in Boston. I am his cousin, Increase Cotton, of the Summer Street Church."

The young woman regarded him with cool eyes. She nodded her consent. I passed the basket to her and stepped to the side where I could observe without notice.

Creasy just stood there, shifting his boots. He seemed not to know what to do. Certainly neither woman offered him any encouragement to speak. When he spoke, he addressed the daughter.

"I have not come to judge her—tell her that for me, if you please."

"Why have you come, then?" the young woman asked. Her pink lips twisted in disdain.

"I have come to find the truth about the accident that befell Naboth Chieves . . . . And because of the prophecies your mother made before my cousin, Mister Mather," he added.

"My mother has no sight for prophecy. She is an old woman. Old women are often accused of these things because they have lived long and know the natures and weaknesses of man."

From my corner I nodded in silent agreement with this observation.

"What has she said that brings upon her a charge of witchcraft?" the young woman demanded of the minister.

Creasy answered this attack with a stammer. "That the ministers of New England would die—one by hanging and one by poison. I only repeat this charge, I do not accuse her."

The young woman turned, addressing her parent in a flow of soft sounds that were like music.

A high, wild keening was the response.

I shivered, I could not help it. It was an eerie noise but, I had to remind myself, only a noise made by a human voice. Creasy's eyes were wider than mine, I noted.

"She says she never prophesied this." The young woman flashed a baleful look at the poor minister.

"Ah . . . ." he hesitated. "I dare say there was a misunderstanding. Does she remember the gentleman who came to see her three days ago?"

The young woman translated his question and a brief answer. "She does."

"Did she not speak to him of the ministers of New England? Did she not say they were the slaves of Satan?"

The young woman translated in the soft, wild tongue; the answer came in a long whine. The old woman fingered her beads, her shoulders were hunched, her head averted.

"She says the gentleman asked her many questions—too many to remember, and he would not let her rest upon her bed. He called her a witch and Queen of Hell, so she called him Satan's whoreson and wished the high and mighty minister a mighty fall."

The old woman whined something more, her bird-eyes glittering.

"She says she wished the minister to hang in her place, and that he spoke poisonous words against her to see her hanged." Deborah Piscopot translated in a wooden voice.

The old woman nattered on.

"He told her she would burn in hell for all eternity because she followed a false God; then she knew he was the Devil himself, the Man in Black, seeking to trick her soul into his power, and she told him to go away or she would throw a stone at him. This frightened him because the Devil is a coward, and he left."

The old woman gave a sharp cackle as her words were translated; I surmised that she understood very well what was being said of her.

Creasy hastened to reassure the old woman. "No, no . . . that was not the Man in Black, 'twas only my cousin, Mister Mather of Boston. He is no one to be frightened of at all."

He turned to the translator. "She is not afraid of me, is she? She must not be frightened of me, I shan't hurt her, please tell her that."

The translator obliged, and repeated the answer.

"No, she is not frightened of you. She says you have a simple mind."

At this statement I had to cover my mouth to keep from laughing. Creasy, oblivious, relaxed in his posture.

"Good," he said. "I don't mean to frighten her, and I'm sorry she was frightened by Mister Mather. My cousin means well, he truly does, but sometimes in his zeal to serve the Lord he forgets the frailty of human beings. Please tell your mother that Mister Mather is as anxious as I am to know the truth about Naboth Chieves' death. I have come at my cousin's bidding for that purpose, and that purpose alone."

He turned his head from one to the other as the words were translated.

Creasy and I had discussed the likelihood that Cousin Cotton has misunderstood the old woman. Her answers had no doubt been garbled in translation by a seaman of questionable sobriety. But then, Cotton Mather often mistook the words of others as personal slights, so morbidly sensitive was his nature.

I spoke up now, unable to stand the shilly shallying of my companion. Why beat about the bush?

"What happened to Mister Chieves? How did he die?" That was the crux of the matter, after all.

"The Devil killed him."

Creasy and I looked at each other.

"How? How did the Devil kill him? Did she see it? Was she there when it happened?" I asked.

Mother and daughter argued; the exchange was sharp; the mother sulked. We waited for the reply; I for one, held my breath without realizing it.

Deborah Piscopot finally spoke in a low voice. "The Devil leaped out from Hell and struck the man down and he died. This is what she says."

The old woman cackled with glee, the black eyes peering at Creasy in particular.

The minister's voice shook as he questioned the old woman directly.

"Did the . . . did you throw a stone at the minister?"

"Yes, to see if he moved, but he did not, so she knew he was dead," Deborah repeated her mother's words.

"So . . . the man lay upon the ground. He did not fall off his horse when she threw the stone at him?"

I recalled my earlier words to the minister: it must be God's design for a stone to kill a man in his prime if the stone came from this shriveled arm. Why, the woman's limbs were hardly more than kindling sticks! If the woman was to escape a charge of murder this answer was most important.

"No, because the Devil pulled him off the horse," the old woman whined. "The Devil killed him."

"What did the Devil look like?" Creasy persisted in his questioning.

"All in black," came the answer, "like the gentleman from

Boston. She was afraid to look at his face, the Devil. She hid in the bushes and said her prayers, like a good Christian."

Deborah scowled at us. "I am translating her words as best I can. You must understand that my mother is confused and frightened by this prison."

"Yes. Ask her to go on, please. What did she do then?" Creasy asked.

"The Devil ran off and she came out of hiding. She saw what he had done but she threw a stone at the body to be sure it was killed, and it did not move."

A shrill cackle accompanied the translation.

"They found her dancing around the body. Why was she happy? Did she have a grudge against the minister?"

The question upset the old woman who cried out in a sharp tongue. Mother and daughter argued back and forth before the answer came.

"She rejoiced when the Devil struck him down because he was a bad man," Deborah repeated, her voice wooden. "He struck at her with a whip and said bad things of her."

Deborah turned to the minister, the first sign of a quiver in her voice. "She is old and confused. What will happen to her?"

"I cannot say. I will see that she is examined by doctors. If they find her insane she will be released into your care."

"Insane?" The young woman stared at Creasy.

"Better that than the alternative," he answered.

Since the alternative was hanging, I agreed with him.

The story about the Devil would not help her in court, I thought.

Consorting with the Prince of Evil was a hanging offense.

Prophecies, poppets and incantations . . . the prospects did not appear healthy for Gammar Pisspot.

Creasy's face was full of pity for the old woman, who returned his gaze with bright, glittering eyes. She spoke in her keening whine, addressing him directly.

"What does she say?" he asked.

Deborah frowned; she looked puzzled.

"She tells the young Puritan priest to obey the tenth commandment," she translated.

I was alarmed by Creasy's reaction; he staggered backwards, his face turned pale as the old woman's cackle unnerved us both. I reached out to steady him. What was the matter with him, did he really think she was a witch? The arm beneath my hand shook.

Deborah spoke sharply to the old woman; what she said I could not tell, but the serpentine eyes grew dim. A trickle of spittle ran down the corner of her cracked, colorless lips. The daughter reached over and wiped off the spittle with a square of linen cloth.

I whispered to Creasy. "She is only a witless old woman. No need to be afraid of her tales. She sees us together," I improvised, "and perhaps she thinks my Mister Henry is still alive. That you and I . . . ." Delicacy forbid my going on.

Creasy's face regained its color. If I had any doubts the young man beside me loved my cousin Abigail, those doubts vanished. I felt sorry for him; I could not help it. I have a soft heart. Both my marriages were love matches. And I knew Abigail loved her husband to distraction, so that was safe.

I called out to the jailer for our release.

My companion pulled himself together. He addressed Deborah Piscopot. "I'll see that the doctors examine her. I'll do what I can to help you. Please call upon me any time. I hope you will!"

I pulled him from the cell, nettled by his wheedling tone.

Deborah gave him no answer. The dark eyes beneath the hood regarded us with open hostility. Yet she remembered her manners, thanking me for the basket of provisions. I added my own offer of assistance, for the old woman's sake.

"Well," I paused outside the jail, drawing in deep breaths to rid my head of the foul stench. "What did you think of the old woman's story?"

"I don't like it," he glared, "I don't like it at all."

"What—you can't believe she killed him, surely!"

"I think the man was ambushed by someone," Creasy growled, "but not by that old woman. I think there is a connection between the two deaths, between Chieves and Lott. I don't like what I think. I think I had better return to Boston." He strode to his mare and pulled himself into the saddle. He looked very much like an angry scarecrow.

"Be careful!" I called.

"And you stay out of it!" he ordered, and rode off without looking back.

I was a trifle miffed at him and his abrupt departure, but I would make my own inquiries, regardless. The orders might come from Boston—I knew what Creasy suspected—but I much feared the murderer came from Rumney Marsh. It had to be someone who knew the area intimately, and knew the two men. This was my community—I was as responsible for it as my late husband Hezekiah,the Magistrate. He would have understood my need to uncover the murderer.

Chapter Nine

I had allies within the Marsh, I was sure. Deacon Lamb was a mainstay of the church. I had also to make a consolation visit to him and to his much younger wife.

(It was a good match; Rachel brought a comfortable property with her which she had neither the interest nor the brains to run. The Deacon was a thrifty, hardy old man who ran the farm with the discipline of Cromwell's troopers, where he had indeed served in his younger days.)

I'd last seem him at Lott's funeral as one of the bearers, holding his end of the coffin and marching as bravely as the younger men. I'd searched the crowd but seen no sign of the Deacon's wife. Possibly she'd stayed at home. Funerals were not to her taste, no doubt.

I was certain he'd be as anxious as I to re-establish order in the community. Loaded with a basket of provisions, I accosted the good old man as he was about to enter the barn. I extended my sympathies as gently as I could. I did not quite know how to approach the subject of his son-in-law's death. My uncertainty made me stuttering and stupid.

"You were well acquainted with Mister Lott, Deacon . . . ."

"He was my son-in-law, my poor daughter's husband," the old man rasped, looking at me as if I were a simpleton.

"It is a sad loss, Sir," I offered.

"Indeed, Mrs. Henry," he answered, "it is a sad loss. We had only the one child, my wife and me. The good Esther Browne that was—my first wife," he explained with care. "Esther was called home to the Lord these fifteen years past, and our daughter Janet joined her in His bosom but five years ago."

"Sir, I am sorry." I lowered my voice.

"The hand of the Lord is heavy upon us, yet must we submit to His will with a good grace."

"Even so," I sympathized, "yet this foul work was by the hand of man."

"Aye, suicide," the Deacon sighed. "Surely the young man's reasoning was disordered to commit such a sinful folly. He is buried in church ground—indeed, my conscience troubles me on the point. I would have supported the decision for burial outside the churchyard. I would not have the young man given special dispensation by his position. A suicide is a suicide, no matter if the sinner's faculties are gone awry. All my life I have agreed with that doctrine."

"But this was no suicide . . . did they not tell you?" I wondered, sorry for him. So he'd not heard the gossip at the funeral! Yet sparing his feelings was not fair to the man.

"Not suicide? Accident, you mean?" he spoke quickly. "Why, that is a tragic happening, yet my mind is relieved! Death by mishap—why, surely that's preferable for his soul's sake, poor Absalom."

"Not mishap, I fear." What could I do but speak openly to the old man? He deserved the truth and would demand no less. "The minister was murdered," I said.

"Murdered!" The old man turned white beneath the hardy pink of his skin. He was unable to speak.

I laid my hand upon the Deacon's shoulder. He stood like an oak. "We'll find the villain," I reassured him. "There will be justice done here."

"How so . . . ." the old man stammered, "Who says it is murder?"

"The coroner's report is conclusive . . . I'm sorry. I'm sorry for being the bearer of such news, but it will be known about town shortly. The magistrates have been notified. I assumed you'd been advised of the manner of his death."

"Nay, nay," the old man muttered, "I was told nothing of this. There is work to be done . . . you will excuse me, Mrs. Henry." With an abrupt turn, Deacon Lamb marched into the barn.

I watched him go with a mixture of pity and admiration. He hid his tears from a woman's eyes. Of such sturdy stuff were made the victors at Naseby (Indeed, many a Cromwell trooper had found refuge in the Bay Colony.) I was certain he would back me in the search for his son-in-law's killer.

I brought my basket into the house and asked to see the Mistress. I was shown into the parlor and greeted very prettily by Rachel Lamb. She patted the chair beside her and called for tea, her yellow curls bobbing about her face with suppressed energy. She wore black silk mourning with a lacy white cap and a matching lace fall so broad it covered her shoulders. White lace cuffs adorned her sleeves. She did seem happy to see me!

I made my condolences and admired the artful draperies of mourning over portraits and the black bows that drew in the shutters.

"I did not see you at Mister Lott's funeral," I remarked, keeping my voice neutral.

"Oh yes, I was much too upset," she breathed in a little girl voice. "Imagine poor Absalom shaming his papa-in-law with such a horrid action! Oh, I could not bear it! I took to my bed, although I assure you I grieve for the poor man. It was such a shock, you know, such a shock and such a shocking thing to do . . . . Why, I never suspected such a thing of him!"

(I did not feel it was my place to inform her of. the truth; that was her husband's privilege.)

"Had he behaved other than usual when you last saw him?" I asked. "Was he angry about something, perhaps?" Or someone, I wondered. Who were the man's enemies?

Tea was brought in on a silver tray by the girl who had admitted me. She laid it out on a small table, which was placed between us.

"Oh no, I should never have guessed," Rachel Lamb

continued as she lifted a silver pot and poured out cups of fragrant, steaming liquid. "Of course we did not see him as often of late. Perhaps two weeks ago he brought some seeds Deacon Lamb requested of him and they went on and on against the government, but that was much as usual. I confess I hardly listen when they begin on that topic!" she giggled.

My hostess passed a plate of dark gingerbread slices.

I helped myself and was pleasantly surprised by its taste and texture. "You have a new cook?" I asked involuntarily.

"Oh yes, she's a gem. Now don't you get any ideas!" She wagged a finger at me. "I haven't been able to replace Zillah since you bought her from me. And I never should have sold her, had the Deacon not taken such a violent dislike to her. I hope you don't find her as saucy as she was to the Lamb. I call him my Lamb, you know . . . . One cannot blame him for reacting to her tongue—she would defy him over the least little order. Indeed, he threatened to whip her several times until I thought it best to separate them, lest my husband have an apoplexy!"

"Zillah?" I asked, amazed. The woman had shown no saucy side to me. She was a good worker, willing to help in the fields those times when we needed extra hands. I had nothing but respect for the woman, who conducted herself with quiet dignity.

"Oh yes, Zillah and the Deacon were at loggerheads 'til it gave me headaches to have them in the same room," Rachel chatted on "I was so glad 'twas you who answered my ad for her . . . . I knew she'd be well treated with you."

I wanted to get back to the subject I'd come to discuss, but one must be polite. "How disagreeable to have a husband and a servant at loggerheads," I agreed. "Tell me, is there anything I can do to help you over this sad period? I believe the Deacon inherits, does he not?"

"Absalom and Janet had no children," Rachel sighed. "How I should have liked nieces and nephews about . . . but we are his only relations. He left no will, so the Deacon inherits after probate. My poor Lamb goes on so about the costs of probate! Why, it's more trouble than it's worth, he says. This is the worst possible time—he'll have to inventory Absalom's goods for probate and there are the fields to plow and more land to be cleared . . . . Why, I assure you, there is very little money left us for all this work!"

I could sympathize with the Deacon's predicament. Probate was another way to line the pockets of the Royal Governor and his cronies "I could lend you Zillah—she's very good at inventory," I offered.

"I taught her to read and write, of course," Rachel beamed, "But I can't believe the Deacon would like her to know our business. Thank you just the same . . . it's most kind of you. Absalom used to tease us to free her because she is so smart, but the Deacon always said she was too smart for her own good. He doesn't believe slaves should read or write—he says 'tis a waste of education meant for their betters. But it was too late, since I'd taught her years before we were married and one can hardly un-teach a body—even a slave—can you?"

I could only nod. "Well, I'm glad you did teach her. It is like Mister Lott to stand up for her. I know my Cousin Mather believes in education for servants and slaves. How else can they read the Bible, he says!"

"Oh, indeed," she agreed. "Why, we learned our letters together as children, since my uncle gave Zillah to me when I was ten years of age and the girl scarcely older. Mister Mather is such a superior man . . . his sentiments do him honor! I should so like to meet him—oh, and that young minister from Boston, his cousin, I believe! I should have been there to hear his sermon were I not laid up in my bed . . . . I asked a friend to take notes—poor Deacon Lamb had not the heart—and I found his words so affecting! Did you not find his sermon affecting?" she prattled on.

"It was well presented, certainly," I agreed.

She leaned towards me in a confiding manner. "I hear he is most handsome and gentlemanly . . . and related to you?"

"Not likely," I snorted, setting down my teacup. "His cousin is married to my cousin, that is all."

"But you were seen with him in the village . . . is there to be news of your engagement, perhaps?" she tittered, giving me what I'm sure she thought was a roguish glance.

My jaw tightened, in spite of my efforts to remain calm. I did not like being the target of gossips. "I assure you, Madame, there is no possibility of any such announcement. As the widow of the local magistrate I was prevailed upon to introduce him to certain citizens of the community. He was sent to interview the old woman.

She knew of whom I spoke. "That horrid old witch," she shivered. "Poor Mister Chieves! Such a charming man—and such a loss to our church! I shall not rest until the old witch is hung! None of us are safe, and so I've told my Lamb. He must see that she is punished, I told him, and so he promised!"

I determined to take my leave at this point and rose. "Well . . . I am sorry for your loss."

"Oh . . . ." She pulled at a yellow curl. "Must you leave so soon?" She jumped up. "It's just that with Absalom gone and Naboth dead there is a dearth of company in this house!"

"Mister Chieves' company is a loss to us all, certainly . . . ." I ventured.

"I shall miss them both dearly . . . . Naboth was such a pleasant man—indeed, almost like one of the family! Now, Absalom was a grave man—of course I enjoyed his visits, but he did not make me laugh, as did Naboth Chieves. Oh, I shall miss their company! So you see, you must come again soon . . . and please bring Mister Cotton with you, I beg of you. We shall be most pleased to make his acquaintance."

"I'm sure he will enjoy meeting you, Mrs. Lamb." I thanked her and made my escape. I felt sorry for her lack of company, but I did not like her haste to hang an old woman. No, the more I thought about it the more I believed the deaths of the two ministers were much more complicated than spells and witchery. There was indeed a malignancy abroad, but its roots lay in Boston. I'd have a word with Elijah about the farm and then run up to Town for a few days. I had contacts there even the Mathers and Cottons would envy.

Chapter Ten

Four-year-old Charity Bezoum lay asleep in the sweet oblivion of those infants deemed worthy of the easiest place in Hell. (No Half-Way Covenanter was the doughty Captain Bezoum; Charity would have to find her own way to Redemption.) The shattering explosion, the flying missile, the sharp shards of glass pierced neither her consciousness nor her tender flesh. The foul curses in the night profaned not the pink ear peeping seashell like from the child's lace cap.

Captain Abraham Bezoum rushed barefoot into the room, nightrail flapping, cap askew. His first thought was for the child, his second to poke his head through the shattered window and seek the source of the unholy ruckus.

"Hold there, you villains!" he shouted at the two dim laughing figures who staggered before his house. Curses and hoots answered his command. Bezoum noted a neighbor's lantern bobbing about in the window of the house opposite.

"Drunkards . . . idle whore masters . . . you'll pay for the damages here!" the Captain threatened, withdrawing his head and raising his candle to assess the effects of the heavy stone which lay in the middle of the room.

"Come out, come out!" came the taunt. "We're not afraid of you, Old Sourpuss!"

Let one of the sailors on his ship speak to him in such a tone and the rogue would feel the lash across his back. "Mrs. Bezoum!" roared the Captain. "Fetch me my coat!"

With the addition of slippers and coat, the captain rushed out into the black night.

"Bezoum," cried the voice of his neighbor, "I'm with you!"

A raised globe lighted the face of fellow seaman, Captain Peleg Moon.

"Apprehend the rascals!" Bezoum shouted, and the two seamen grimly marched towards the jeering figures before them. Dogs barked, candles flickered in windows along the street, arms and legs flailed in the inky night, and two surprised Captains, Bezoum and Moon, found themselves alone, sitting on the cobblestones, nursing stab wounds that seeped dark blood onto collars and coatsleeves.

"Ho—murder!" Bezoum cried in a shaky voice to the neighbors who gathered around him.

Word of the attack upon Captains Bezoum and Moon spread like a conflagration across the Town. I had an interesting gossip about it with two business colleagues over tea the next afternoon. (I kept my rooms over the warehouse in Boston, the same that Jack and I shared as a young couple new married and making their way in the world. Oh, what tender memories!)

"Well, we could not help but overhear," said my merchant friend, leaning his corpulent person forward until the chair creaked. "We were sitting right there when something crashed against the wall behind us! Why, I jumped from my seat!"

His companion nodded. "Broke a vase," he frowned. "Heard it crash."

"Why, whatever caused such a display of temper?" I questioned, pouring tea into china cups. I offered each man a plate of cakes.

"Temper, Madame—you may well call it a display of temper." My corpulent friend helped himself to the cake. "The language, why I could not repeat it before a lady's ear! 'Twas shouted so loud we could not help but make out the curses . . . ."

"Ungodly," his companion agreed, disapproval writ across his spare face.

"Why Sirs, I shudder to think what must have provoked such behavior!" I poured myself a cup of fragrant liquid.

"Oh, the Secretary was most angry, I assure you. 'Dolt! Idiot!' Those were but a few of the names I may repeat!" My corpulent friend helped himself to more cake. At my delicate shiver of dismay at such behavior he continued: "I'm afraid he spoke ill of your respected uncle, Madame—how Mister Mather escaped to cause trouble in London though this man was supposed to stop him, and now he'd stabbed two Boston men which would cause a great trouble in the Town . . . ."

"Mercy!" I cried, setting down my teacup.

"Stabbed," the spare companion confirmed. "I heard him say the words."

"And what did the man reply to that charge?" I asked.

"Oh, that we could not hear so well. It was Secretary Ruckenmaul that yelled so loud. 'Drunken Lout!' he shouted, 'one of my excise officers throwing stones through windows— attacking unarmed men—a pack of ranting parsons on my back!' These were words we heard clear as a bell."

"A bell," confirmed the other.

"Then we heard something about the Kennebec settlements and trying his tricks against the Eastern savages . . . . Then he ordered the man out."

"Gracious! And did you see this rogue?" I leaned forward in suspense.

"No," my friend shook his head; the curls of his periwig danced. "He must have gone out a different door. We heard the Secretary shout for his servant and not long after we were called in."

"I saw the servant leave with pieces of a vase," the spare man observed.

"How did the Secretary receive you? Was he in a state?" I asked.

"Oh, he was most cordial—most friendly," my rotund guest leaned back in his chair.

"Hypocrite," the other snorted.

"That's as may be," my friend turned to his companion, "but you must admit he received us with the utmost courtesy.

He shared some very fine brandy and could not have been more agreeable."

I intervened. "I take it the business went well. You got the contract?"

The two men looked at each other.

"Oh, you've nothing to fear from me, Gentlemen." I reassured them. "I may not like the man, but business is business. We are in no competition here—I have no timber lots. The navy must have masts, after all. I would rather see good colleagues of my late husband receive the contract to provide them—I know you capable of fulfilling the contract." I sipped at my tea.

The two men relaxed at my words.

"That is what we told the Secretary, Madame. 'We can fulfill the contract, Sir,' I said to him. 'We have prime wooded lands.'"

"I know that well," I nodded at my New Hampshire colleagues, "and at a fair price, too, I'll wager. Thirty-five thousand pounds?" I hazarded a guess.

The two men exchanged glances of satisfaction.

"You know the value of timber, Madame," my rotund friend beamed.

"I own ships, Sir, I must know the value of wood."

The companion nodded in silent approval.

"But what did it cost you to procure the contract? You will excuse my blunt questions, Gentlemen," I apologized, "but as a widow woman in business I should like to know how these contracts are obtained." I have often found it helpful to feign ignorance. It is expected in a woman.

Neither gentleman was overset by my frankness. I passed around the plate of cakes.

Upon a signal from his spare companion, my rotund friend beamed. "Why it cost us nothing, Madame, that is the beauty of it!"

"Oh?" I did not believe in something for nothing.

"Now you would not repeat this, Madame . . . . We may count upon your discretion?" My rotund friend leaned over and pressed my hand, his eyes on mine.

"You have my word—your identity in this matter is secret."

"The Naval Commissioners allotted forty thousand pounds for the purchase. It was suggested by the Secretary that we rewrite the bid for that amount . . . ." My friend let go of my hand and leaned back in his chair.

"A gift to him of the difference?" I suggested.

Both men smiled.

I was not surprised in the least. For a gift of five thousand pounds my colleagues gained a lucrative contract. I should have done the same myself, could I bring myself to do business with the lying, cheating bully of a Secretary! These two gentlemen were from New Hampshire. They'd not yet encountered the tyranny, graft and corruption that infected Boston in the persons of Edward Ruckenmaul and Edmund Andros.

"Business is business," my friend beamed. "The Secretary was most complimentary. He wished the merchants of your town were as accommodating as the merchants of New Hampshire."

"The way of the world," the other muttered

"More tea, Gentlemen?" I smiled with all the sweetness I could muster. I'd learned that one of the miscreants was an exciseman banished to the Kennebec, no doubt before he could prove an embarrassment to the Royal Governor. It should not be difficult to ferret out the name of the latest recruit to the settlements there.

Poor Abigail must have her hands full right now. As soon as I rid myself of my visitors I prepared to go prod Cousin Cotton Mather into some sort of action. At least he could write a statement condemning the outrages against poor Captain Bezoum and Captain Moon. My blood boiled in my veins at the thought of two citizens of Boston being attacked upon the streets—two worthy, honest seamen!

Abigail Mather did have her hands full, as I discovered scarce an hour later. The only trouble was that the dainty digits were clasped hard upon the wrong man. I could not help being witness to the unseemly display—the front door stood wide open to the street, for all to see. Good thing it was me coming up the walk and not some other prying eyes. I hastened to pull the door shut and latch it secure from interruptions. These two would not have noticed had the Reverend Whitestone ridden in on his brindled ox.

Abigail was sobbing on the shoulder of Increase Cotton's best black coat. "Oh, Creasy!" I heard the mournful cry.

Creasy held her with both arms. His face alternately paled and crimsoned in my sight. "Abigail . . . what is it? Shush, shush, my dear cousin," he crooned.

Such sentiment, thought I!

Abigail, responding to him, stifled her sobs. She lifted **tear-starred eyes, artlessly brimming with hope. (Lord forgive me the envy I felt at her ability to cry and keep her beauty!) "Creasy," she breathed, 'you've come just in time! oh, how I have prayed for your return! I couldn't help myself—when I saw your face at that door . . . ."** The little hands plucked at the ivory buttons of his waistcoat. "You think me a silly goose, I know . . . ."

(Nothing of the sort, thought I.)

"No . . . no . . . ." he protested, squeezing her in a bear grip.

"Well I am," she smiled through those artless tears. "I didn't mean to weep like a baby. It's just that I've been so worried! I'm so happy you're back! Oh Creasy—whatever should I do without you!"

(I could have told her but they were oblivious to my presence and I wanted to find out what had upset her to the point of neglecting her good name.)

The young man responded with a smile of idiotic bliss.

"No need to question that, my dear, for I'll always be here when you need me," he promised.

Isn't that what they all say? She did look pretty in her neat lace cap, soft honey-gold curls peeping out, eyes starry with tears. I could understand the young minister's infatuation, not that it was right.

"Now that you've come, I needn't be frightened anymore," she confided.

"Frightened?" Creasy echoed my apprehension aloud. "What ever has frightened you, my dear girl?"

Visions of an ominous, shadowy figure made me shudder. Had the murderer of two ministers of God dared approached the Mather household?

"Oh, Creasy—you don't know what's been going since you left!" Tears threatened to spill.

I moved a step closer.

"Dear Abigail," Creasy cried, "what is it? Has anyone threatened you? Who is it? Did you see the scoundrel?"

Horrid thoughts filled my brain. They'd tried to arrest Uncle Increase to enforce his silence—might they not attempt to harm Cousin Cotton? And what of this woman's danger? I must protect her at all costs! "Abigail!" I cried out.

She turned to me, forcing Creasy to loosen his hold. "Why, Cousin Hetty! I did not hear you come in!"

"Mrs. Henry!" Creasy exclaimed, not without alarm, I thought.

"Who is it? Who threatens you?" I insisted.

"Threaten me? Why should anyone threaten me?" She pulled herself apart from her comforter. "Not I . . . attempted murder!" she explained.

"What . . . who . . . ?" Creasy croaked.

I held out my hand and drew her away but she kept her eyes on the young man even as she explained.

"Two Boston men—seamen and neighbors—stabbed by the Governor's excisemen! They were recognized by Captain Bezoum . . . . Abigail's eyes shone with excitement. "They all came here to take council with Cotton, only Cotton has taken again to his bed with nerves, and oh, Creasy, the borage tea doesn't work anymore."

She would have moved back to him had I not held her arm in an iron grip. If she so forgot herself to the gossips of this town, I did not.

"I prayed and prayed for you to come back and calm him," Abigail appealed to him. "Oh, I am such a hindrance to him as a wife!" This judgment was addressed to me. "I am not worthy of him, Cousin Hetty—indeed, I am not!" Two tears spilled down the curve of her cheek.

I refrained from uttering my opinion on the subject, given her real upset. I merely patted her arm.

"Abigail," Creasy frowned, "listen to me. Has anyone tried to harm you . . . or Cousin Cotton?"

"Me?" She arched slender brows in surprise. "Why should the excisemen harm me? We were sound asleep in our bed. Anyway, the fight happened over on Fish Street, not here. But they all came here—Mister Oliver, Wait Winthrop, Samuel Shrimpton—they asked Cotton what to do. He told them he would pray on it, but then he took to his bed . . . . Oh, Creasy—they expect him to speak to the Governor and to that horrible man, the Secretary!" she burst out.

I put my arm around her before he could.

"Oh, Cousin Hetty, it was awful! They've got him in such a state . . . . I fear for his health!"

"The talk is that the attack was Mister Ruckenmaul's doing," I explained to a puzzled Creasy. "He uses the excisemen to do his dirty work. There was a brawl last night and two men, **Captain Bezoum and his neighbor Captain Moon, were stabbed. The town is rife with rumors . . . .**"

"They say the Governor is to betray us to the French," Abigail interjected with gloomy eagerness. **"They will send the Indians down upon us to slaughter us in our beds!"**

I shushed her, intending to reassure her concerning the gossip spreading like wildfire through the town.

"Abigail," Creasy interrupted, ignoring me as best he could. "Is that all? Cotton has taken to his bed, there's been a brawl, the French may send the Indians . . . that's all? You are unharmed?"

"Isn't that enough to frighten her?" I said. "Two good citizens of this town attacked upon our streets . . . are any of us safe?"

"I meant only . . . ." he began, then hesitated.

"Well, we must do something," I insisted, "and not just stand about hugger-muggering. A protest must be made!"

"Yes...." The young minister's face burned. "I must speak to Cousin Cotton."

"Oh Creasy, I knew you'd help!" Abigail broke away from my grip, caught his hand and pulled him to the staircase.

I sighed.

Chapter Eleven

"It's insupportable, that's what—insupportable! Bursting into my room and dragging me from a sick bed!" Cotton Mather fumed. He was seated in a sedan chair, being carried to the Governor's residence by two burly men. (Creasy had called for a chair, making that concession to his cousin's health.) "It's a wonder I'm not expected to crawl upon my hands and knees to the Governor! I'm not a well man!" He shouted over the din of horses hooves, peddler hawkings, construction hammering and carriage rumblings.

Creasy strode by his side with a look of grim determination. Cotton knew that look of old. "You. are the one sent me to bed . . . . Told me I must look after my health . . . said you'd take care of everything!" Mather grumbled.

"This can't be put off—and you are the one they came to, not me." Creasy's mouth was set in a hard line. "Citizens stabbed on the streets of Boston—a protest must be made! I'll make it myself, I tell you! I'll gladly tell the Governor what I think of him and his murdering henchmen!"

"No, you mustn't!" Cotton cried in alarm. "They'll arrest you, Creasy, then and there—just as they arrested the minister of Charlestown for preaching such thoughts!" Mather leaned perilously over the edge of the chair. The bearers grunted, shifting weight to compensate for their cargo's shift.

"Sit down!" Creasy barked.

"You'll bring us both to disaster with your intemperate zeal . . . ." Mather groaned, falling back in the seat. "You must let me speak, Creasy. Indeed, you must curb that hasty tongue of yours and let me speak for us both!" Beads of sweat broke out upon the high Mather forehead.

Creasy strode along, considering, his brow furrowed.

"Give me your word," Mather insisted.

"Oh very well," Creasy growled, "but only because you are better at this kind of thing than I am."

"Yes, I am," Mather was frank. "That's why they came to me—I am known for my conciliatory abilities."

"They came to you because of Uncle Increase, that's why," Creasy interrupted with a bitter twist of his lips. "Just remember that Uncle Increase stood up to them, Cotton, and so must you. There comes a time when conciliation is cowardice."

"I am no coward, Increase Cotton, though you may imply such." Mather answered the impertinent interloper with pale dignity. "I am not a well man. You've never truly concerned yourself with my health, Cousin—you who have never known a day's illness in your life. You don't know what it's like to suffer a roiling in the gut or a blackness of the mind or a throbbing in the head which paralyzes you like a trapped animal!"

"'I know what a heaving gut is like," Creasy remarked, remembering the Atlantic swells. "And a throbbing head, too."

"No doubt from intemperance," Cotton Mather snapped.

"No . . . 'twas intemperance that cured it," Creasy grinned. His companion did not share in the humor.

"I know you suffer from nerves, Cousin," Creasy attempted to pacify his companion. "If I have been abrupt, I apologize." He'd just been scolded by Mistress Henry. Rightly so, he admitted to himself, but none the less, the itch to feel his fingers around that slender neck had caused him to flair out at his companion. "I'm sorry to make you undertake this journey, but we shall keep the meeting short and return you to your bed as soon as may be."

"I know whom I represent, Cousin Increase—my father taught me my duty. I know my health is of no consequence when it comes to safeguarding those civil rights we have always enjoyed." Mather stiffened his shoulders, sitting straight in the chair.

"Well said," Creasy approved. "Just tell it to Governor Andros like that."

"You give me your promise you won't open your mouth," Mather insisted as the bearers set the chair before the gate of a fine, three-storied brick house.

The two young ministers were paraded down a mahogany-paneled hall of liveried servants to the library door. Creasy's mouth fell open at the glitter of paste buckles, sparkling tiered chandeliers and glimpses of gleaming silver pitchers and bowls.

Cotton Mather disregarded the ostentatious display, leaning upon his cane and relying upon his dignity to carry him through the ordeal. His head pounded and his bowels cramped. Only the formidable Mather will denied his feeble constitution its craving for rest and repose.

"Cousin, you are in the right," he murmured to his companion, whose resolve seemed in danger of wilting. "A complaint must be made to the Governor, who must learn that not even the King's emissary can go about stabbing the godly peoples of New England. Is it not by God's own providence that an Indian wilderness was irradiated and those evangilical churches erected here, renowned for the degree of reformation they attained? There are always those men of power who seek to stop the progress of that reformation with vexatious persecutions . . . ." Mather's voice rose.

His fulminations were interrupted as the two ministers were shown into the presence. of Governor Edmund Andros. The curling wavy locks of a black periwig framed a full-jowled face with heavy lidded eyes, a strong nose and pouting, mean-lipped mouth. Andros made a striking figure in a scarlet, gold-laced coat. The curved hilt of a gold rapier gleamed upon his left hip. Martial and commanding appeared this Governor of the Provinces.

Creasy took his cue from his cousin. Cotton Mather studiously ignored the square-jawed man slouched upon a chair to the Governor's right. Edward Ruckenmaul; vilifier, traducer, harpy in the Mather flesh, that man received no bow from Cotton Mather. Creasy could not help admiring the man's coat of rich tobacco velvet; the garment stood open, exposing a waistcoat of silk ivory embroidered with floral gold leaf.

Cotton Mather straightened his back and set aside his cane. He called upon the dignity of his Mather and Cotton ancestors to sustain him against these, his enemies political and ecclesiastical.

Neither minister was offered a seat. The Governor stepped from behind a long mahogany desk to greet them, an expression of affability upon his well-fleshed face.

"Gentlemen . . ." he began, "I am set to meet with the council at this time. Perhaps you would care to schedule another meeting with my clerk? I regret I am not able now to give you my full attention, as I should wish . . . ."

"Sir . . ." Mather began in a frigid tone, "we will ask but a few moments of your time to discuss an injurious attack upon our citizens that I am sure you agree must not be repeated."

"Indeed, young Mister Mather . . . . I believe I know of the incident to which you refer." The Governor glanced at Creasy. "I'm afraid I don't have the acquaintance of your colleague . . . ?" Edmund Andros arched his brows in inquiry.

"This is my cousin, Mister Increase Cotton, who serves the Summer Street Church," Mather introduced Creasy with a grave gesture.

Creasy bowed, his back stiffened.

Governor Andros nodded his acknowledgment; he turned his attention to the young scion of the Dissenter leader. "Mister Mather, I am aggrieved by the ruffianly behavior which took place last night—regrettable, highly regrettable. And I do agree that such incidents must not be repeated. An employee of this government has been attacked, and this is not the first time our excise agents have been reviled and publicly cursed by the citizens of this town! I am glad you have come to me about this. Perhaps between us, we may arrive at a peaceful solution to what has become a very grave problem, indeed!"

"Sir!" Mather corrected; he cast a warning glance at Creasy, whose face was turning red. "I think you have been misinformed as to the circumstances of last night's attack. I refer to the unprovoked assault by an inebriated exciseman and his companion upon the persons of Captains Bezoum and Moon."

"Bezoum and Moon . . . those are the names of the guilty parties, I believe?" Andros looked at Edward Ruckenmaul for confirmation. "I fear the two seamen held a grudge against the officer for carrying out his duties and took the opportunity to retaliate. My man—who is in your King's service, may I remind you—was forced to defend himself for his life! Oh, Sir, you must control your peoples! These attacks upon authority, they cannot be condoned." Andros shook the ponderous black wig.

"I say again, Sir," Mather answered, "you have been misinformed. Captain Bezoum had a stone thrown through his window, endangering his sleeping child. The stone was thrown with deliberation by two men who were carousing in drunken idleness upon the streets of Boston."

"Ah, Sir—there we are agreed somewhat," Governor Andros interrupted. "It is the reason why I have not issued warrants for the seamen's arrests. The man admits to enjoying a friendly glass of wine at a nearby tavern, from which he and his companion were returning to their homes when set upon. It may be that drink clouded the judgement of the two men—they may have disturbed the peace with loud talk—who is to say nay? Secretary Ruckenmaul has convinced me, for the sake of peace in this town, the exciseman should be removed from service here. Fortunately, the fellow has volunteered for the Eastern frontier—he'd heard of the need to protect the Kennebec settlements from the savages."

"And his companion?" Mather pressed.

"His companion is a private citizen. He has not come forward to press charges against the captains—unless he does so, we have no concern with him." Andros was short.

"He probably high-tailed it back to Rumney Marsh—no doubt he'll stay clear of town in the future," Edward Ruckenmaul drawled in a voice heavy with amusement.

"Rumney Marsh?" Creasy questioned, forgetting his promise to remain silent. He received a vicious jab from the cane of Cotton Mather as a reminder.

"The companion is a farmer from Rumney Marsh," Governor Andros answered. "He does not concern us, since the exciseman admits to defending himself with a knife."

"Nonetheless—this man is sought by the magistrates upon a complaint from Captain Moon, upon whom he laid violent hands," Mather contended.

"A brawl . . . a man come to the aid of his companion, as any stout man would," Ruckenmaul drawled in protest.

"Perhaps this farmer's testimony will convince you that you have been misinformed as to a near fatal incident," Mather spoke to the Governor, ignoring the other man.

"Perhaps pigs will fly," came a jeer from the figure slouched in the chair.

The Governor shrugged scarlet clad shoulders. "I will, of course, hear his testimony . . . but it is the larger issue of your people's disobedience which concerns me. You ought to instill in them a proper respect for authority! They look to the church for their example! That's why these problems arise."

"Sir, I have never advocated attacks upon person or property . . . ." Mather began.

"Your father, young Sir—your father! When he speaks against the policies of this government, he enflames the ignorant to acts of violence!" Governor Andros spoke in reproach.

"My father, Sir," Mather spoke calmly, placing a hand upon Creasy's arm to forestall any reply from that quarter, "my father seeks only to restore to us those ancient rights and privileges which we have enjoyed since the founding of this colony—until the charter was taken from us—rights and privileges that belong to the poorest and meanest of Englishmen!"

"Rights and privileges!" the Governor snapped, his jowls reddening, "Do you speak to me of rights and privileges, Sir?"

"Rights and privileges do not exist for traitorous libelers,"

Ruckenmaul sneered from his chair. His thick brows formed a bushy line.

"These rights do not follow you to the ends of the earth," the Governor scowled, "although you in New England think you have founded your own kingdom! Your rights and privileges come from the Crown, which I represent! And I tell you this, Sir—you have this privilege from me," he paused, "that you are not bought and sold as slaves."

Creasy gasped at Cotton Mather's elbow.

Mather turned to him and warned him in a whisper: "This provocation is deliberate." He squeezed Creasy's arm to emphasize his words. Aloud he said, "Come Cousin, let us not keep the Governor from his Council. *Nulla quaesita scelere potentia diuturna.*"

"What does he say?" Andros asked his Secretary, puzzled.

"It's French," Ruckenmaul drawled, brushing a speck from a velvet sleeve. "I think he says he'll never return here."

"Drat his impudence—he shan't be invited!"

The Governor's voice followed them from the room as a liveried servant escorted the two men past a line of footmen to the front door, which was shut upon them with a resounding thud.

Chapter Twelve

"*Nulla quaesita scelere potentia diuturna*, that's what Cousin Cotton told the Royal Governor, can you imagine? *Nothing achieved by wrong doing is lasting.* Right to his face, and they thought it was French!"

Creasy's face split into a wide grin as he regaled Abigail and me with the details of his meeting with Royal Governor Edmund Andros and his hated henchman, Edward Ruckenmaul.

"I tell you, I held my breath at Cousin Cotton's daring, then I could hardly keep a straight face when we left. As soon as I got out the door I burst out laughing."

Cotton Mather, ensconced in his chair and wrapped in shawls, nodded his head with a tight smile while Abigail's eyes were round as shillings.

"I am all admiration for the way you stood up to them, Cousin," Creasy addressed Cotton Mather. "I confess that I had all I could do to keep from smashing my fist into Ruckenmaul's face. He sat there looking so smug and satisfied with himself . . . see how smug he'd be then."

"I also felt the sting of that obnoxious presence," Mather answered with a weary calm. "You will note that I maintained my discipline. I could not be drawn into their web, for that's what it was, a trap set by two glutinous spiders. Nor must you allow your emotions to overcome your discretion, Cousin Creasy. That way lies disaster. They would have arrested us and thrown us in prison without a thought."

Even as he chided Creasy, I noted how Cousin Cotton lapped

up Creasy's praise like a kitten with a bowl of milk. He insisted upon sitting up with us while we took a light supper. Abigail fussed about him like an old hen. Honestly, sometimes her devotion gets on my nerves.

When the two men ended their tale I took the opportunity to relate the relevant point of my conversation with the men from New Hampshire. (I did not mention the bribery—I had given my word on that.)

"Now we know who stabbed Captains Bezoum and Moon," I said. "These excise men are dangerous. Would I be premature in speculating that these men may have had a hand in the deaths of our two ministers?

Abigail grasped her husband's hand with a cry of dismay.

"You would be premature in such speculations, Cousin Hetty." Cotton Mather frowned. "I beg you will not frighten my dear consort with such wild surmise. Abigail, my dear, will you not prepare me some of that excellent India tea Cousin Hetty procured for us?" He patted her hand. Abigail sped out of the room.

I realized he had sent her away on purpose so I waited until she was out of hearing. "I don't think it's so wild a surmise," I protested. "Both ministers preached against the government."

"We have no proof, no connection," Mather said.

Creasy spoke up. "The Secretary said one of the men who attacked the captains is a farmer from Rumney Marsh. Do you know who that might be?"

I shook my head. "Our people are law-abiding, our farmers honest men," I protested. I would not accuse any of my countrymen until I had time to make inquiries. "What are we to do next?" I looked at each man in turn.

"Creasy, you will manage things for me, I'm sure." Mather rose from his chair. "Come—your hand, Cousin. If you'll help me to my bed, I should like to take my tea there."

Creasy jumped up, nearly as anxious as Abigail to please the man.

"What am I to do?" I called out.

"Stay home," Creasy grunted.

Mather, leaning heavily upon his cousin's shoulder, smirked. "My dear Cousin Henry," he said, "we appreciate your concern . . . 'tis womanly concern that does you honor. We hope we shall soon dispel your fears. I shall send my cousin Increase to you so that he may discover the identity of the second miscreant. I'm sure you will see to his comfort with your usual hospitality. If you'll excuse me, my dear . . . ." He hobbled from the room upon the arm of his obsequious companion.

Oh yes, I thought, I'll see to his comfort. I'll put burrs in his bed; I'll feed him toad, I'll pour molasses over him and stake him near a beehive . . . . Cheered by these thoughts, I took my tea with Abigail while the two scions of the Saints plotted upstairs.

"Dear Abby—you're looking uncommonly well these days," I observed. (In truth, she was.)

My cousin blushed with her usual modesty.

"Yours is such a sweet nature—why, 'tis no wonder your husband's cousin is devoted to you!"

She looked up in innocence. "Creasy? Why, he has always been a comfort to us. He is the only one my husband can turn to in his adversity, what with Father Mather away in London."

"And you depend upon him, I know."

She blushed roses. "If you mean to rebuke me, Cousin Hetty, I do reproach myself for what must appear to be undue familiarity with Creasy . . . Cousin Increase. It's just that we have been so overset lately . . . ." Her pretty eyes began to tear.

I reached over to pat her hand. "No, no, Cousin—I could not rebuke you. I have no doubts at all upon your devotion to your husband." (I almost wished I had.) "It is hardly your fault, so lovely and sweet as you are, that a young, impressionable bachelor like your husband's cousin should admire you." (Lest her face catch fire, I hurried on.) "And it's hardly to be wondered that you send for him. Creasy does indeed work miracles upon your husband's spirits!"

Her eyes shone. "Yes, he does—they spent summers together as children, you know. They are really close as brothers," she confided.

"But I am also here for you to call upon, Abigail, should you need me," I assured her. "Perhaps it would be wise to turn *to* a woman's counsels, rather than to encourage the admiration of a young, single gentleman, unwitting as that may be."

"Oh, Hetty!" Abigail cried in real distress.

"No, no, I do not scold, Abby—not in the least. I just think it wise that you should call upon me in the future, rather than Cousin Increase. There are those tongue-waggers in this town . . . ." I hinted. "Do you not agree with the wisdom of this course of action?"

She nodded, unable to speak.

"I am only in Rumney Marsh, you know. You have only to send a message and I will fly to you. Tell you what . . . ." I had an inspiration. "You must write to me daily with the news of Town— who comes to see your husband, what they speak of, what plans are made to catch the rogues who attacked our good citizens . . . . And I shall help Increase Cotton in his investigations in Rumney Marsh. If we women work together, Dear Cousin, we can relieve your poor husband of much of his burdens. Would that not please you?"

Abigail threw me a look of gratitude. "I should like that, Hetty," she whispered.

"Good," I smiled. "That's settled."

We'd just see who'd discover what about what.

Back at the Royal Governor's grand home the two young ministers were not forgotten. Edward Ruckenmaul slapped a brown leather glove against the arm of his chair. Behind heavy lids, his eyes were keen upon Andros.

"So . . . . I may assure the man he has your protection?" The Royal Governor gave a curt nod. His plump fingers were busy tying a ribbon around a packet of papers. "If the rogue has done us service, as you say . . . . I'm not in the habit of abandoning my people, no matter what lies these contentious Dissenters preach of me."

"He's removed several impediments in our way as it is,"

Ruckenmaul purred. "One may count upon the creature for any kind of vile work. Yes, he is definitely useful to us."

"Then tell him he has my protection, so long as he is discrete. I'll have no more stabbings. You understand me?"

"Oh, he'll keep his mouth shut and his knife sheathed, I'll see to that." Ruckenmaul took up a three-cornered hat, fingering its band.

"If only I could shut the Mather mouth," the Royal Governor sighed. "Here's a new one to plague me, the insolent cub! Spout French at me, will he? They think I would betray my King and sell these colonies to the French . . . hah! I must say, it was your idea to use the Jesuit priests as intermediaries with the Eastern tribes." Andros glared at his Secretary. "Here I am, trying to solve the Indian troubles through negotiation and all I get for it is an accusation of treason!"

Ruckenmaul shrugged. "The use of the priests makes sense. They have a great deal of influence with the bloody savages."

"We're not dealing with sensible men," Andros complained. "These Dissenters are more afraid of the Jesuits than they are of the Indians."

"Then leave them to the hatchets of the heathen, Governor, and small loss. As to the Mathers . . . that lot is as slippery as eels. Still, I'll think on it. I'll think on it." Ruckenmaul turned the brim of his hat, considering all three corners.

The Governor rose, collecting the packet of papers from the desk. "Come, Mister Ruckenmaul, we've kept the council waiting.

Ruckenmaul hauled himself to his feet. "I'll speak to the rogue from Rumney Marsh. By the way," he drawled, "the lout has a pretty sister to plead for him."

"Has he indeed?" The Royal Governor, a widower, pricked up his ears. "Tell me . . . do you think an introduction might be arranged—"

Life was lonely for a Governor in the hostile territory of Boston. He'd far rather face the dreaded Iroquois in the forests of the New York colony than these Dissenting rogues. At least the natives of the Five Nations were polite and well mannered in conference and would listen to reason. They understood the protocol of governing, those fearsome allies of the English crown. Nor did they spout French at a fellow. Sir Edmund Andros sighed aloud. This town was full of saucy-tongued rapscallions. No respect, not even for their King!

Chapter Thirteen

Creasy found himself once again on the road to Rumney Marsh He'd left Cotton Mather to rest with the consolation of India tea, a plant whose balsamick and medicinal virtues Mather must expound upon to his cousin before Creasy could escape. They'd agreed that Creasy should make this trip; if he could connect Edward Ruckenmaul with the attacks upon Captains Bezoum and Moon by this planter's testimony, a magistrate's warrant for Ruckenmaul's arrest would put an end to the man's machinations. It might even lead to the murderer or murderers of the two ministers.

He'd had a time convincing Cotton that neither devils nor witchcraft were responsible for those deaths; he had not totally convinced his cousin that Ruckenmaul was behind the murders, although the actual hand might not be that villain's. He'd had no problem, however, convincing Cotton that his own life might be in danger, that he should stay indoors and wait for Creasy to come back.

As he urged his mare to a dignified trot, body rising and settling in the saddle with easy grace, Creasy frowned at the memory of the square jawed, caterpillar-browed Ruckenmaul. Who had more reason to silence the poor Ipswich minister than the Secretary of the Provinces? Absalom Lott dared attack the man in a printed pamphlet, accusing him of graft and publicly vilifying him. Lott had stirred up a veritable insurrection when the town of Ipswich refused to pay the illegal taxes Ruckenmaul levied. Neither Ruckenmaul nor the Royal Governor could allow that kind of insubordination.

Look what happened to Uncle Increase! He'd attacked the Secretary from the pulpit of Second Church and Ruckenmaul sent his spies to arrest Increase Mather, Boston's leading citizen. Uncle Increase only escaped arrest by donning a disguise and fleeing into the night. And who provided the sloop that carried him to a ship bound for London? The minister of Rumney Marsh, Naboth Chieves, who was found dead weeks later with his head bashed in. Coincidence? Even that saucy swineherd Hetty Henry spotted the connection.

Not that she was stupid, Creasy tolerantly conceded. Hetty had a brain as sharp as her tongue. No, Cousin Cotton had an ingrained reluctance to point a finger at an officer of the Crown— well, that could lead to hardships, granted—but who had more reason to silence his opponents than Edward Ruckenmaul? He would lose his lucrative position, his contempt for the men of Massachusetts Bay was open, and any man who set his minions to stab honest citizens was evil enough to set them upon two defiant ministers. What he needed was proof, however—proof strong enough for the magistrates to arrest a powerful official. Proof so indisputable the Royal Governor could not intervene. He hoped to find that proof in Rumney Marsh.

Creasy found himself reining in beside the neat, five-rail fence of Deacon Lamb's farm. The hardy old man was in sight, chopping away at a fallen tree trunk. "Hi—Deacon!" Creasy called.

The old man whacked away at the log, making deep cuts in the wood with a sharp bladed axe. White chips flew in all directions. At Creasy's third call he suspended his swing and turned around. His face was a deep pink; sweat beaded his forehead. He screwed up his eyes to locate the source of the call.

"What is it?" he asked. "Oh . . . Mister Cotton, of the funeral. Will you go inside the house, Sir? I'll be done with this log in no time." He pointed with the axe to a neat pile of wood.

"Thank you no, Sir," Creasy called over the fence. "I ask only a moment of your time."

Deacon Lamb set down the axe. He took out a square of white linen, pausing to dab at his face before he walked over to the fence, a look of inquiry in his shrewd blue eyes. "Won't ye come into the house?" he urged. "Why, my wife will draw you a mug of cider and set out a plate of cakes for you. There's not a goodwife keeps a prouder table than Misses Lamb."

"Thank you, no," Creasy repeated, tempted by the offer of refreshment and the company of Mistress Lamb, a woman reputed to be most amiable. "I won't trouble you . . . ."

"Why it's no trouble at all. She'll be glad of the company. My wife's an exceptional friendly woman, Mister Cotton."

"Yes, I'm sure she must be, but . . . ."

"She sets a fine table," Deacon Lamb continued, ignoring Creasy's polite attempt to decline the invitation, "and she's handsome to look upon, with it all. Her price is above rubies."

"Oh, I'm sure your wife is a gem," Creasy agreed, "but I only wanted to ask . . . ."

"She was most impressed with the funeral sermon," the Deacon remarked. She was not there herself—womanly nerves, you know. She had her friend take notes for her. She said as she'd like to meet the author of that sermon."

"That's kind of her. I trust you completed your business with the estate?" Creasy resigned himself to a chat with the good old man, although he must resist a visit to the house. It was time to locate and speak to the witness, if he could only keep the Deacon's attention.

"There's a whopper of a probate fee for the estate," the Deacon complained, wiping his face and folding the handkerchief into a neat square. "Those royal scoundrels have raised the fee fifty-fold—it's unfair, but we'll have to pay it. My wife will be glad to see ye—why don't you go within?" he pressed.

"Why, that's very hospitable of you, but I'm afraid I have business to attend. Perhaps on the way back . . . ." Creasy hemmed.

"All right, then I'll tell her that you'll stop by. Now, how can I help ye?" He leaned against the fence, eyeing Creasy.

At last, Creasy sighed, the old man had come to the point.

"I'm looking for a planter from Rumney Marsh—one who

took part in a brawl in Boston the night before last. I must talk to him. Do you know of anyone here who might have been involved in an altercation in town?"

The Deacon shook his frosty head. "No honest planter would go brawling about the town—but it might be young Tom Pisspot. He's neither a planter nor honest, the shiftless scoundrel, and as like to spend a night in the goal as any quarrelsome whoreson."

Creasy thought of the old woman. "Gammar Piscopot's son?" he wondered.

"Like as not," the Deacon frowned in disapproval.

"Could you give me directions to his home?" Creasy asked. "I have to speak to the man."

"The witch's spawn?" the Deacon frowned. "Best not go near him, Mister Cotton—he's a liar and a villain." Deacon Lamb pounded his hand against the fence rail to emphasize his disdain.

Creasy shrugged as if it could not be helped and repeated his request for directions.

"I'd best go with ye," the Deacon grunted. He tramped back to the woodpile for his coat and cane while Creasy waited.

Creasy followed on horseback as the old man strode off, his walking staff thrust forward, pointing the way. Flocks of pigeons circled high overhead, the meadows shone with new grasses, carpets of tiny blue pissabeds softened banks on both sides of the dirt road. The air was soft and sweet with spring. Creasy was touched with pity at the thought that the two ministers, cut down in their primes, would never know such wonders again.

"Where did it happen, Deacon?" Creasy called out, curious. "Where was Mister Chieves's body found?"

"Why, on this very path. about a league from the witch's den. I'll show ye," the Deacon answered without turning his head or pausing in his march.

This fellow—the brother of Mistress Piscopot—he sounded like an idle rascal. If he'd taken part in the brawl, could he be persuaded to testify against Edward Ruckenmaul's man? It was obvious that Ruckenmaul had sent his exciseman off in a hurry, to avoid the law. If he could only prove a connection between

Ruckenmaul and the stabbings . . . . Creasy felt sure he was close to the key that would unlock many mysteries.

Ahead of him the Deacon made a sudden stop; he swung his stick in an abrupt arc. "Here 'twas," he scowled.

Creasy leaned forward in the saddle. There was nothing here but a few trees, some bright budded bushes and patches of yellow cowslips. This was marshy land, hardly the desolate deep forest he'd imagined as the scene of the attack. True enough there was no shelter close by, yet neither was the road beneath him hard and rocky. Where, he wondered idly, was a rock big enough to smash in the side of a man's head to be found? There were small stones on the road such as an old woman's weak hands might manage . . . . He shrugged and dug a heel into his mare, following the Deacon's onward march.

The Piscopot homestead was a long, low building of weathered clapboard; the roof sagged, exposing gaps of missing shingles. Unkempt bushes surrounded the house; a few chickens scratched about the large rock that served as a front step. Yet clouds of pink and white outlined the building from a profusion of sturdy apple trees in blough. With a little shoring and proper care, Creasy thought, the place might be made very cozy a spot. He dismounted, tying his mare to a bush.

Deacon Lamb stood on the dirt path and hollered lustily: "Tom Pisspot, ye rascal, come out, Sir! Come out, I say!"

"Who is it wants me?" came a belligerent cry from the dim interior of the shack.

Creasy stepped back a pace, unconsciously distancing himself from his companion. He had thought to knock upon the door first. Perhaps these were country ways.

Deacon Lamb pounded his walking stick upon the ground. "Don't argue with your betters, ye idle, thieving whoreson! Come out at once!"

Silence. Creasy gazed about.

"Cowardly lout," the Deacon sniffed.

Was the man going to appear at this impolitic summons? Creasy wondered whether Tom Piscopot was indeed as cowardly as the Deacon seemed to believe. He shifted his weight from one foot to another. A missile whizzed past his ear. The family trait must include throwing rocks at people, he thought in annoyance, spinning about to catch sight of the lout who greeted visitors in so unneighborly a fashion.

A green-coated, hulking giant emerged from the bushes to his right. The giant had a long face with a hooked nose and bold eyes; he had long arms and long hands that held a long wooden truncheon.

"Aha! So there ye be, ye thieving, skulking dog." The Deacon bristled like a terrier. "Brawling again, are ye? Where were ye but two nights last? Answer me that, will ye?" he demanded.

The giant raised his truncheon in a greeting that made clear his dislike of such summary questioning. "Get off my land," he ordered, with a trace of brogue that reminded Creasy of the old woman's whine in the Rumney Marsh jail.

As the giant advanced in slow, threatening paces, Creasy retreated three steps.

Deacon Lamb stood his ground, growling: "Don't be a fool, ye great booby. We'll have the law on ye."

Creasy, eyeing the oak club in the giant's hand, attempted to mediate. The Deacon's manner was a trifle abrupt, after all. "I have only come to ask you some questions," he called out, "I did not mean to disturb your peace."

"Get off my land," the giant repeated, the green-sleeved arm raised even higher.

The Deacon waved his own walking stick, a pale shaft of solid hickory. "Be nice to the gentleman," he commanded, "or we'll have the law on ye!"

"Be nice to the gentleman," the giant mimicked, turning his attention to Creasy. "I'll answer the gentleman's damned questions with this," he threatened, with a wave of the truncheon.

Creasy raised his fists, crouching in a defensive position, awaiting the rush. The green clad giant lumbered towards him, unswerving. Creasy dodged a clout, feeling the breeze from the truncheon's arc. He butted in with his head against a dirty waistcoat, his arms grappling around the giant's huge waist. He attempted to plant his feet for a throw. The giant's great legs did not budge, even with the full force of Creasy's body. Creasy felt himself being lifted from the ground. There was a sensation of weightlessness, a rush of air, a sharp cry that sounded high and shrill, and Creasy knew no more.

Chapter Fourteen

"Now see what you've done . . . ."

The woman's scolding penetrated Creasy's consciousness. He tried to apologize for whatever it was he'd done to vex her but couldn't get the words out. A strange ringing in his ears interfered so that he couldn't hear what he was saying.

"He's coming around," the voice murmured. "You may go now."

Creasy opened his eyes. Go? Go where? He couldn't seem to move and his breath came in wheezes.

Two dark eyes looked down upon him; he saw the heavens reflected there. "Are you an angel, Madam?" he managed to croak.

The heavens smiled down upon him.

"You've broken no bones, only had the wind knocked out of you." The vision spoke with angelic calm. Dark tresses framed a face carved from ivory. "Do you know me, Sir?" she asked.

"I believe so," Creasy said, bemused.

"Who am I?" the vision pressed.

"Persephone, come to bring beauty to the earth once more." He was content to gaze in open wonder at the stars that shimmered from the black depths of her eyes. Oh, brown comets circled black planets there . . . .

"Mister Cotton, collect yourself, please," the sweet voice urged. "Tell me, what is my name?"

"Why, not gentle Persephone?" A winged brow rose in mock dismay at her questioning. "Helen, then . . . beauteous belle of

Troy. They say she is fair, but I think her hair is black as a raven's wing and her eyes . . . dark as the sky over Delphi." Creasy reached up, capturing a dark curl upon his finger and twirling it in wonder.

A slender hand swept the curl away from her face. "Your wits are addled, Sir." She shook her head in pity. "I cannot let you leave in such a state."

"Ah, wise Deborah, prophetess and leader of armies. *Sing me a song, oh Deborah, a song of thanksgiving,*" Creasy quoted Biblical text. He struggled into a sitting position, an involuntary groan escaping from his lips as his stiff limbs responded with resistance.

"Where am I?" He rubbed his head and discovered a bump as large as an egg there.

Deborah Piscopot stood before him. "You are in my mother's house," she said. "I'm sorry my brother was so rough with you. I'd have prevented it, if I'd known you were coming. Why did you not inform me?"

Creasy rubbed his sore head, wincing at the pain his own fingers caused. "I didn't know I was coming here. Deacon Lamb brought me. I only wanted to ask your brother some questions. Where is the Deacon?" he asked, suddenly reminded of his companion. He squinted in the dim light, seeking another injured body.

"He took your horse and rode for the constable," Deborah said.

He noted her indifferent tone and calm demeanor. She must be used to the consternation caused by her brother.

"I'm sorry, I didn't mean to make trouble like this," he apologized.

Deborah shrugged slender shoulders. "My brother will survive another night in jail." She reached over and produced a pewter mug, which vessel she offered to Creasy.

He thought her fingers like ivory vines as they twined around the handle.

"Brandy," she said. "Drink it."

Creasy accepted the mug and took a long sip of the liquid. A golden warmth spread from his throat down through his limbs.

"This is good!" He looked up in surprise.

"My brother has a few bottles hidden away. It's the least we can offer you, to make amends."

Creasy glanced around the room in sudden unease. Where was the big oaf, anyway?

"Tom's gone," she said, understanding his look. "They'll have to catch up with him before they can arrest him."

Creasy took another sip from the mug and relaxed. "I didn't mean for this to happen," he said. "Someone from Rumney Marsh was involved in a brawl in town the other night. Deacon Lamb thought it might be your brother. I only wanted to question him, to hear his version of the events that took place. Do you know if it was him?"

"I don't know. It's a likely possibility." Deborah spoke with indifference

"Perhaps he'll cooperate when he's put in jail," Creasy grumbled, touching his head with sensitive fingertips.

Deborah took his mug without comment and refilled it.

"Thank you." Creasy accepted the mug with gratitude. His aches seemed to have lessened, his guts to have stabilized with the infusion of good brandy.

"Sit and recover for awhile," Deborah said. "I'll go tell the constable he's too late for Tom."

"What, is the constable here?" Creasy had not heard the arrival of the rescue party.

Deborah touched him lightly upon the shoulder before she moved away, her skirts rustling, leaving a scent of roses in her wake.

The light was dim in the room. Creasy nursed his drink, staring at tiny blue flames that crept along a charred log in the hearth The house smelled of smoke and mold, with the musty damp of an abandoned building. Missing here were the sounds of sizzling meats over the hearthfire, the heady aroma of baking breads and pies, the banging of pans, the clatter of spoons. Still, he reflected, the brandy was quality. Who'd have thought the big oaf had such discerning tastes? A glow of well being filled him. He might as well stay here with Deborah until his head recovered its wits . . . which might not be for hours. Then he'd claim his mount from Deacon Lamb and go to Boston for an arrest warrant. He hoped Deborah would understand; he had to question her brother, it was essential.

Creasy could hear voices outside now. Perhaps they've captured Pisspot, the lout, he thought. He'd make the great booby sit in jail until he returned from Boston, that's what he'd do. Pisspot deserved to sit in jail and ponder his attack upon a minister of the Lord. Creasy's body jerked at the notion: if Pisspot did not hesitate to attack one minister, might not he have attacked two others?

Creasy forced himself to rise and drag his stiffening limbs over to the window by the front door. With his coatsleeve he smudged a space clear in the dirty glass and peered out.

Deacon Lamb stood upon the road, holding the reins of Creasy's horse. The Deacon's face was pink from shouting.

"Ye can't arrest him, it's the wrong man!"

The Deacon stood defiant before an English trooper in scarlet and blue uniform. The trooper sat upright in the saddle of a brown horse coated with sweat.

"We have our orders," the trooper answered in an icy voice.

"Show me the warrant, then," the Deacon demanded.

"Who are you?" The trooper raised haughty brows, daring the country lumpkin to challenge his authority.

"I am Deacon of the church here," Deacon Lamb snapped. "This man's the constable of the town. He has the authority to arrest that man there."

Creasy followed the Deacon's gnarled finger, which pointed to Tom Pisspot, standing behind the trooper. The bully was nearly blocked from Creasy's sight by the trooper's mount. Pisspot stepped around the horse and grinned at Deacon Lamb.

"This man is under our authority, he is not subject to yours," the trooper sneered, looking down his nose at the old man.

"And I tell ye, Pisspot is the man who attacked us. Laid the minister in the dust, near killed the poor man, he did, the heathen scoundrel. We've come to arrest him." The Deacon's face deepened into a scarlet hue, his voice became shrill. He turned to a man who stood beside him.

"Constable, arrest that man!"

The constable of Rumney Marsh took one nervous step forward.

"Halt!" the trooper ordered. He made a motion and two men-at-arms moved quickly to block the constable.

"We have a warrant for the arrest of this man. It will be served." The trooper's voice was as grim as his face.

"But it's that man, there, that Pisspot," the Deacon insisted, shaking his fist at the green-coated giant. "Pisspot, ye thieving whoreson, ye'll not get away from me!"

The giant placed a broad thumb against a broad, hooked nose and waggled his fingers at the old man.

Creasy was tempted to chuckle but this was the oaf who waylaid him, who'd outweighed and outreached him and dropped him like a sack of flour.

The constable attempted to mediate with little success. The Deacon jabbered, the trooper sat like a statue, Pisspot lounged grinning by the horse. As he watched the scene, Creasy felt a strong tug upon his coattail. He turned to behold a flushed Deborah Piscopot.

"Come, you must leave here now, this moment." She kept hold of his coattail as she advised him. "There are troopers out there who have come to arrest you."

Creasy attempted to release her grasp with gentle fingers. "No . . . no . . . it's your brother they've come to arrest. They are fighting over who gets to do it. I'm sorry, but . . ."

"It's you they've come for," she insisted, dropping his coattail and grasping his sleeve. She pulled at the sleeve with such urgency that he fell forward. "It's something about 'treasonable utterances,' I overheard them. Now come with me!"

He stumbled after her, cursing as he went: "False

villains . . . Ruckenmaul and his dogs . . . face them with their perfidy . . . ."

She led him into an ell black as coal. He could not see a thing but followed her like a mole on a string. When she opened a small door, light flooded his eyes and he squinted. He faced a massive wall of brambles.

Deborah pressed her hands upon his shoulders and forced him to kneel. She swept down beside him, placing her mouth against his ear. "This is your chance to escape while they argue over you. Do you see this opening?"

He nodded, spotting a small arch in the prickly brush. Her sweet breath tickled him all the way to his groin; it felt a pleasant sensation.

"Go on through the brambles," she whispered. "You'll come out on the other side of the orchard. There's a path—you'll see it—that leads into the woods and comes out through the marsh to the ferry road. Get to the ferry. If Bob's not there, find your way to Mrs. Henry. I'll put a word in the Deacon's ear so they'll be on the lookout for you."

She withdrew her mouth; he wished she would put another word in *his* ear and leaned forward for that purpose. Instead he received a shove that sent him scrambling into the brambles.

Ignoring the thorny barbs, he turned back to her. "Perhaps I shouldn't run off . . . perhaps I should face them!" Why, would she think him a coward? He was no coward.

"Go on," she urged, frowning at him. "Take your freedom if you can. Too many have lost theirs."

On his hands and knees Creasy crawled through the bramble tunnel as quickly as he could. He ignored snags and scratches. He was not satisfied with this course of action but she, Deborah, had urged him on. He was in no condition to think for himself, between Pisspot's rough treatment and the strong, but oh so soothing drink! He should have expected to be arrested, after defying the Royal Governor with Cousin Cotton Mather. Cousin Cotton would be safe as long as he kept to his bed. Yet this attempt to arrest him came as a shock.

"Treachery," he mumbled, "toads . . . tricks," Yes, they'd tried their tricks upon Increase Mather and Uncle Increase outfoxed 'em. The thought cheered Creasy. Deborah was right to urge his escape; what could he prove against Edward Ruckenmaul from a prison cell?

Creasy emerged from the brush and picked up the path into the woods. He trotted along what was little more than a deer trail; it twisted and wound through a ravine filled with decayed brush. He jumped a tiny creek and climbed over logs, all the while dodging branches and listening for sounds of pursuit. English troopers were easy to hear; their jingling spurs and clanking sabers gave warning as they crashed through the woods. Only the warble of the thrush and the harsh cry of the jay broke the forest silence.

The trail left the safety of the woods and led into the marsh; tall stalks of brittle age-yellowed grasses and shoots of new green reeds towered over Creasy's head as he bent, parting the grasses before him. His boots left puddles of water as he crept forward past whorls of straw made by bedding deer. Keeping his head down, he snaked through the grasses. How brave of Deborah of warn him, to help him escape! She had her own troubles to consider . . . . He had not asked her how her mother fared, but perhaps the old woman would have the company of her son in jail.

Recalling Tom Pisspot and the fall he'd taken at that giant's hands, Creasy felt indignant. He could take care of himself in a fair fight, but the giant had his advantage in weight, height and reach. The wrestling holds he'd learned in his Plymouth youth were useless against legs like tree trunks and a waist like an oak barrel. Even giants had their Achilles heels—or their Goliath foreheads, in David's case. If he ever learned Pisspot's weak spot, how the mighty would fall!

Creasy crouched before a wall of reeds. He heard noises beyond; instinct urged him to caution. This must be the ferry road. The less people who saw him there, the better. He'd trust Bob Stubb to get him away to Ipswich, where he was sure the Selectmen would stand by him until he could get the warrant for his arrest quashed. The Boston magistrates would see to it; they were no friends of the Royal Governor.

The whoosh of a horse's muzzle broke the silence. Creasy froze. Someone was on the road ahead. He crouched down and wiggled through the reeds, parting the screen with care.

A trooper in scarlet and blue stood upon the road, leaning against his horse. One gloved hand rested upon the animal's thick brown mane. The other hand raised a leather flask to the trooper's mouth. It was obvious that the man had been posted upon the road long enough to become bored The road to the ferry was blocked, unless there was a way to sneak past. Creasy thought it the wiser course to head for Hetty Henry's and confer with her there. Perhaps she could think of a way for him to escape; she knew this country well. She would have noted the trooper posted here; she would know if other troopers were abroad. How badly did the Governor and his toad of a Secretary want to arrest him, anyway? He'd hardly said a word to them. His crime was keeping the company of Cotton Mather. Creasy beamed at the recollection of his cousin's bravery. It took courage to stand up to Tyrant Andros.

Creasy squatted upon his haunches, patient and willing to wait for the trooper to move on. Perhaps the man would get so bored he would ride to the ferry, then Creasy could cross the road. He could find his way to Hetty's farm, if he could only get to the other side of that road. He'd remember the way from his first encounter with that woman. Creasy's head felt fuzzy; he should not dwell on his first meeting with Hetty Henry, he decided. Better off to just wait and watch the road and not think at all.

The trooper seemed content to nip at his flask. The horse swished its tail and made another whoosh through its nostrils. As he watched, Creasy saw the reeds across the road quiver and shake. Was someone watching from that side? Friend or foe? Was this an opportunity to cross? Creasy felt a swell of excitement; he crouched, balanced on tiptoe, ready to move at a second's notice.

The reeds swayed like an ocean wave then exploded apart as a horrid snarl rent the air. A huge, tawny hide hurled itself straight at the unsuspecting trooper. The horse reared in fright, jerking the reins from the trooper's careless glove. The gallant mount thundered down the road towards the ferry. The trooper found himself sitting hard upon the dirt, his flask extended like a torch in the air, while a snarling, red-eyed monster descended upon him. The trooper reacted instantly, rolling to his knees, finding his footing and stumbling after his mount. Clumsy boots and clanking scabbard hindered his flight; he turned and threw his flask at the beast, which was hard upon him. Fortune favored the trooper, for the beast stopped to sniff and to lick at the liquid puddle that spread out upon the dirt.

Stifling his laughter with an effort, Creasy leaped across the road and dived into the opposite reeds. He whispered blessings upon his savior, Priscilla the Pig.

BETHLEHEM HISTORICAL ASSOCIATION

Susan Leath, Corresponding Secretary

Thursday, March 17, 2005 7:30 PM
"Naughty Puritans & Saintly Sinners"
Marilyn Kemp Rothstein
Author and Lecturer

Meeting at the Cedar Hill Schoolhouse
1003 River Road, Selkirk

NON-PROFIT
ORGANIZATION
U.S. POSTAGE PAID
DELMAR, NY
PERMIT NO. 52

BETHLEHEM HISTORICAL ASSOCIATION
Cedar Hill Schoolhouse
1003 River Road
Selkirk, New York 12158

RETURN SERVICE REQUESTED

Carol & John Dana
39 Elm Avenue E
Selkirk, NY 12158

Chapter Fifteen

I hid in the ell while the fugitive from arrest lingered in plain sight in my barnyard. I fumed. Was the man mad, coming here in plain daylight? What should I do? So many lives would depend upon my action . . . I watched him in growing dismay. There he stood, by my milk cow, which was tethered only feet away. He seemed to be contemplating the cow, which placidly chewed upon new green shoots of grass. I prayed and my prayers were answered. The unsuspecting felon turned his back upon me; he was now close enough for me to strike.

"Where have you been?" I reached out and yanked at Creasy's coattails, pulling him bodily into the ell. He stumbled backwards into me. I admit to letting out a curse as he stepped upon my toe, but I hope I may be forgiven because the man had caused me so much worry, I was in a distressed state.

"What . . . ? Who?" he gasped.

The ell was black as pitch; I had brought no candle with me as I certainly did not wish to be seen with him. "It's me, Hetty Henry," I hissed. "We've got to get you hidden." I switched my grasp from his coattail to his sleeve. He stumbled after me in the dark, his clumsy boots causing the rats to run for their lives. I heard their tiny scratch-scratches as they scrambled away. Creasy heard them, too, for he made a fearful noise in his throat.

"Better these rats than the ones who are after you," I noted. If there was a hint of bitterness in my tone, why who could blame me? He'd brought trouble right to my door. Still, it was my duty to save the poor man and I intended to keep him from the clutches of that villain, Edward Ruckenmaul.

Creasy started to speak but I shushed him, hurrying him along the passage to the kitchen doorstep, where I stopped, reached to open the door and moved aside, whispering to him:

"Watch the step, mind you." I shoved him through. He made the step but bumped his head upon the low lintel and let out a cry of pain.

Zillah looked up as she stood over the table making pie crust. I placed a finger over my mouth to silence her and bundled my prisoner over to the staircase and up to the little bedroom that was Zillah's own. We had done this before, days ago; I was tempted to smile at the recollection but too much of a serious nature had happened since his first visit here. Instead I slammed the door to the little room shut and turned to face him.

"Where have you been?" I repeated, crossing my arms for the interrogation. "We've been waiting for you. The troopers are swarming around here like bees to a hive—we expect them any minute and you stroll across the yard as if you were out smarming with your sweetheart! Have you any idea what's going on here?"

"I looked before I came into the yard," Creasy began.

"Don't try to defend yourself, I saw you," I interrupted. "You stood around by the barn in plain sight for anyone to see. Honestly, Increase Cotton, have you no sense at all? Do you wish to be arrested like a common felon? Are you hurt? Did you lose your way? What took you so long to get here? I was afraid they'd captured you!"

"Hetty . . . Mistress Henry . . . ." Creasy batted away the finger that waved in his face. "You're making me dizzy. I am unhurt, although that great lout Tom Pisspot knocked me down. The road to the ferry is blocked, that's what delayed me. How did you know to look for me?"

I took his hand in mine and pressed it, relieved that he was safe. "Deacon Lamb came by," I said. 'You don't know what a worry it's been, not knowing whether you were captured or not."

"Where is the Deacon now?" Creasy patted my own hand with his free one, as if to reassure me.

"Gone to Boston on your behalf, and to have Tom Pisspot arrested. He left his wife here with me. Did the big lout hurt you?" I could see an unusual bump on the side of the gentleman's head. He backed away as I reached up to touch it, snatching his hand from mine.

"I'll survive. No bones broken," he said. "How long has the Deacon been gone?"

"Nearly thirty minutes, I think. Are you sure you're not injured? Can I look at that bump for you?"

"You can help me get to the ferry," Creasy said, fending me off with his hand. "I've got to get word to Cousin Cotton. Is there another way there?"

I lifted a finger to my lips. I had excellent hearing and I thought I heard a grumbling outside. Creasy stiffened; he looked pale. I judged that the adventure was taking its toll upon him. I ran over to the window and stooped down to look. He followed and knelt by my side.

Three troopers in scarlet and blue coats rode into the yard, scattering my ducks and chickens. My resolve hardened at the sight. Creasy must be saved at any cost.

"Stay put. I'll handle this," I ordered. I laid a hand briefly upon his sleeve to reassure him, then I rose to leave the room. "I'll send Rachel Lamb to you with some food as soon as it's safe," I promised.

I ran out of the room and down the stairs. slamming the bar across the door and locking Creasy inside. I paused to shake out my petticoats and to pull a few curls loose from my cap. I nodded to Zillah; she knew what she was to do. I took a deep breath and stepped out the kitchen door.

The troopers dismounted with a great deal of jingling of spurs and clanking of sabers. There is something attractive about military men, I thought, as I pasted a smile upon my face and floated across the yard to greet them. I managed to show a glimpse of ankle as the breeze stirred my skirts; the gentlemen noticed, I am sure. They bowed, all three, as I reached out my hand.

I curtsied. "Gentlemen, it's such a relief to see you!"

The sergeant of the troop moved forward, his gait awkward and rolling, like a man who spends much time on horseback.

"Ma'am?" he said.

I curtsied for him alone, raising my skirts just a token. I thought a simper appropriate.

"Sir, we are two weak women here, with no husband about to protect us and we've heard such horrid tales of dangerous men loose . . . . I cannot tell you how pleased we are that you have come!" I looked up into his face and batted my lashes; the gentleman had the grace to blush.

"Mistress Hetty Henry, Sir." I offered my hand, which he accepted and bowed over.

Zillah came up beside me; she carried a tray with a foaming pitcher of ale and three tankards balanced there. The troopers accepted the brew with obvious relish. They'd ridden far and hard, they said, as they introduced themselves.

"Sirs, will you take a little supper before dark falls? Some cold beef and cheese, perhaps? Oh, do say you'll join us for a bite . . . . You must be hungry and tired, I dare say, and thirsty, too. My servant Zillah, here, brews the best ale of anyone in the county, I'm sure." I noted how fast they'd quaffed their ale. Zillah refilled their tankards twice—and it was true about Zillah's talent.

"Sergeant?" I tilted my head with my prettiest smile, waiting for his answer.

Creasy watched from the window, incredulous, as Hetty Henry motioned the men towards the house. Yes, she was actually inviting them in! What was wrong with the woman? Was he betrayed? He hadn't trusted her from the first. Creasy glanced around the room for means of defense but there was only the wash basin, which he might break over someone's head before they subdued him. He returned to the window. One trooper led the sweating horses into the barn. The other two followed Hetty into the house.

Creasy folded his arms with dignity and stood, waiting. He listened. No assault upon the stairs followed, no clankings and janglings of sabers drawn . . . . Why did they delay? He pulled off his boots and crept in stockinged feet down the staircase. Of course, they had ample time to decide how best to attack him, since he was helpless in a trap, thanks to that woman. He'd heard the solid clank as the bar fell into place locking him in. Caught like a rat in a basket, he thought, a knot forming in his gut. He placed an ear against the door.

A woman's voice came sweet and clear to him—it was not Hetty's bossy tone, it must be the Deacon's wife.

"Oh Sergeant, I am so glad you could join us. You must be hungry and tired, I dare say. It is such a comfort to have a man about the place. My husband is from home just now, and here are we poor, weak women . . . ."

Creasy wrinkled his nose in disgust; Hetty Henry was not his idea of a poor weak woman. He didn't know about Mrs. Lamb.

Hetty's voice rang out loud and clear. "Let me refill your mug, Sir. Zillah, please draw another jug of ale for the gentlemen." There—that commanding tone, that was more like the Hetty Henry he knew.

Creasy heard the scraping of chairs, the clatter of pots and pans, with more female simperings. He couldn't make out the words but he could hear the simperings. What was Hetty thinking, inviting the troopers who were out to arrest him, into the house to dine? Was she strengthening the men to attack him? What was wrong with that woman? He pressed his ear against the door in frustration.

The troopers kept a civil tone, although he not hear their words. They did not seem ready to seek him out yet.

The melodic tones of the Deacon's wife danced about the kitchen hither and yon. "Oh Sergeant, how kind! La, Sir . . . . More meat, Sir? More of that pie?"

Meat and pie? His stomach bean to churn. What next, 'Oh Sergeant, surely you'll help yourself to a little of that prisoner trapped upstairs?'

He heard Hetty direct Zillah to carry a platter of food and a fresh pitcher of ale for the trooper left in the barn to care for the horses. Oh certainly, he thought, consider the poor trooper's welfare. Here was he, stuck behind the door, while they ate in shameless and merry abandon! Women's laughter rang out like bells. He could hear the rustle of skirts and petticoats. They approached the other side of the door and stopped. He held his breath—was it come then, the moment of betrayal?

Chapter Sixteen

Creasy, his ear glued to the door, grew tired of listening to silly giggles and hearty male guffaws. The two women cooed with shameless flattery over the two troopers; they would give him away by overdoing it. His feet were cold upon the floorboards. His head ached. The troopers were not about to leave, but he seemed in no immediate danger . . . unless it was from dyspepsia caused by the women's false simpering. He turned and climbed noiselessly back up the stairs.

Creasy sat down upon the black and green checked coverlet. His head throbbed. He leaned back with care for his wounded head. 'Might as well rest a spell,' he thought. No way of knowing how long he'd be cooped up in this room. He'd just recruit his strength in case he had to defend himself; no harm in that.

"Mister Cotton! Increase Cotton!"

Creasy mumbled his annoyance; someone was shaking him; his shoulders bounced up and down. Couldn't a man take a nap? He forced open one eyelid. Above him was a pointed little chin and lips that curved like a cupid's bow. Who was she? Where was he? Two sparkling blue eyes laughed at him as she rudely shook him awake.

"What cool courage," the vision cooed, "falling asleep while the enemy dines below."

Creasy's brain felt befogged. Why was he here? Oh yes, he'd been trapped—he recalled the circumstances now.

"The troopers? Where are they? Who invited them in to dine?" He could not hide his indignation.

"Mrs. Henry," the woman above him giggled.

"Why did she do that? Where are they, anyhow?" He rose on one elbow, peering about the room, expecting the troopers to pop out from the under the bed, sabers bared.

"They are safely tucked away, Sir," The woman's laughter sang out like sleigh bells. "You needn't fear them."

"What has she done with them? What does she intend for me?" he asked, sitting up. No doubt the Delilah had fed the troopers with the sole aim of giving them the strength to arrest him. Most likely they were stationed upon the other side of the door, waiting for him in grim silence.

The woman read his doubts: "Don't worry about the troopers. It was Mrs. Henry's idea to fill their stomachs with food and drink! We plied them with libations until they became too drunk to chase you!"

"Thank the Lord they're gone!" Creasy sighed with relief.

She smiled smooth as pudding, satisfied as a cat with a bowl of cream. "Actually, they're bedded down in the barn for the night. Mrs. Henry insisted."

"What?" Creasy sat bolt upright.

"Mrs. Henry says we can keep an eye on them there. The woman giggled. "That way you won't bump into them on the road."

"I don't see why that's preferable," Creasy argued. "Now I won't even be able to get on the road. I'm trapped here, thanks to Mrs. Henry. What am I supposed to do?" He slumped back upon the pillow, feeling dejected. It was all too much!

The woman leaned over, patting his shoulder in consolation.

"Mrs. Henry says you are to wait until midnight. You can slip away then."

"But that won't be for hours yet," he protested, glancing at the dusky light out the window.

"Mrs. Henry says I am to keep you company. My name is Rachel Lamb, by the way. I have so much wanted to meet you, Mister Cotton! I've heard so much about you." She turned and stooped, lifting a cloth-covered tray from the floor.

"I've brought you some food and a bottle of wine." With one hand she whipped off the cloth and set the tray under his nose.

The smell of roast fowl made his mouth water. He settled the tray upon his lap without further argument and dug into the tender slices of chicken. There was a piece of minced meat pie to go with it, and several chunks of fried bread.

Rachel Lamb poured wine into an etched glass and handed it to him. She settled herself at the foot of the bed, watching Creasy eat without comment. When he'd polished off the contents of the tray, she reached over to the side table and handed him a bowl of corn meal pudding with molasses. She nodded in satisfaction as he dug into the bowl to the last spoonful He even licked the spoon.

"I had to set aside a plate for you or they'd have eaten everything in the kitchen," she said. "They ate all the beef. We've got a nice haunch of ham left at the house . . . I'll send Zillah for it in the morning."

"Well, whose fault is it if they did eat everything?" Creasy grumbled. He was not ready to forgive Hetty for that. "Who invited them in? 'Oh Sergeant, you must be hungry, a big strong man like you . . . . Oh Sergeant, I'm only a weak woman . . . .'" He mocked with savage humor.

"Could you hear us?" she giggled in delight. "Mrs. Henry thought you were there by the door, she thought you would guess what we were doing."

"It was a disgraceful performance," he growled.

"Well, the men were quite taken with me . . . and Mrs. Henry, of course," she said.

"More fools they," he snapped. "I would have been suspicious of you from the start, your simperings were so absurd."

"Mrs. Henry says there's not a man alive she can't charm into doing her biding. Give them a belly full of food, tell them how strong they are, and they're yours." She paused to reflect upon this, adding: "I must say, I have always found it so."

Creasy sniffed audibly. "I would have seen through that preposterous behavior, I assure you. But then, I am a minister, trained in logic."

Rachel Lamb pulled her knees together and tucked her feet

beneath her skirts. She eyed Creasy with fascination from the far end of the bed. "Mrs. Henry says that ministers are the first to succumb to flattery."

Creasy drew himself up, prepared for a sound disputation upon the topic. He set the tray aside.

"I don't agree with her, except that there are some ministers who are too unworldly in their innocence. Such good men may be drawn in by a woman's meekness, but not by flattery, no. Are we not trained to be humble, to examine our flaws? Such a young man—or an older man, for that matter—is so innocent in his belief that women are good creatures and faithful servants of the Lord, that they may be taken in by a woman's insincere praise."

"Mrs. Henry says it is a minister's very nice sense of his own self-worth that fools him." Rachel Lamb waited for his response.

Creasy only sighed. "Mrs. Henry . . . Mrs. Henry. It's Mrs. Henry who has put me in this bind, and you listen to her?"

"I think she is a very learned woman, Mrs. Henry. She has read many books, you know." Rachel settled back against the footboard of the bed. "Anyway, the troopers never suspected you were here, so her plan worked beautifully. She asked me to show you this." She pulled a sheet from her apron pocket.

Creasy reached out his hand to accept a worn broadside that was folded into quarters.

"They've orders to confiscate any copies of this and to arrest anyone they find distributing it," Rachel Lamb said. "I think it must be very important."

Creasy unfolded the sheet, which was weathered and stained from many handlings. His brows rose as he read it.

"Where did you get this?" He peered over the top of the paper.

"Mrs. Henry stole . . . she borrowed it from the Sergeant," Rachel amended with haste. "She said you would like to see it."

Creasy grinned. "I think this is one sin for which Mrs. Henry may be forgiven. I understand why Andros does not want this distributed in Massachusetts Bay. Did you read it?"

"I'd no chance to read it." Rachel gave a pretty shrug. "Why? What does it say?"

Creasy smoothed out the paper with his hand. "It's a document proclaiming William of Orange as the rightful King of England." His voice swelled and lifted as he spoke.

"Can it be true? What does it mean?" she asked.

"A Protestant Prince upon the English throne, that's what it means!" Creasy's dark eyes sparkled, his lower lip quivered with excitement. "There have been rumors, but . . . . Just imagine, Catholic James' own daughter Mary has turned against him! Her Dutch husband has taken the throne. A bold move!" He raised his etched glass in the air "Here's to the health and long lives of William and Mary! Oh," he gestured, "you must take a glass, too, Mistress Lamb. Please join me."

Rachel unfolded herself from the bed and took a second glass from the table. First she refilled Creasy's glass to the brim, then she poured into hers and raised her offering to clink gently against his. She stood poised by the bed like a young sprite.

"Here's to the success of the Protestant Princes! Oh, I feel quite giddy, Mister Cotton!"

Creasy downed his wine in one long drink and lowered it for another. "May we prove ourselves as bold and as brave," he toasted.

Rachel peered at him over the rim of her glass. "What do you mean, Increase Cotton? Do you mean to act against *this* government? Is that why they want to arrest you?"

"Creasy," the young man admonished with a smile. "My friends call me Creasy. And yes, I believe the time has come to strike at the Tyrant, Andros, who forbids us our churches and steals our lands . . . ."

"Oh, Creasy," she breathed. Her eyes shone in blue wonder. "That is bold of you, and brave!" She sat abruptly upon the bed, by his side.

"As soon as I can get out of this house I'm going back to Boston. Andros and his iniquitous henchman Edward Ruckenmaul have gone too far." He leaned towards her, lowering his voice in confidence "They have illegally detained our ships, harmed our trade and prevented us from selecting our own government. Now they are guilty of murder . . . I'm sure of it! That is the only way they could silence the leaders of the people."

"Murder?" Rachel shivered; her blue eyes stared at him in helpless alarm.

She looked, he thought, like a sweet little rabbit cornered by a dog. The urge to protect her grew hot within him, yet he could not lie to her nor lessen her fright. There was danger ahead.

"Murder . . . just so," he affirmed. "Absalom Lott and Naboth Chieves were their victims. I'm sorry, but the connection is inescapable." He reached out to touch her shoulder in comfort.

"Both ministers opposed the government and both men died for it. Other ministers have been jailed, harassed and threatened. Andros condones this treatment, Ruckenmaul carries it out. Oh, he may have creatures like Tom Pisspot to do his bidding . . . ." Creasy touched his sore head; the lump had receded but the pain remained. "Edward Ruckenmaul is behind it all. He set Pisspot upon me."

"Oh, Creasy!" Rachel cried out, "You might have been killed by that big brute!"

Creasy dropped his hand. "Yes, I might." He screwed up his mouth. He'd not considered it as anything but a scrap, such as men will indulge in a bout of fisticuffs. Now a cold knot of ice formed in his guts. He had warned his cousin to take care, but he'd neglected his own safety. Tom Pisspot could have killed him! It may well be that he intended to, although to be fair, Tom had no forewarning of his arrival. There was that.

He forced a smile for the worried little face regarding him with such shimmering blue eyes. He must not frighten her any more than necessary.

"I escaped harm, though. And I've escaped arrest with your and Mrs. Henry's help."

"Oh, you are brave! I knew you were brave!" The Deacon's wife, overcome with admiration, threw herself upon him.

Creasy dropped his glass upon the coverlet. Drops of golden liquid spilled, dripping over the edge of the bed.

With two plump arms around him and a rosy face with cupid bow lips quivering over his, Creasy succumbed to a long, sweet kiss. Ah, artless outpouring of gratitude . . . . That is all she meant, he assumed, a simple sharing of emotion at the successful revolution of a new King!

Rachel Lamb pinned him back upon the bed with her breasts and her hips; her compact little body held him prisoner, her soft mouth demanded complete surrender. And he was tempted, oh so tempted! With a supreme effort of will, he tore his lips from hers, twisting his head upon the pillow.

"Oh, Creasy . . . ." she crooned into his ear. She nibbled on the shapely lobe.

Creasy squirmed; a warm tickle teased his loins. Her hips moved against his. He felt as if he were drowning in golden honey.

"Dearest of men . . . boldest . . . bravest . . . dear Mr. Cotton!"

The sweet poison of her breath poured through his ear canals into his bloodstream.

"Rachel," he croaked, managing to free one arm, which he waved like a helpless turtle.

"Brave leader of the Lord's army . . ." she crooned, "oh take me, my Archangel, I long for your mighty rod!"

Her little hands unwound from his neck, lifting his head up to a wondrous sight. Her bosoms heaved free of their lacy constraints, his feeble protests were muffled by living flesh, his senses swooning with the perfume (lavender) and the silky caress of the globes that pressed softly upon his lips. A drowsy bliss flowed through his body, his Ebenezer was raised in glory. Was this not the perfection of God's blessings upon man, the loving embrace of a wife? But whose wife . . . ?

A vision of hellish import flashed before him; the beady eyes of old Gammar Pisspot, her grainy cackle to beware the tenth commandment! Oh, she was a witch!

Desperation gave him the strength to free himself from the embrace of the Deacon's wife. His hands shook visibly.

"Oh, I admire you so, I do, Creasy," she pleaded as he scrambled away. "I can only find release through a man like you! Help me, Creasy . . . help me!" She grabbed his sleeve, holding tight so that he dragged her with him across the bed.

"He's too old to give me babies . . . . I want a baby, Creasy," she sobbed. "You can give me that gift, is it so much to ask? A little one, strong and brave like you . . . . How can our coupling be a sin when we are commanded to multiply? No one need ever know . . . . Oh," she groaned, "I am on fire for you!"

Her words spoke to his soul, twining around his heart like the serpent in Eden. He felt frantically under the bed for his boots.

"A baby, Creasy . . . a fine little man . . . ."

The plea tugged like a child on the coattails of his reason. A little one in his image! Creasy closed his eyes. With a ragged cry he broke the temptation, thrusting her away.

Creasy stumbled down the staircase and out the kitchen door. Heedless of whether the troopers saw him or not, he raced across the yard, out the gate and down the road as if the hounds of Lucifer bayed behind him, nipping at his heels with their fiery fangs.

Chapter Seventeen

I searched around the tiny room, totally bewildered. It's occupant was missing. Rachel Lamb lay sobbing on the bed, a wineglass shattered on the floor.

"What has he done to you?" I rushed to the bedside, ready for murder. She was a pretty woman, he was a moron. I should never have sent her to keep him company!

Rachel lifted a face blotched and red-nosed. "N . . . nothing."

I could see she made a brave effort to collect herself. "Where is he? Where did he go?" My voice was sharper than I meant it to be.

"I . . . I don't know. He j . . . just ran off," she sniffed. "H . . . he didn't want to wait!"

I stamped my foot in annoyance. "Headstrong," I sighed. "Isn't that just like a man? It's a good thing the troopers are snoring away in the barn."

A timid smile peeked through her tears: "We did fool them, didn't we?"

"Men are easily fooled, Rachel," I agreed.

"Creasy . . . Mister Cotton said Tom Pisspot killed Absalom and Naboth." Rachel swallowed hard.

I had to admire her attempt to be brave. So that was what upset her! Leave it to Creasy Cotton to blurt out the news, without regard for the poor woman's feelings. She had known both men, after all.

"I'm sorry, Rachel—but it's best you know the truth." I patted her shoulder. I'm awkward at comforting people.

"But why would Tom Pisspot kill Absalom?" Rachel asked, dabbing at her cheek with a lace handkerchief "To my knowledge the rogue had no acquaintance with Absalom. Now, I can understand why he might hold ill feelings against Naboth Chieves, but why Absalom?"

"Oh?" I asked, trying to muster a casual tone. Why would there be ill feelings against Naboth Chieves?"

"Why, over Pisspot's sister, you know. Didn't you know?" Rachel searched my face, her eyes lit with interest. "Naboth was engaged to Tom's sister once, but he broke it off when he found out who she really was . . . .

I must have registered my puzzlement.

"The Pisspots are Papists," Rachel explained, "and, well . . . not the best people. Of course Deborah isn't a Papist exactly—she was raised by a Reformed family in Roxbury. That's where he met her. He told me he was misled by her into proposing marriage so he felt no obligation to continue the engagement." Rachel leaned forward as she related this gossip. "He could never countenance connection to a Papist. That's what he said."

"So . . . . There was some personal ill will between Tom Pisspot and the minister!" This was news to me. Naboth had never so much as hinted at this engagement, although I knew he'd been dismissed from one church for fighting over a woman in an alehouse. How diverting if the hoity-toity Miss Piscopot were the woman in question!

"But that doesn't explain why he would murder poor Absalom," Rachel objected.

"It doesn't mean he did. There was another man involved with Tom in an attack upon two Boston citizens—one of Ruckenmaul's toadies."

"Well, why should that man want to kill poor Absalom?"

It was a reasonable question. "We think they were paid by the government—probably by the Secretary of the Provinces."

"But why?" she persisted.

"Because they were leaders in the opposition to the graft and corruption of this government," I explained.

"Oh, it is a political matter, then," Rachel concluded. She pushed wisps of hair from her face.

"That's what I think," I said, emphasizing my own belief. "If you think it, it must be so, Hetty, for you are quite the wisest woman I know."

What could I say?

She rose from the bed, primping at her curls with a soft hand. "May I borrow your hand-glass, Hetty? Gracious, I must look a fright! It's getting late—I wonder when my Lamb will return? It is nice of you to take me in. The Lamb would not hear of my staying alone with the soldiers about. They are really rather nice, though, aren't they? I haven't had such a time in ages!"

She chatted away as I led her to my bedroom, marveling at her recuperative powers. She borrowed my looking glass, my new starched cap and a lace whisk. "For I had not time to pack a thing, the Lamb was in such a rush to leave, and I would hate for the Sergeant to see me in my same old dress . . . ."

The sergeant and his fellows would not see anyone but the militia's muskets, I sincerely hoped. I did not tell her that I'd sent word to the local militia captain about the landing of William of Orange in England and that I'd a prize for the boys to collect. Militia units from other towns were on the march for Boston to arrest the Royal Flunky and his corrupt Cronies. (So my sources had informed me.) 'Twas impossible to keep such news as Protestant William and Mary ascending the English throne from my countrymen, try as Andros might! The tyrant's time had come.

And while I did not doubt Rachel Lamb's loyalty, I did not trust her idle tongue. I was thankful for her assistance in handling the Sergeant and his men—she quite shone in the art of flirting. I did not hold a candle to her, although I thought I'd acquitted myself well. However, her soft heart might find pity for the three men. (Witness her grief at the news of Pisspot's dastardly deed, poor thing!) We'd made the soldiers drunk as Lords before Zillah locked them in the barn.

As for Creasy's abrupt departure, perhaps he'd gone off to join with the militia. I, too, felt the urge to go to Boston to see what was progressing there, but I could not leave 'til my soldiers were collected. Three of the enemy captured! My Jack would have been proud. And without a drop of blood spilled! My wise Hezekiah would approve of that.

I could not help but feel jubilant! There was danger in our actions—these were officers of the King, after all—but the excitement made me feel I could walk on water! We would fight for our rights, and in the course of that fight the truth about the grafting, scheming, murderous Tyrant must out!

"Hetty, what are you smiling about?" Rachel Lamb considered me from my table where she sat pinching at her cheeks.

"I was just thinking about the soldiers in the barn," I answered, "and hoping Mr. Cotton manages to reach Boston in one piece. That young man seems to bring chaos in his wake. I hope he didn't upset you too much—he has a blunt manner of speaking."

Rachel kept at her primping.

"What did you think of him?" I asked, curious.

One slender hand paused in mid air as she considered. "Oh, he is a man of most high principles."

"It is Creasy—Increase Cotton—of whom I speak."

"Yes," she said, resuming her repair.

"Oh. Well I suppose he is loyal to the ideals of our rights and liberties."

"Oh yes," she agreed.

I could see she was not interested in discussing the man. The fool must have upset her terribly.

Turning away from the hand glass she suddenly announced: "Hetty, I think I should like to go home now. It's been kind of you to take me in, but I do not feel myself in any danger at all. The soldiers were most gentlemanly."

"If you're sure . . . ." I hesitated.

"It's just that we rushed off and I was in the middle of my spring wash . . . . I hate to think how soggy my linens must be, and there's cloths to be pressed . . . . Well, you know how it is," she appealed. "Perhaps Zillah could see me home? I shouldn't be in the least afraid with her by me."

"Yes, of course," I agreed. To tell the truth, I was relieved. I didn't particularly want a weeping female around when the soldiers were taken from the barn. And she was perfectly safe, I was sure of that. "Let Zillah help you with the wash," I offered. "Send her back to me when your husband returns.

Her face beaming, she came to me and embraced me lightly. "I knew you'd understand," she said.

I called Zillah, gave her instruction and sent the two of them off without preamble. "Better you should reach your home before dark," I called from the gate.

Rachel Lamb turned to give me a brief wave, a small brave figure upon the road.

Chapter Eighteen

"Oh no, not again!" Cotton Mather sat upright as a madman invaded his bedroom. The man's coat was stained, one sleeve torn; his dark hair hung in lank strands about his face; his boots left a trail of prints across the handsome turkey carpet that was a wedding gift from Colonel Phillips, Abigail's father. Into what difficulties had the young man ensnared himself this time? Mather held the bedclothes tight to the linen neckpleats of his nightrail.

By the chamber door his dear wife hovered, sweet face aflame. As if she could have stopped the importunate fellow! Cotton, still recovering from his exertions to the Royal Governor, remained in bed.

"What is it?" he cried out in sudden fear. "Where have you been all this time? Have they come to arrest me? That's it, isn't it? They've come to arrest me!" He threw the bedclothes over his head.

"Far from it, dear Cousin, come out of there!"

Cotton Mather poked his head out from under the blankets.

"Why have you come here then, in such disarray? You look so . . . so . . . ." He could not finish.

Creasy grinned. "I had to walk all the way back from Rumney Marsh," he said.

At Abigail's soft cry of concern, the intruder blushed. He looked away, avoiding her eyes.

"Walked?" Mather lowered the blankets and sat up.

"Yes, well . . . . They did try to arrest me, but I escaped and Deacon Lamb took my horse when the brute Tom Pisspot beat me. That's the old woman's son," he explained, "the one in

Rumney Marsh jail, and he's Ruckenmaul's man, I'm certain of it. I think he may be the man we're after."

Mather shook his head in confusion.

"Oh, Creasy!" Abigail uttered another soft cry and reached out to touch him.

Creasy moved away in haste. "I was thrown by the great oaf, that's all."

Mather motioned Creasy to move closer to the bed; he made a brief examination.

"Nonsense, Abigail," he said. You can see for yourself he stands before us in good health. Of course, Cousin," he addressed Creasy "you were not the real target of their persecutions. A warrant for my arrest was issued as I was told, but I foiled them by keeping to my bed." He held up one hand to stop Creasy from interrupting. "As you advised, Cousin, as you advised. Yet I am heartily sorry for your troubles, for I fear I am the cause. Had I known they were after you I would have spoken to Magistrate Winthrop about it. You see, when they could not tear at me with their horrible talons, they sought to hurt me through you."

"I have my own thought on that," Creasy grinned.

Cotton Mather's mouth tightened. Cousin Creasy was too pleased with himself. There must be trouble afoot. He grunted.

"Well?"

"I think they are after me because I have come close to proving that Secretary Ruckenmaul ordered the murder of the two ministers. A charge must be held for the moment, I'm afraid. Other matters have arisen of a more immediate nature . . . ."

"More immediate than murder?" Mather's cry was sharp with disapproval. What was the young man thinking?

"I did not walk back to Boston unaccompanied, Cousin. The country people are up in arms—they are swarming in like bees to the hive. The time has come—we will deal with the tyranny of Edmund Andros right now. I think you had best get dressed and prepare to give the people some leadership."

"Why me, Oh Lord, why me?" Mather howled, drawing up the bedclothes again.

Creasy thought it a good sign that he did not hide underneath this time.

"You are your father's son, the grandson of John Cotton and Richard Mather," Creasy said, his voice stern.

"So are you," Mather grumbled, thrusting a handsome chin at Creasy. "You're my father's nephew and John Cotton's grandson. You've as much right to claim the leadership as I. Oh, why can't you do it? This is rebellion—you know what that means, Creasy? We could all be hung! Treason! Treason . . . that's what it will be to King James. Not even my father will be able to save us from the charge." Mather began to pant.

"Look, Cousin Cotton, it was your father, Increase Mather, who preached that ministers must stand first in the line of battle, even if they fall first. Your own father!" Creasy remained inflexible.

"Yes, but my father is safe in London. At least I pray he is safe," Mather amended. "What if they have clapped him into prison, Creasy? What if Protestant William fails to take the throne?" He began to pray: "Good Lord, deliver my father safe from his enemies and keep him in favor with the King . . . King James or King William, whomever Thy will favors. Let not the King take out his wrath for this rebellious colony upon our beloved ambassador . . . ."

"You're not in this alone, you know," Creasy interrupted. "Look, there is no time to waste. We have to act now. They've taken Captain George into custody. They say the Governor planned to escape in the captain's ship, *The Rose*, and that he's fled to the fort to wait for rescue from that frigate."

"Do you mean the people have arrested Captain George?" The bedclothes fell from Cotton Mather's hands.

"The South Enders did," Creasy explained. "The North Enders are gathering at the Town House. We have to get over there, Cousin. There is an escort waiting for us outside the house."

"An escort?" Mather reached across the bed for his robe. "Abigail," he gestured to his wife, "lay out my clothes, if you will. I must dress in haste."

"An armed escort," Creasy said.

"And the Governor's troop?" Mather looked up as he thrust his arms into his robe and dropped his feet over the side of the bed.

"Holed up inside the fort. Don't worry about them, Cousin. The escort is to move us through the crowds. You can't imagine the crowds, Cotton. I fell in with the Ipswich Company on the road and asked them to convey us to the Town House."

"Well, why didn't you tell me all this at the first?" Mather grumbled as he stood up, reaching for the wash basin. "If you'll excuse me, Creasy, I'll only be a moment."

If Cotton Mather doubted his cousin's estimate of the crowd, he was soon disillusioned. The Ipswich militia had to use their muskets to forge a path through the mob before the Town House.

Men, women and boy; farmers, merchants and slaves; black faces, red faces, complexions from pink to pale; people thronged the streets with a loud hum of conversation that mingled with the sharp tattoo of the militia drums.

Cotton Mather was hustled through the mob, Creasy right behind him, guarding his back. Mather heard angry cries:

> Conspiracy with the French priests . . . plot to fire the city . . . rights of Englishmen . . . ."

Sticks, cudgels, spades and axes waved in the air; Mather found it exhilarating and frightening at the same time. It was clear the people needed leadership, and gratifying that they responded to his sight:

It's Mister Mather . . . Young Mister Mather . . . ." A ragged cheer went up as the Ipswich militia forced a path through the mob to the pillars of the Town House.

As they clambered upstairs to the council chambers they collided with Samuel Shrimpton. Mather waved him through the door while Creasy dismissed the militia members. Mather walked in the chamber to find the first gentlemen of Boston assembled there: venerable old Governor Bradstreet, magistrate Wait Winthrop, Danforth, Richards, Cooke, Addington—all the officials of the former charter government, in fact.

Mather's mind clicked into political gear, certain his father would approve his plan: resume what was in place before the Tyrant, Andros, arrived; bring charges of corruption against the Tyrant; make it clear that this was no rebellion against the Crown but against Andros' oppression, which was the cause of much misery to His Majesty's subjects . . . whichever Majesty sat in London at the time.

"Gentlemen," Cotton Mather declared in ringing tones, "we need a declaration of the wrongs which we have undergone."

"Cotton," cried out a voice behind him, "we need to act. *Now*, before the people riot!"

Mather ignored Creasy's voice. He addressed the august company before him, standing so that he could be seen and heard by all members of the council.

"We must make a list of our grievances," he continued.

"We must appeal to the King and to Parliament for justice . . . ."

"Aye . . . ." Heads nodded in agreement.

Creasy moved up beside him, impatient as ever: "A list? This is no time to sit around making lists! We must fight, as William of Orange is fighting!" He pulled a worn broadside form his coat pocket and waved it in the air. "Let us take our destiny into our own hands!"

"And what of the blood that will be shed if we go off willy-nilly, without direction or cause?" Mather rebuked his cousin in sharp tones. "Will you have us all hung, Sir?"

A voice on the far side of the table mumbled. "It's a plot to sell us out to the French . . . ."

"It's a plot to destroy the Protestant religion . . . ." Another voice chimed in.

Samuel Shrimpton, seated near Mather, voiced his concern. "We must lead the people before they degenerate into a mob."

"We must have order," Mather nodded. "We must have sound reasons for our actions . . . ." He feared the lust for vengeance that came from the crowd and from this table.

"Reason? We all know the reason . . . ."

Mather could not see who spoke.

"Yes," he agreed, "we know them, and we must list them for England—for King and for Parliament!"

Magistrate Wait Wintrop backed him with calm, good sense. "Mister Mather means that a declaration is necessary for King William, who may not know our situation. His Highness must understand that we act as loyal subjects against those men who are our oppressors, who deprive us of the rights of all Englishmen."

Mather felt a measure of relief at these words. William or James, whoever the monarch, he must be dissuaded from hanging them all for treason!

"I doubt the people will wait around for you to write a declaration." Creasy challenged his cousin, his brows twisted like jagged bolts of lightening. "Piddle with paper while there's a revolution going on? We don't have time! Go out there and speak to the laborers, Cousin Cotton . . . you'll see their mood."

One or two heads nodded in agreement. "Perhaps Mister Mather can calm them . . . reason with them . . . perhaps he should address them . . . ."

Did they expect him to reason with a bloodthirsty mob? Cotton Mather stood by his resolve, even though his voice was a bit shrill: "I'm not going out there without a declaration!"

"Yes . . . yes . . . we must set down our reasons . . . ." Other voices rose to back him.

Cotton Mather turned to admonish his cousin, but Creasy was all ready out the door. Someone thrust a pen into Mather's hand. The touch of quill upon his fingers released a spill of thoughts to be set down upon paper. He took a seat, found a sheet of paper before him and began to write:

The charter taken away . . . falsehoods . . . trade spoiled . . . fees extorted . . . illegalities . . . imprisoned without habeas corpus . . . design for the extinction of the Protestant religion . . . .

The words flowed like wine.

Chapter Nineteen

Creasy made his way towards the Common, drawn by the flow of the crowd and by the whir of the many drummers whose nimble fingers beat out a tattoo-buzz loud as a giant nest of angry hornets.

In front of the old burial ground where rest the bones of that intrepid rebel, Governor John Winthrop, Creasy was halted. "Sir—" he gritted his teeth, "kindly step aside."

But the gentleman in the broad brimmed hat blocked his way, thrusting his cane against Creasy's chest with this challenge: "Is not your soul worth saving?"

"I know you not, Sir—we have not been introduced." Of course Creasy recognized the Quaker, Foxy Gabriel, who stood before him with appearance as grave as the carved slates that marked the burial ground.

"Is not your soul worth saving?" the Quaker repeated, punctuating each syllable with a poke from the cane.

Creasy, who felt he must answer this indignation, put out a gentle but firm hand to turn aside the walking stick. "I pray I am regenerate, Sir," he said with an equally serious demeanor.

"And I pray ye to give me a public hearing—whither thou wilt, Preacher of Boston," the Quaker challenged. "The doctrine ye preach to the people is false and pernicious—I know this from the Spirit of God in my heart."

Any other time Creasy might welcome a public debate over doctrine, but they were in the middle of a revolution! This being neither time nor place for disputation he answered with a firm yet courteous response. "Sir, my answer must be as the Apostle John: *If there come any to you and bring not this doctrine, receive him not into your* house, *neither give him* God-speed."

"0 ye of but little heart," the Quaker frowned with blond brows so light as to be invisible. "In like manner did yon preacher of Charlestown answer me, and he died. Thus spake the haughty preacher of Rumney Marsh, adding violence and curses to his response, and he also died. Alas for poor Gabriel! The deluded preacher of Ipswich—they say he took his own life rather than face me in open, agreed debate."

"What—" Creasy exclaimed, "did Absalom Lott agree to a debate? Ah, Sir . . ." he added at the other's solemn nod, "you bring misfortune in your wake."

"It is the judgment of God upon the Independent preachers for false and unsound principles," Gabriel intoned. "Nabal of the Bible—did he not die from drinking wine? And

Naboth was stoned to death. And Absalom was hung from an oak tree—'tis the judgement of God!"

"Nay, Sir—" Creasy cried out, face reddened in anger, "Nabal Clapp died of apoplexy—and it was man's violent hand that killed the two young ministers, not God's judgment. Why, where were you when those cruel murders took place?"

The Quakers had a history of civil lawlessness and violent interruptions of Puritan church services. Foxy Gabriel knew and had spoken with all the ministers who died, except perhaps for Mister Brock, the minister of Redding—and Brock's was a natural death. Had he been lax in disregarding this madman as a suspect in the murder of the two young men? Creasy stared into the glazed blue eyes with the pale lashes.

The Quaker did not waver. "Adulterous priest," he charged with scorn, "beware the fate of thy brethren!"

A roar from the Commons drew Creasy's attention. He looked up in astonishment as a great ball of flame brightened the morning sky. Billows of sulphurous smoke rolled like black clouds over the heads of spectators.

"They've lit the beacon!" he exclaimed, jubilant, for now the signal would call in militia from miles around. "The Revolution has begun!"

He turned to confront the mad Quaker but Foxy Gabriel was nowhere to be seen. Creasy looked about for him in vain as men, women and children **swarmed towards the Common.**

"Ho there, Mister Cotton, Sir!"

Creasy turned around to stare at the silver haired little man hopping towards him. Deacon Lamb grinned, his eyes sparkled like cracked ice.

"I'm glad I found ye, Sir—Mister Applegate of Ipswich said as ye were arrived safe in the town. My wife was full worried about ye when I told her what that great lout Tom Pisspot had done to ye. But we've got him now, Sir—we've got him now!" The old man hopped from leg to leg in his excitement. "I've a company of men to arrest the rascal, that's what! We'll throw the devil's spawn into the same cell as his dam, the old Queen of Hell!" A cackle of glee accompanied this revelation.

"That will be company for her," Creasy nodded, scanning the crowds. "Did you see the Quaker, Gabriel, as you came up?"

"The Quaker? What do ye want with that ranting blasphemer?"

"Have you seen him?" Creasy repeated. "He was here a minute ago—he seems to have disappeared . . . ."

"No, I've not seen him, and it's well for him. He'd better stay clear of Rumney Marsh—I'll have him tied to a cart and whipped from town, that's what!" the old man frowned. "We knew how to deal with his like when I was a young man. They say we'll have the old charter back, now that the Governor has fled and Ruckenmaul is taken—we need to return to our former godly ways under the old government!"

"What?" Creasy interrupted, "Ruckenmaul taken? When? Where?"

"He's in jail," the old man answered with satisfaction, "where Tom Pisspot is bound. I came to fetch ye—your horse is stabled near. Won't ye like to see the lout in his proper quarters? With your testimony we'll have the great booby hanging from the gallows, and his dam swinging beside him, the old witch! What a pretty sight!" the old man cackled, rubbing his hands in anticipation.

"Ruckenmaul in goal?" Creasy repeated. "What an opportunity this is . . . . I must speak to the man." He turned.

The Deacon pulled at Creasy's sleeve. "Won't ye come and see justice done?" he demanded.

"Oh, I'll be along soon—don't hang anyone until I get there." He placed a warning hand upon the old man's sturdy shoulder. "Edward Ruckenmaul is the key to Tom Pisspot's violent behavior—I think the Secretary paid Pisspot and his friend to assassinate the two ministers. I'm sure of it! That's why Pisspot attacked me. Perhaps I can get them both to confess . . . to convict one another." Creasy had a thought. "By the way," he **warned, "be watchful. Three troopers stabled in Henry's barn last night. Mistress Henry thought it best to let them in so she could keep an eye on them."** He did not want the old man to walk unsuspecting into a trap. **"No doubt they've left by now, but it's best to be watchful."**

"Oh, so ye did reach the house, then?" the Deacon questioned. **"How did ye escape the patrol?"**

"Mistress Henry hid me, with the help of your wife," Creasy explained. **"I slipped away when the troopers were settled for the night."**

"Aye, she's a clever one, Mistress Henry. She was fearful you'd be taken upon the road." The Deacon lifted silver brows, as if questioning the relationship.

"It's likely I would have been, had she not hidden me away." Creasy spoke in a curt tone. Never mind Hetty, he preferred to forget his encounter with the Deacon's wife.

"Aye, I thought you'd find your way to Mistress Henry's house," the Deacon nodded, **"and so I told my wife. Mistress Lamb was much concerned for your safety as well. She's a softhearted creature, is my wife. I took your horse to ride for help, our old mare being fit for naught. I'm glad there was a man by when those troopers came. 'Twas a comfort for my wife, surely."**

"She was in no danger," Creasy assured the old man. He concealed his doubt that a few troopers might frighten Rachel Lamb. Rather were the men lucky to escape her with their breeches intact!

He watched as the Deacon marched off to his company of militia. Would one company be enough to handle the giant Pisspot, he wondered idly? With the Deacon giving orders they wouldn't dare let the great oaf escape. Creasy shook off his thoughts and headed with a long stride for the town goal.

He shoved his way through an unruly crowd and was only allowed into the jail when a carpenter of his congregation recognized him. The man, Scates, pulled him through the door. "They've put me in charge here," he said. "We've locked the jailer in his own jail—see how he likes it!"

Creasy was ushered past members of the militia, merchants and mariners. He was shown to a cell where several of Andros' officials huddled in a corner as far from the angry Boston men as the limited space would permit. Lounging upon the sole cot was the Secretary of the Province. At sight of Creasy, he raised himself upright and gestured for the intruder to sit beside him. The bushy brows raised in a sardonic greeting.

"I'm sorry my accommodations are so poor—I cannot offer you a chair." He waved a bare, beefy hand. Except for a small rent in the lace that flowed over the front of a silk waistcoat he was dressed with the same elegance Creasy had noted in the Governor's study. "Have you come to pray with me, Sir?" The bushy brows formed a line like a huge woolybear. "Mister Cotton, isn't it? How kind of you to visit me. Has young Mister Mather sent you to save my soul?

Nice of your cousin to think of my welfare."

"I have not come from my cousin, nor have I come to pray for you. My prayers are for New England's deliverance." Creasy made an effort to put aside the animosity he felt for the man, although the muscles of his mouth stiffened, his voice became stern. "*And Naboth said to Ahab, the Lord forbid it me that I should give the inheritance of my fathers unto thee.*"

"Why Sir—your inheritance comes from the Crown. 'Tis treason to usurp that which was given by His Majesty. Treason! I hope you will remind your friends of the penalty for what they have done." Ruckenmaul addressed him with deliberation, his voice carrying beyond the cell.

"My hope is that you will speak freely to me, Sir. I beg you to answer my questions with frank and open courtesy. An honest confession will stand you well, I think I can promise that much," Creasy began.

"Confession to whom, Sir? I do not recognize the actions of yon traitorous pirates." He gestured with contempt to the Boston men. "I serve His Majesty, King James—I am a representative of the Crown, and the legal authority of the Crown protects me."

Creasy shook his head in an impatient negative. "I am not here for your civil sins, Sir . . . though they be many. No, I fear for your soul, Sir."

"Ah . . . you claim a higher power, like your Quaker brethren, do you? And what sins have you in mind, I wonder? Lust . . . intemperance . . . gaming . . . I fear I've overindulged in all the vices," he boasted. "I know your people derive much elevating tittilations from these public confessions . . . . Well, I am prepared to amuse them, I suppose, if that will procure me safe passage to London. Can we strike a bargain then, Sir?" Edward Ruckenmaul sneered. "My confessions of the flesh for a berth, unhindered, upon *The Rose.*"

"They'll be passage for you in hell, I think."

"Such vehemence, Sir!" Ruckenmaul tempered his sarcasm. "On the whole, I'd prefer London."

"Your levity is out of place," Creasy warned. "Even the Crown will not protect a murderer."

"Sir?" Ruckenmaul's caterpillar brows crawled upwards.

"Hast thou found me, O mine enemy?" Creasy charged.

"I beg your pardon?"

"And they carried him forth out of the city and stoned him with stones that he died."

"Sorry . . . ?" Ruckenmaul inclined an ear, as if he could not hear the charge.

"I cite *Kings 21:20* . . . . The story of Ahab, King of Israel," Creasy scowled at the man's obvious incomprehension. "Were you not taught your Bible?"

Ruckenmaul shrugged. "Mister Ratcliffe keeps me tolerably informed—that is how he earns his salary. If you wish to question me on King's Chapel doctrine I must refer you to him, Sir. He will no doubt refute your attacks upon the church you have worked so hard to deny him."

"No—this is not about doctrine, though any child in the Bay Colony would know my reference." Creasy's voice held a subtle condemnation of the English church's neglect. "Do you not recall the fate of Absalom, son of David?" he continued.

"Ah, this I know. Absalom rebelled against his King and died a traitor's death. Take warning, Sir!" Ruckenmaul's throaty voice rose. "Treason—your uncle preached it, your cousin continues to preach it, and I have no doubt its vile advocacy runs in the Mather family!" He poked Creasy's arm to include him. "His Majesty will view my imprisonment as nothing less than treason."

"We do not act against the Crown—we act against those few men who violate His Majesty's laws, who deny us the rights all Englishmen enjoy." Creasy remembered his cousin's advice and vowed to keep his temper; the man's baiting would do him no good. He would not be distracted from the issue, which was the murder of the two ministers.

"Do you recall, then, the manner of Absalom's death?" he continued.

"No doubt he was drawn and quartered—such is the manner in which traitors are displayed for all to witness the perfidy of men who rebel against their King!" Venom dripped from the snake's mouth as he hissed; the dark eyes glittered with malice.

Creasy drew back with an involuntarily start. Perhaps the man was feigning his lack of scriptural knowledge, but Creasy did not think so. He examined the unsullied brocade waistcoat and the satin breeches—here was a viper who would coil hidden behind a rock while others struck the dastardly blow. He kept on with his questioning. "You do not deny that you held a grudge against Mister Absalom Lott, late the minister of Ipswich?"

"Ah . . . the author of that libelous pamphlet against me. He was fined for his impudent lies." Ruckenmaul's voice returned to its usual husky growl. "He was dealt with."

"So he was," Creasy agreed, "and you knew Naboth Chieves?"

"The name is not familiar—I don't believe I've met the gentleman." Ruckenmaul brushed a speck from his waistcoat.

"Naboth Chieves, the minister of Rumney Marsh," Creasy prompted.

"Oh . . . another of the Dissenters." Ruckenmaul's heavy lids drooped, the mask of indifference descended.

"Was he known to you?" Creasy pressed.

"I don't number many Dissenters among my acquaintances, Sir."

"Mister Chieves helped my uncle to escape your warrant of arrest, Sir."

"Did he?" Ruckenmaul suppressed a yawn. "That information will be noted when you are all arrested for treason." He removed a delicate white handkerchief and pressed it to his mouth.

"Mister Chieves is dead, Sir—as is Absalom Lott. Both men opposed you, and both men are dead. Murdered, Sir. What have you to say to it?"

Ruckenmaul's jowls flushed red. "So that is your game? Destroy my reputation with a false charge to hide your own corruption and stinking rebellion! Well, Sir—you shan't get away with this! I have no connection with those men other than the action for libel against the one, and the courts found in my favor against him. I know how much your animosities were enflamed against me by that decision, and so His Majesty will see the proofs in the hateful pamphlets that spouted their vile propaganda against me . . . ." Ruckenmaul paused, drawing upon his determination to regain control over his voice and features.

He continued in a soft, dangerous growl. "Your charges are base and unfounded—and fallacious, Sir. If I were to slink about in the night murdering Dissenting priests, surely the Mathers would be my first victims, as my most vocal opponents—yet your own presence here refutes your specious reasoning." The thick lips twisted in disdain.

"Perhaps . . . perhaps not," Creasy argued. "As the leaders of this town, the death of either my uncle or his son would produce an outcry heard in London. Revenge against those who aided my uncle's escape would serve as a strong message of oppression."

"That is ridiculous." A snort of contempt escaped from the broad nostrils. "There is no way I can be connected to any deaths, fabricate what lies you may. My secretary keeps a diary of all my appointments. You name a date and I can prove exactly where I was, with whom and what transpired. The man is meticulous . . . and to think I used to mock him for it! Well, well . . . I shall see he is rewarded, in the future."

"I'm sure you can prove your whereabouts. I don't accuse you directly—you have your creatures to do your bidding for you. I was attacked by one of them. Why did you send your exciseman away in such haste?"

"Oho . . . so we're back to that, are we? That stabbing—which I did not order, by the way—was in self-defense, and it produced no fatalities. You cannot say that it did, for Captain Bezoum himself stands large as life over yonder. His opponent in the brawl, an exciseman named Steele, volunteered to fight the Eastern Indians. He may be sent for and questioned, with my approval. Go and send for the man!" Ruckenmaul taunted, "If the fellow is guilty of murder, 'twas not by my order nor my encouragement. I'll see him hanged myself, damn the fool!"

The good Captain Bezoum, having overheard his name mentioned, wandered over and stood at the door to the cell, listening.

"What of the Rumney Marsh villain—Tom Pisspot? Do you deny he is your creature?"

"What—the great Irish ox? Have I given him employment,

upon the recommendation of the exciseman, Mister Steele? I'll not deny it. There are jobs when strong arms and brawny shoulders are needed."

"Do you deny that you sent him to attack me, to stop my investigation of the murders?"

"My dear Sir," Ruckenmaul hooted, "I'd no notion of your existence until the other day, when we met in the Governor's study. You flatter yourself!"

"Yes, well the attack occurred shortly after that meeting, when your troopers came to arrest me."

"Ah—well, that was the Governor's decision. You and your cousin Mather—you made seditious statements. Arrest warrants were issued. I have no knowledge other than that. I certainly had no idea you were investigating any murders! I had no idea there were any murders to be investigated. If the fellow attacked you, as you say, it was on his own initiative, not mine. A great brawling fellow, as I recall . . . ."

"You deny that you sent your creatures to silence your opponents?"

"I deny it."

"And that you sent away the exciseman, Steele, is it? To keep him safe from charges of murder?"

"I deny it. The man's a fool, and quick with a knife, but that's not my responsibility. Send for him. If he is guilty of stabbing your precious ministers I'll see him hanged, myself." Ruckenmaul's features hardened.

Creasy paused to think; Ruckenmaul's words rang true, reluctant as he was to admit it. The man did not know his bible—Gabriel for instance, recognized the significance in the manner of those biblical deaths.

"Do ye speak of the death of that good man, Mister Lott, of Ipswich?" Captain Bezoum raised his voice from the cell door. "Then 'twas not a suicide?" he demanded.

"No suicide—the man was murdered." Creasy face was grim.

"I could not think it of him. I knew the man. He was no coward, to take his own life. This man," he pointed a bandaged hand through the bars, "is a villain, and he employs villains to attack honest men . . . ."

"A brawl by stupid fellows . . . ." Ruckenmaul sneered.

"But upon the day Mister Lott died all three of the villains were in court with me—Mister Ruckenmaul, the exciseman, and a big, brawny fellow—the same who attacked Captain Moon, the one called by that vulgar name, Pisspot. Two mornings before, on the tenth that was, they'd boarded my ship and confiscated my cargo . . . ." The Captain's ruddy face reddened further.

"That was the day Mister Chieves died," Creasy noted aloud, turning his attention to the mariner.

"The records will bear him out," Ruckenmaul interjected. "The Irish lout was hired to unload . . . they worked a day and half the night at it."

The Captain gave the man an ugly look. "And my best brandy stolen," he remarked. "I brought them to court for illegally boarding my ship and won my case, but my brandy was never returned. I'm here to press charges against this man for the theft."

"My dear fellow . . . am I to blame if an idle rogue gets into your warehouse and helps himself to a dram or two? You should hire honest help, you penny pinching old buzzard."

The Captain let out a roar of rage, causing heads to turn and Scates to scurry over.

Ruckenmaul smiled sweetly.

Creasy intervened. He rose from his seat and went over to calm the mariner, whose face shone a mottled purple. "Now, now, Captain . . . don't let him bait you. You are an honest man, while he is behind bars, where he'll not harm anyone. I should like you to verify that he and his henchmen were indeed occupied aboard your ship on the tenth of this month."

"They were, the sorry scoundrels!" the captain scowled.

"And when were you in court with them?" Creasy asked.

"That was upon the twelfth, but two mornings after."

"And so you were all in court upon the day of April twelfth— what about the evening of the twelfth?"

"Court ran late . . . I missed my supper, I can tell you that," the Captain growled.

Creasy sighed. He motioned for Scates to open the cell door. As far as he was concerned, the Secretary was cleared of murder. While it was true Ruckenmaul could have hired other villains to do his dirty work besides the exciseman and Tom Pisspot, Creasy did not believe he had any knowledge of the crimes. All his theories were confounded by an honest sea captain! So who, then, murdered the two ministers?

He thought it best to retrieve his mare and ride back to Rumney Marsh before an eager Deacon Lamb hung the wrong man. With luck he'd get back to Boston before the Revolution ended.

Chapter Twenty

Next morning, with my groggy captives safely delivered into the hands of the local militia, I thought it time for a womanly chat with Mistress Deborah Piscopot. I would not trust the task to Mister Increase Cotton who had all the tact of a charging bull. And who was impressed with the beauty of the lady like any country bumpkin. So, Mistress Piscopot had been engaged to the late Naboth Chieves and Chieves had—admittedly with a lack of gallantry—broken the engagement. Now that was cause for family concern. Most honest families would resort to a breach of promise suit but the Pisspots were not known for their honesty, nor their concern for the law. So there might be other reasons for Chieve's death mixed up, I had no doubt, with political chicanery.

I wondered if Absalom Lott had made the acquaintance of the mysterious Deborah. Lott was a widower, after all, and a frequent visitor to Rumney Marsh through his connection to the Deacon. Had their paths crossed? Had the beauteous Belle of Roxbury stolen his heart, as well as Chieves? Alack aday for both men. What if she was a spider in the web of Secretary Ruckenmaul? Lure in the poor insects with her cold, compelling charm, then toss them for the finishing to her great lout of a brother.

She'd ensnared poor Creasy in her silken web and he'd been attacked by Tom Pisspot. Well for Creasy the old Deacon was witness to the attack or he might have. gone the way of the others. I could not but feel a pang of indignation at the thought. Yes, someone who was immune to her cold heart decidedly should question the woman.

Of course it might be all gossip, that engagement between Chieves and Deborah Piscopot. Yet I knew Chieves had an eye for the ladies and was in want of a wife—he'd approached me soon after my poor Hezekiah's death. I took a moment to meditate upon the brevity of our days upon this land and to hope my two husbands were clasping hands of friendship in a Better Land . . . .

Mistress Piscopot was not best pleased to see me, but as I'd a basket of provisions for her mother as an excuse, she agreed to let me walk with her to the jail.

I began by prattling away about the excitement of the news that the militia had converged on Boston and were reputed to have The Tyrant cornered in the Fort like an angry black bear. I glanced at her for a reaction but there was none. "Oh," I feigned concern, "perhaps I should not run on so. There are those whose sympathies lie with the Royal Governor."

"Mine do not," she answered shortly.

"Oh, but is not your brother in the employ . . . ?" I left my question unfinished.

"My brother is employed by whomever cares to pay him a shilling. He has no head for political matters," she added.

"A great brawling fellow . . . ." I hinted.

Tom is that," she allowed, her face a mask.

"A rogue," I continued.

"That also," she admitted.

"A liar . . . .

"No, that he is not. He has not the wit." She spoke with cold judgment.

I admired her objectivity. "A murderer, they say," I pushed.

She jerked to a halt. "They say that of my mother." Her face was cold as marble beneath a black French hood. "But it is not true." She walked on with a brisk pace.

I kept in stride with her. "I'm sorry," I said, and meant it. To be old and addle-witted is a fate that awaits us all. "I shall speak for your mother if need be," I offered. "She did suffer provocation from Mister Chieves, I understand."

Deborah glanced at me then, but I could read nothing in her dark eyes. She did not speak.

"Your engagement, for instance. Mister Chieves treated you most shamefully in breaking your engagement."

"Is that what people say?" She did not break her stride.

"Is that not what happened?" My curiosity was genuine. I was discovering facets of Naboth Chieves' character that were not to my liking.

"Let people say what they will," she spoke crisply.

"But you were engaged, that much is true?" I watched her face openly.

"That is so."

"And he discovered your family ties and broke off the engagement?"

"I released him, willingly."

"Well, it would have been a good match for you," I considered. "There was cause for resentment."

"If you think Tom killed him for that or any other reason, you are mistaken," she snapped. "Tom did not kill him."

"You must admit your brother has a proclivity for violence," I argued. "I don't accuse him of murder—it may well have been an accident. The great lout doesn't know his own strength. And if he did have a fight with Mister Chieves, it may well be that the Secretary of the Provinces set him to it." There, it was out. I could not pussyfoot around any longer.

"Tom did not kill him," she declared with certainty. He was in Boston that day. I saw him there myself."

It was my turn to halt in my tracks. "But you are his sister . . . you would protect him."

She gave a bitter laugh. "There were many who saw him besides his sister. He was unloading cargo on a busy wharf."

"If Tom didn't kill him, who did?" I exploded. She was confounding my nicely held notions!

"I do not know, but you may tell Mister Increase Cotton that Tom did not. Had he asked me himself, I should have told him."

"Increase . . . ." I muttered, vexed. "What has Creasy to do with it?"

"Did he not send you to question me?" she threw back her hood and peered at me.

I shook my head. "Why would he send me?"

"My brother threw him down in the dirt . . . . I would have stopped Tom had I known, but it was too late." She sounded regretful. "I could not blame him if he never came near our home again."

"Men will brawl no matter how we scold," I agreed. My Jack loved a good fight. He died in a battle at sea, but not before he'd secured his prize; a Spanish treasure ship. I was glad Hezekiah was well over that phase of manhood when I married him.

"We were raised in different households and in different faiths, Tom and I, but Tom was raised to fear God's wrath, just as you or I. He would not take a man's life at another's bidding, no matter what the payment offered."

She spoke in so positive a tone I was inclined to believe her. I'd have to look elsewhere for the murderer of Naboth Chieves. "Mistress Piscopot, forgive my impertinence, but did you ever meet Absalom Lott? He is—was—Deacon Lamb's son-in-law."

"No. I knew of his protests against illegal taxation and honored him for it, but I never met the gentleman. Nor did Tom." She glared at me, daring me to contradict her.

"Well I had to ask." One must be practical.

"Mistress Henry, why do you involve yourself with these matters?" It was she who was frank.

"Hetty," I said. (I do not like to stand upon ceremony.)

"This is my community—I care for its welfare as did my late husband. I will see justice done here."

"But you are a woman . . . ."

"As are you. Do you not want to see the murderer punished?" I asked.

"Of course," she frowned. "But you may be resented . . . you may place yourself in danger with your questions. Is it not best to leave these matters to the magistrates?" She spoke with calm curiosity.

I sighed. "We have no magistrate here, my husband dead. All they have sent us from Boston is Increase Cotton—and your brother showed just how effective he is in questioning people. Oh, oh," I paused.

"What is it?"

"I suspect they've gone to arrest your brother," I said. "I'm sorry."

"Not for the first time has he been inside the jail," she noted. "There are witnesses to clear him."

She was right—the lout had an alibi, yet I felt guilty for pushing my ideas on Creasy and on Cotton Mather, both of whom would act on my assumptions. I'd voiced my opinion that Tom Pisspot was connected to the deaths of the two ministers.

"I fear I am to blame if he is accused of Mister Chieves' murder. I'll send word to Creasy to let him go," I offered.

"Tom should not have been so rough with Mister Cotton," she shrugged. "A night in jail will not harm him. Leave it in Mister Cotton's hands. He'll find the truth."

I'm afraid I could not hide my skepticism.

"Why," she examined me, "do you think Mister Cotton capable of vengeance towards Tom because of that fight?"

"Oh, I have no doubt that justice weighs more with him than a knock-down." I thought of the tactless clod who'd left poor Rachel Lamb in tears and of the coward who quivered in fright at my sweet Priscilla. Was this the man to bring down the murderer of two ministers? Creasy needed all the help he could get, although he would not admit it.

The path we trod became wider and smoother as we neared the village. I could smell the scent of sulfur in the air. Two urchins pushed past us, brushing my skirts and almost knocking the basket from my arms. They ran off down the path, ignoring my reprimand.

"Children today have not the manners we were taught," I grumbled. Yet I caught something of their excitement; I could hear the faint rattle of drums. Perhaps the militia were training on the Commons; perhaps the village was celebrating the downfall of The Tyrant! The thought made me giddy and I picked up my pace. The capture of the Royal Governor and of his detested Secretary, Ruckenmaul, would clear up their complicity in the murders, I was sure. I was convinced of a local connection and no doubt that would all come out. It vexed me that any of my fellow townsmen would take part in such a hellish venture as murder. It vexed me even more that I could not think who, besides Tom Pisspot, would commit such a heinous deed.

"Are there any Quakers in your family?" I asked abruptly.

Deborah only arched her brows in surprise.

"Well, you were raised in the Reformed Faith and your mother's a Papist—it was just a thought," I said, knowing what troublemakers Quakers were. Now Foxy Gabriel I'd thought to be harmless, but he had challenged both ministers to debate. There was that for a connection, and there were several Quaker sympathizers in Rumney Marsh.

The buzz of a crowd reached my ears; more boys rushed past us. Something was going on at the Common; the tat-a-tat of the drums stirred my militant soul. I put aside my musings. I'd tender my basket to the old woman and join in the celebrations!

"I've wronged you, Madam," I gasped out, increasing my steps to an unladylike trot. "I thought you were a minion of Secretary Ruckenmaul! I apologize," I added at her darkling look.

"I detest the man." Her shoulders shuddered beneath her cloak. She kept to my pace.

"He's the cause of your brother's troubles," I shouted to be heard, for the din increased as we neared the Common. We could see people milling about. Puffs of smoke billowed in the air.

"Tom needs no cause," she said, framing her mouth with her hands. "Oh," she pointed ahead, "what is that?"

I peered though a smoky haze and spied an odd feathered

creature break loose from a ring of spectators only to be chased and surrounded by the greater crowd.

"Oh, it must be a menagerie! Come, let's go see!" I ran, forgetting my dignity and reverting to the little girl who loved novelties, especially exotic animals.

Whoops, laughter and jeers spurred my anticipation. Men were holding their sides in mirth, children darting beneath long legs to get a better view of the creature.

Ignoring a stitch in my side I pushed my way into the crowd. "What is it?" I gasped to onlookers. Broad shoulders blocked my sight. "Deborah, can you see?" The woman beside me craned her neck and shrugged.

I pounded upon the shoulder of a mud-caked farmer; the smell of manure assailed my nostrils, an honest smell. The man was straight from the fields. I hoped none of my hired help neglected their work so. "What is it?" I demanded.

A ruddy face smiled down at me. "Just some sport, Missus!"

"What animal are they baiting?" I prompted, "What kind of creature?" The glimpse I'd caught promised an unusual rare bird.

"Creature you might say," the farmer beamed. "'Tis the Hell-creature from the jail and Deacon's gone to see her son do the gallows dance."

Whether the scream that pierced my brain came from my own mouth or from Deborah near me I shall never know. My mind went numb. I butted and shoved my way past men's bodies, Deborah clawing her way beside me 'til we stumbled onto the green to see clouds of feathers and smoke and an odd creature hopping about seeking frenzied escape from the men who were pouring sacks of feathers over it and retreating with hoots of laughter.

"Mother!" Deborah screamed.

The basket fell from my hands and we two ran forward, but the creature vanished into the crowd on the far side of the green.

"Stop it! Stop It!" My voice grew hoarse with shouting. Bodies blocked us, feathers floated around us, tar pitch burned in my nostrils, smoke blinded my eyes. We fought our way towards the elusive creature, Deborah white as death, me shouting in vain, "Stop it! Stop it! Stop it!"

My limbs moved as if made of lead; I flailed away like a drowning swimmer, unable to make headway against the wave of brutish bodies that loomed over me. I pushed and lost my footing, stumbling over heavy boots but Deborah grabbed my arm and wrenched me upright. "There," I sobbed for breath, pointing to a space in the undulating crowd. We shoved and pushed towards a glimpse of the green until we scrambled onto the grassy sward. Tears came unbidden to my eyes at sight of the poor creature hopping about before us. Hands held me back; I could not make myself heard over the jeers and mirth as I commanded the grinning idiots to release me. Deborah pulled two big men with her every dragging step forwards. I despaired.

'Twas then methought I saw the Angel of Death all dressed in black on a dark foaming charger. The seas parted and the Voice of Judgment thundered: "Sinners!" The tumult stilled. Fiery condemnation lashed o'er the inhuman waves, whipping their brutish souls to stormy tears. And Deborah and I ran forward to drag the old woman from beneath the very heels of Death. I was never so glad to see Creasy Cotton in all my life.

Chapter Twenty-one

Creasy had a difficult time dragging himself away from the excitement of the Revolution, but the prospect of seeing a pretty, dark-eyed lady made it bearable. Perhaps she would feel some kindness for him if he reunited her with her oafish brother. He would have to do something about the old Gammar as well. If only he could produce the real killer of the ministers! He must begin over again. Both Tom Pisspot and Secretary Ruckenmaul's whereabouts were verified. With those villains eliminated, who could have been so filled with hatred, so unrelenting in their mockery of the Lord, that they would murder two men of God? There must be another motive for this blasphemy.

The Quaker, Foxy Gabriel, for instance. Did he so hate the doctrine that he'd silence the preacher? These Quakers did mad things—painted their faces black and invaded the churches, rushed naked down the aisles disrupting the services—and they recognized no legal authority, refusing to remove their hats before the magistrates. A radical lot; yet so far their violence had been contained to shocking acts against the church and verbal debates with the ministers. The Quakers had courted martyrdom in the olden days, and received it at the hands of the older generation of Massachusetts Bay. Would they take revenge for the hangings of so long ago?

It was Gabriel who brought to his attention the correlation between the ministers and the biblical manners of their deaths. The significance had not escaped him completely, rather had it gnawed at his mind like a mouse at a paper-wrapped cheese.

Jezebel, that wicked Queen, had Naboth taken from his house and stoned to death, just as Naboth Chieves was stoned. Absalom in the Bible rebelled against King David and was found hanging in an oak tree, where David's general planted three darts in the rebel's heart. Hence those three blue pinpricks, unexplained, in the corpse of Absalom Lott. Creasy shivered with the horror. And Nabal Clapp had died while drinking wine, but that was from natural causes.

Creasy's musings were interrupted as he neared the village of Rumney Marsh. He heard cheers and shouts of laughter as he rounded the bend that led to the commons. There upon the green a great crowd was assembled. Perhaps they were celebrating the overthrow of the Tyrant Andros! He spurred his mare forward. Rising in the stirrups he could see the cause of the commotion.

A strange sort of bird hopped about in the center of the crowd. The bird was muffled in a hood of loose cloth, like some giant gyrfalcon. Feathers flew in a snowy cloud as the creature flapped about amidst the hooting of the spectators. Weird croaks issued from the downy hood.

"Catch it!" A smocked farmer shouted as the bird flopped into the crowd. Men held their sides with laughter as people fell back before the confused creature's feathered floundering. Creasy reined in beside the green. He craned his neck to find the menagerie from which the exotic bird must have escaped but there was no cage upon the green and no frantic mountebank attempting to capture the exhibit. Where had the creature come from?

He noted that the bird was hobbled about the knees; it hopped in circles, green worsted stocking loosened about its thin, stick legs.

Creasy let out a roar of anger; he plunged the mare through the crowd, heedless of scattering bodies and frantic cries.

"Savages!" He placed his horse so that it blocked the helpless creature, which stumbled and fell beneath the mare's hooves. Creasy held the mare still with an iron hand. He shook his fist at the crowd.

"Savages!" he repeated. "Are ye no better than animals?"

He used his voice like a whip. "Are ye worse than the wildest Indian of the forest, to torment a poor creature for your sport?

Can ye dare call yourselves followers of Jesus Christ? Do ye dare?" he demanded of the audience.

"She killed our minister. She is a witch," a laborer in a worn smock explained.

Creasy glared down at the hapless fellow. "We rule by law here. We are New England men. This woman will stand before the magistrates for judgment, and so will every man, woman and child here that denies the law!" He raised his voice in thunderous displeasure. "We'll have no anarchy here in Massachusetts Bay! Now go—get out **of my** sight! Go back to your homes!" He pointed a gloved finger toward the **road.**

And they went; all but two women who rushed forward to **the aid of the** stricken creature, pulling it from beneath the mare's belly. Creasy stood grim guardian over them all.

Hetty Henry pulled a knife from an apron pocket; she knelt **next to the creature and sawed** at the **ropes of the** hood. Deborah Piscopot, with a face like white marble, lifted the hood from the **jerking** form **as feathers flew about the air.** She brushed them away from the dazed, blinking black **eyes of the old** woman; uttering soothing sounds **as she** cradled the old head against her bosom.

"Where is Deacon Lamb?" Creasy addressed a curt question to Hetty Henry, who **was slicing at the hobbles around the old** woman's skinny legs.

"They've taken Tom Pisspot away to **hang** him," the woman answered, not bothering to look up.

"Where?" Creasy demanded.

"At the giant oak, I think—where they used to hang witches." Hetty pointed the way with the blade of her knife.

"I know it." Creasy's face set in grim determination. "Will you be safe?" he asked Deborah, sidling the mare away with care from the little group huddled upon the grass. She nodded, still crooning to the mother in her arms. Her eyes were wide and black with grief, although no tears traced the marble contours of her face.

The dark eyes of Deborah Piscopot burned into his soul; he spurred his mount across the common, bootheels digging into the mare's flanks with unaccustomed severity. Slather dripped from the animal's mouth, sweat flew from its flanks as Creasy galloped towards the cloud of dust in the dirt road. Shouts and raw hootings led him to the spot where a dozen men struggled to subdue one bear-sized man. Like so many terriers they leaped and snapped at the bound bruin, who kicked at them with great boots and shrugged them off with brawny shoulders. In spite of a valiant effort by the growling Tom Pisspot, his attackers had succeeded in wrapping a noose around his burly neck. Two men were pulling upon the end in a vain attempt to jerk the raging giant over to the nearest tree.

Creasy thundered straight into the dusty cloud. Bumps, groans and bodies diving from his path only brought a fierce pleasure that warmed his gut. He pulled up short, forcing his mount to turn, ready for another onslaught.

"Stop!" he roared, the rhetorical power of his lungs fueled by white-hot anger.

Men fell back; heads turned to face the intruder, whose wrath resembled the Archangel Michael upon his snorting steed. All actions suspended except for the two men, who took advantage of the lull to tug at the rope anchored around the bear's hairy neck.

"Stop!" Creasy commanded, a finger of doom pointing at the two men, one of whom promptly fell away, hands behind his back.

The silver haired old Deacon was left holding his end of the rope.

"This is ill work," Creasy warned the Deacon in a loud, solemn voice.

"Why, Minister . . ." the whine came, "did ye not tell me the villain murdered two men of God, one of them my own daughter's husband?" The Deacon gave a sharp tug at the rope, to little effect.

"Drop the rope," Creasy ordered. "I was mistaken."

The Deacon's lined face twisted with skepticism. He retained his hold upon the hemp.

"Leave it," Creasy frowned. "There is an honest witness to this man's whereabouts at the time the murders occurred—an honest sea captain and court records vouch for his innocence."

"Innocent, ye say?" the Deacon argued, "Pisspot is not innocent—he is a great rogue and a villain, with a string of infamies . . . ."

"Yet he is innocent of these crimes. He was engaged by the Secretary of the Province to unload cargo from the ship of Captain Bezoum—the captain saw him there on the tenth, and in court upon the twelfth. You cannot hang him for crimes for which he has not been charged." Creasy's face was stern and set.

"Then we'll hang him for something else." The Deacon thrust out a pointed jaw. "For attempted murder of a minister—I saw him attack you with my own eyes, ye'll not deny it!"

"We are New English men," Creasy rose in the stirrups, his voice carrying an appeal to each and every farmer in the crowd. "We live by English law. If you have other charges against this man you will bring them to the magistrates. Our fathers established a code of laws in this wild, new land, so that we would live in harmony. It is Satan who urges you to acts of anarchy! Satan who tempts you to hang a man without trial by English law! Deny Satan, I say . . ." he boomed, "deny Satan and return to the Godly ways of our fathers, the Saints! Release this man!"

A smocked farmer with a barrel frame loosened the heavy knot on the noose around Pisspot's thick neck.

The bear of a villain threw off the hemp, shoved out his great paws to scatter those around him and lumbered off down the road.

The Deacon gazed after the man with a wistful expression. He looked down at the limp rope in his hand. "Now ye've done it," he whined. "Ye've let the devil go! You've only yerself to blame for what happens."

Creasy regarded the little man with cold eyes. "I will see you before the magistrates, Sir, for usurping the authority of the court." Creasy knew this argument would weigh more with the magistrates, who guarded their positions with jealous industry. The public torment of a poor addled creature, an accused witch, would not appear as serious a charge.

Creasy waited until the crowd had dispersed completely before he turned his mare and trotted back in the direction of the Rumney Marsh green. After he'd reassured himself of Deborah's safety, he would return to Boston and the Revolution! It was as well he had come straight to Rumney Marsh, he thought.

Creasy felt a sense of responsibility for the Deacon's hasty actions, since he was the one who'd convinced the old man of Pisspot's guilt, but he'd made reparations for that error and two lives had been saved.

The energy that kept him erect in the saddle suddenly deserted him; his shoulders slumped, his eyelids grew heavy The mare was in a similar state, its head lowered, its hooves plodding. The animal needed watering, as did its rider. There was a stream not far down the road; he'd noted it even in his gallop to Pisspot's rescue. He clucked encouragement to his mare.

Creasy dismounted amidst clumps of fern and sprouts of green skunk cabbage. The mossy soil was spongy under his boots. The spring vigor of the stream overflowed its bank and spread out to cover the ground in a swelling pool. Creasy released the mare to wade into the water and lap its fill.

He sank to his haunches where little rills of water swirled around his boots with a gentle gurgle. He leaned over, plunging his hands into the current, gasping at the pleasant shock of winter's icy legacy. Cupping his hands together, he splashed droughts of crisp fresh water over his face. He shook his head like a puppy, droplets flying into space, energy restored.

Creasy watched tiny tadpoles dart about in shallows of golden dirt. He looked up at the bark of a long necked goose and saw a doe step daintily through a strand of young saplings, which formed an island caught in the middle of the overflow. The doe nibbled upon delicate green buds on branches that arched over her head, stretching her graceful neck and pulling with a gentle mouth. He dared not move lest he frighten the deer, even though rills swerved in their course and flooded his boots.

From the corner of his eye he saw a bronzed frog perched upon a stone near his right boot. The frog watched him unblinking, and as steadily as he watched the doe. Creasy grinned, recalling the time he'd taken his sickly cousin Cotton Mather out to the swamp to catch frogs—Cousin Cotton spent summers in Plymouth—and the older boy had fallen into the water when a frog jumped out between his legs. Cotton Mather, slime-covered and dripping wet . . . how his mother had scolded! Cotton came to them scrawny and pasty-faced and left with rosy cheeks plump with sunshine and country cooking. Venison roasts, cranberry puddings . . . . Creasy sighed remembering them.

The doe vanished from sight as silent as a ghost. The bronze frog slid from the rock into the water, stretching its long, speckled legs in an easy glide. Creasy leaned forward.

A high squeal of rage filled his ears while lightening blasted through his skull. He felt himself flung into the water like a straw doll. His mouth and nose suffocated beneath icy, dank water while frothy black bubbles swirled around his head in spirals. A heavy weight upon the small of his back pinned him under; his hands sank into soft muck. He grasped mud and dead leaves and thrust his arm up in desperation.

His fingers closed upon a line of strong hemp that tugged him free of the weight. The line pulled him up and out of the muck; he clung blindly to the line, his lungs aching. Sunshine burst upon his face like a blessing, mud squished beneath his body as he was dragged out of the pond, the stench of skunk cabbage smelled sweeter than roses in his nostrils. He vomited yellow slime into the broad leaves of the green cabbage, each retch splitting his head. His fingers closed over a fistful of fern tendrils, living green wonder, before a black curtain obliterated his senses.

Chapter Twenty-two

I was on my way to fetch Zillah when I heard Priscilla's squeal of distress by the creek. I'd know her squeal anywhere. Almost at the same moment I saw Creasy's horse and a man crashing through the brush—I caught a glimpse of silver hair; it was enough.

I found him, Creasy, prone in the skunk cabbage, retching, while Priscilla stood next to him, squealing away, snout raised, eyes red with rage. I didn't stop to think what happened, I just ran. His clothing was sodden and icy cold, his hair muddied and wet with clumps of green slime hanging like cobwebs from his head.

I pounded upon his back. He gasped like a fish out of water, which is what he resembled, his body flopping about helplessly uncoordinated. I leaned with all my weight between his shoulder blades. Bile and noxious substance oozed from his mouth. He moved his face an inch away and groaned.

"Increase! Increase Cotton!" I yelled. "Increase Cotton! Speak to me! Speak!" All the while I pounded upon his back while praying fervently that he would respond.

"Stop . . . hitting . . . me," he gasped.

I fell back upon my heels, hands clasped in relief. "Thank God! Oh, thank God!"

"I . . . do," he gasped.

'Twas then I saw the blood oozing through the muddy hair. I'd have to see to that. Priscilla poked her snout into my shoulder as if nudging me to action. I ran to the creek, dunked my kerchief in the icy water and used it to sponge away mud from a rapidly swelling bruise on the back of his head. Once cleaned, I could see it didn't look too serious. He'd have a sore head, no doubt. In this case it was a good thing the man was so hardheaded.

Clumps of pigweed were close at hand so I grabbed fistfuls, scrunched them in my palms and thrust them against the wound. Zillah knew more than I about such cures, but needs must . . . and the Devil was certainly driving. Creasy jerked his head, groaning as I worked.

"Hold still," I ordered. "I'm doing the best I can."

I left him moaning and ran back to rinse off my kerchief, which I must use to bind the poultice in place. His groans were pitiful to hear. "I'm coming," I called back. "I'm here!"

Priscilla snuffed gently down at him, moving aside with delicate understanding as I returned to finish my handiwork. I twisted the kerchief into folds. Slipping it beneath his neck proved too painful for him so I pressed it against the gooey leaves. "Don't move," I commanded, ignoring his cries of pain.

"Oh Lord," I prayed aloud, "what am I to do?" There *was* the old woman near death, and here was Creasy, sadly injured! I'd left the old woman in the care of her daughter and of the jailer, whom I'd freed from being locked in his own cell. I could not carry Creasy by myself, nor could I leave him in such a state— danger threatened him, he was cold and sick . . . . I doubted he'd fallen into the creek on his own; the bump upon his pate proved otherwise. Would his attacker return? But I must fetch Zillah for the old woman and get Creasy to safety!

As I considered my plight, I grabbed great leaves of the skunk cabbage and placed them over the noxious effluvium near Creasy's mouth. The smell of skunk cabbage was not pleasant, but it was better than vomit.

Creasy began mumbling. I leaned over, placing my ear as close to his face as I could without pressing into the skunk cabbage. "Creasy?" I questioned. "Can you hear me?"

"0, Hope in mortal pain," he gasped, "am I called to Salvation?"

I could not help snickering. I suppose it was a form of mild hysteria.

"What Wild Angel is this?" he mumbled.

"No angel, Creasy—it's me, Hetty Henry." I patted his arm. "Now don't move. I'm going for help."

He cried out, his fingers flexed weakly as if he would clutch my skirts.

"Don't worry," I reassured him, "I won't leave you alone." I placed my hand over his; the fingers were alarmingly cold. The man needed to be moved to a warm bed. I glanced around me but there was just Priscilla. Priscilla! I stood up. "Priscilla," I ordered, "stay here! Guard him!"

The pig trotted over and took up her post.

"Good pig," I said. I wished I had a cloak to cover the man but it was such a warm day I'd worn none. I'd a good warm petticoat, however, so I slipped out of it and placed it over him. "You're safe," I spoke softly. "Sleep if you can. I shall be back for you soon as may be."

He mumbled something about the Seat of the Elect.

I brushed away tears of exhaustion, emotion, pity, anger and fear. Then I set off for help.

Zillah's instructions were to remain with Rachel Lamb until the return of that lady's husband. (I did not believe that would be soon.) Lamb's plantation was near. I grabbed Zillah and two of Lamb's men and hurried them back to the creek. Zillah made a cursory inspection of Creasy's head; he moaned at her slightest touch. "He will recover," she pronounced.

"Good. Carry him to my house," I directed the men.

Zillah put out a hand, softly touching my arm. "Mistress Lamb is near—he should be warmed as soon as possible," she spoke in a grave voice. "Put him to bed there."

"But . . . ." I protested, thinking of his attacker.

"Put him to bed there—he will be safe."

Zillah must have read my mind. I did not have time to argue— the healing woman must be sent where she was badly needed, to the poor old woman. I nodded. I'd have to see that Creasy was properly protected. I walked over to Priscilla, giving her broad sandy back a pat.

"Take him to Mistress Lamb," I ordered the men.

Zillah stood. The woman had expressive eyes. With her look she requested permission to go to Gammar Pisspot's aid.

"Go," I said, "quick as you can."

Zillah strode off with her long limbs.

The men transferred Creasy onto a blanket. Rather than respond to his cries of pain I turned to Priscilla, who was rooting around in the edge of the water. She flipped up a long stick with her pink snout.

"Priscilla," I scolded, "this is no time to play." Curiosity forced me to bend over her. She nudged the stick towards me. I reached out, ignoring the icy water soaking my sleeve. Cold water dripped onto my skirts as I held the stick aloft; a stout hickory stick with knobbed handle.

"Men," I cried, thrusting forward the stick for their inspection, "can you identify this?"

The two men paused in the act of lifting the blanket with its heavy burden sagging on the ground. One nodded. "Yea, Mistress.

"It's the Deacon's stick, isn't it?" I could not keep the triumph from my voice.

"'Tis," the man confirmed tersely.

With surprising gentleness the men lifted the blanket, corners wrapped securely around rough hands.

I saw Creasy installed under the covers of Rachel Lamb's own bed. The woman would have fussed over him but I pulled her from the room. "He needs sleep. Zillah will see to him when she comes back." Mistress Lamb's eyes were pale with tears but I had no time for pity. I was enraged by her husband and ready to take it out upon her. Before I could lose my temper, I sent a boy to fetch Elijah from my farm. I needed someone I could trust to set over the patient.

I found Rachel Lamb hunched on the settle by the kitchen fire. She raised a woeful face to me.

"Make us a pot of tea," I ordered a woman who hovered near her mistress; the cook, I assumed.

"What has happened to him?" Rachel's voice quavered.

"Do you mean to Mister Cotton or to your husband?" My own voice was cold and sharp. I could not help it.

"I know my husband has done great wrong . . . ." Rachel whispered. "They told me of his mistreatment . . . ."

I snorted in contempt. Mistreatment, she called it!

"I never meant any harm to the old woman!" she cried.

"You would have her hung," I reminded.

"But she is a witch—he said she is a witch!" Tears gushed forth from her pale eyes.

"That was for the court to decide, not your husband. "I was stern. She did not answer for sobbing. There was no talking to the woman in this state, and talk to her I must. I motioned to the cook. She brought cups of fragrant brew. I sniffed mine; the scent of pennyroyal filled my nostrils.

I gave a nod of approval. Pennyroyal is known to clear the brain.

Rachel Lamb sniffled over hers, but she drank and became somewhat composed.

"Mistress Lamb," I began, "I must lay a charge against your husband. Do you understand?"

Her eyes were red-rimmed saucers peering over her cup but she did not say nay.

"Before I leave here I must ask you some questions. You will do well to answer truthfully." I spoke in a firm voice, sure of my command over the woman. "Has your husband been here since I came for Zillah?"

"No," she whimpered.

I did not think he had, since I'd seen him crashing through the brush in the opposite direction. I must be sure, however, and I could not leave until Elijah arrived to relieve me. "When did you last see him?"

"I have not seen the Deacon since he left me to stay with you. He hasn't been home since my return." She stared at me with the fascination of a bird watching a snake.

"You knew nothing of his intention to tar and feather the old woman and to hang the son?"

"No . . . no, other than his wish to hang them both, which he often spoke of." She held the cup next to her breast with tight fingers.

I believed her.

"What happened to Creasy? Was it the Deacon who harmed him?" She searched my face with anxious eyes.

"Your husband struck him from behind and threw him in the creek to drown." I spoke the stark truth, my anger blinding me to her feelings. Of all the cowardly acts, this deed came second only to the harsh treatment of the old woman. Tom Pisspot, at least, was a great brute who could defend himself.

"Oh, this is my doing!" Rachel cried, shaking her hands as if they were wet. "I have brought him to this!"

"How is this your doing?" I snapped. Silly woman—some people think the world revolves around them.

"I am punished for my wanton wickedness," she sobbed, "for my lewd, lascivious behavior . . . ."

I sat there, amazed. "Go on," I urged, confession being the first step to repentance.

"For my adulterous urges . . . . Oh, I am punished, and that good, honorable man lies broken upstairs! Oh, that I was ever cursed with this lusty body . . . ."

"What?" I interrupted, "You and Creasy . . . Increase Cotton? You told me you never met him before! Are you telling me you know him now—in the biblical sense?" I could not believe my ears.

"I tried," she sobbed harder, "but he wouldn't let me."

"Oh," I relaxed. "Oh!" Understanding dawned. So that's why she was crying on the bed. It wasn't Creasy's fault at all. Perhaps I owed the man an apology. I examined Rachel Lamb with new regard. Her eyes were red, cheeks smudged with tears, cap askew with untidy wisps of straw sticking out, but she had a full bosom and wide hips. Some men would not be able to resist her ample charms.

"Still," I went on in an attempt to calm the woman, "no harm done. You had no way of knowing what your husband would do to Mister Cotton." I held out my cup for more of the pennyroyal infusion. Only the Lord knew what I'd gone through this day.

Rachel leaned forward on the bench, hiding her face in her hands. "I should have known . . . Absalom, Naboth, now Creasy . . . ." she groaned.

"Calm yourself," I ordered. "Drink your tea." I motioned to the cook, who picked up the cup from the settle and freshened it with steaming brew. Questions flooded my brain but again I waited, with commendable patience, if I may say.

"Now," I resumed, "What should you have known—and why? Did you have cause to believe your husband would harm Creasy . . . Mister Cotton?"

Rachel took a long sip from her cup, closed her eyes for a moment and collected herself. "I should not have expressed my interest and admiration for his funeral sermon, nor of my desire to meet Mister Cotton to my husband. He has fits of jealousy . . . strange fits," she added, "not only of me but of all his possessions. He argued with Absalom over Janet's bride-portion, with me over Zillah, with Naboth Chieves over the wood lot . . . . I should not have praised Mister Cotton to him—it may have set him off!"

"He was jealous of Absalom Lott, his own son-in-law?" I asked.

"Yes, and that was ridiculous because I did not care for Absalom above half—he was far too serious, always ranting over some injustice or other. Yet the Deacon was forever hinting about this or that sign of attachment. I swear he badgered poor Absalom until he rarely visited us." She grimaced.

"And Naboth Chieves—what of him?" I knew Chieves could be a very agreeable man.

"Oh," she replied, setting down her cup again and leaning towards me, "that was strange! Mister Chieves was always charming and attentive to me. The Deacon did not seem to mind it one whit. Naboth was quite flirtatious, in fact . . . ." A spark of animation lit her face. "He made professions of love to me and twitted my husband for it! The Deacon only laughed at his jibes."

"And . . . your feelings for Mister Chieves?" I hinted.

She had the grace to blush. "I enjoyed his company, I don't deny it, but his own reprehensible behavior ended our friendship!" She straightened suddenly, her stance rigid.

"Reprehensible behavior . . . ?" I prompted. What had come between them? An improper advance, perhaps? Yet I could not quite see this woman as helpless to deal with such an event. Not after attempting to seduce Creasy in my bed! Well, practically in my bed.

"Naboth Chieves so far forgot himself as to attack Zillah in the barn." Her lips tightened in disgust.

"Zillah?" She caught me by surprise.

"Can you believe it?" she agreed, "Zillah! My slave! After all his attentions to me!" She shook her head in bewilderment.

"Poor woman," I cried. "Is that when you decided to sell her?" I was not best pleased at this thought, but I could not blame Zillah.

"Oh no, you must not think it. Nothing came of it. Zillah screamed and my man heard her—he frightened Naboth off," she explained. "The Deacon went after him and laid him out in lavender, I can tell you. Of course we refused him the house after that." Her features improved with the animation of her speech. One hand swept back the stray hairs escaped from her cap. "But that did not prevent him from quarreling with me over my servant," she continued. "Zillah was mine, given me by my uncle when I was just a child, and so I told him. He claimed his right as my husband to chastise the slave. Well, I could not agree to that because I knew he would beat her for her saucy tongue. Oh yes, she did not hide her dislike for him. You can imagine what a position that put *me* in, and so I sold her. That was that." Rachel spread wide the fingers of both hands, as if to stop further discourse.

Much as I relished the prospect, I did have a few more questions, which must be asked. "Where was your husband when the two ministers were killed?"

"Oh, I don't know—I don't remember . . . ." She stuck a finger in her mouth, scowling in childlike concentration. "Oh," she brightened, removing the finger and suspending it daintily in the air. "I do recall when they brought the news of Naboth Chieves—yes, he was here. They were all working in the fields, the men and the Deacon. He likes to get in a spring crop of peas. The Deacon has to be first to serve green peas at the table—I don't know why. He takes considerable pride in the achievement and boasts of it to everyone within hearing. So much fuss over so little! Men do take their pleasures in the strangest things; don't you find it so? It is quite incomprehensible to me . . . ."

My heart sank, at her blathering and at the thought that I had lost my prime suspect for murders. "The men will vouch for his whereabouts upon that day?" I interrupted.

"Oh yes. Why, I brought out cider to the men mid-morning and in the afternoon, and of course he was in the house for dinner and for supper, when the news came about the witch . . . the old woman killing Naboth Chieves."

I sighed. Preparing the fields was an arduous task. Still, I would check with the laborers myself. Was he here when Absalom Lott died?" I asked.

She looked at me, eyes wide, brows raised, face vacant of understanding.

"Where was your husband on that day?" I kept my temper with commendable patience, I thought.

"Mmmm. . . ." she considered. "Well, he had his crop in by then. No," she shook her head, releasing more straw curls; "It was a day much like any other. I'm afraid I can't remember."

I rose from my seat on the settle and asked for paper and ink. I did not believe I could glean any more from the sterile field that was her brain and I had instructions to issue.

Chapter Twenty-three

The pig's bulk slammed into him, knocking him clear off his feet into the reeds. The squeals of rage rang in his ears, the vicious little eyes promised to stomp him with her bulk and her sharp trotters.

Deacon Lamb rolled into the reeds and scrambled for his life. The pig came down upon him as an instrument of destruction, but it was God's will he be spared. He fled into the quaking bogs—few would dare follow him here. There were places where a man could stay safe and dry. You could survive very well upon fish, upon duck eggs, and there were the crisp heads of ferns and cattail shoots tender as white asparagus. You could survive very well.

They'd come looking for him, he knew, and he lay in wait. He set a trap to give him warning of their approach—set a deceptive clump of bog grass over a watery hole. You'd have to know enough to hop across, or into the treacherous swamp you'd fall.

The young minister shouldn't have interfered, the sniveling hypocrite. He recalled with satisfaction the thwack of his cane across the young man's head. *Thou shalt not suffer a witch to live.* The Deacon scowled. It was Jehovah's will! He'd had the old hag tarred and feathered. The Deacon snickered at the memory of the grotesque figure hopping about on the Green like a giant bird.

It was snippy Mister Cotton's interference that saved her; the Deacon fumed in silent resentment. *Thou shalt not suffer a witch to live!* It was The Word! He was only obeying The Word! He'd meant to hang the old hag, a warning to all other witches. What did the young minister know of Rumney Marsh? The black arts— they were practiced daily, if only they'd listen to him.

He'd convinced the men to hang Pisspot on the site where Chieves was killed—hadn't the young fool accused the big oaf of the murder? It was Mister Cotton's own stupidity that nearly hung Tom Pisspot. And the sniveling young hypocrite deserved to be pushed into the pond. As if he didn't know what Mister Cotton meant sniffing 'round his wife. The Deacon shook his head. Did they think he was too old to protect his own property? He'd caught the young rascal alone, taking a drink, and thwack! He'd hit him over the head and pushed him in. Would've held him there, too, but for the pig. Sniveling young sneak, sniffing and snuffing 'round his wife . . . .

'Zillah's put a curse on me,' he thought, his heart heavy in his chest. The slave was a friend of the old hag. Hadn't Zillah come to him in a dream, taking the form of a snake? She'd lain on top of him so that he could neither move nor speak nor hardly breathe, and the very next morning as he mucked out the barn he'd seen the snake. It lay in serpentine curves on the pine floor boards, watching him with its evil eyes. Nor could he move, paralyzed as he'd been in the dream.

When it slithered down a hole in a brown pine knot, only then could he lift the shovel in his hand. He'd known it then; Zillah's put a curse on him with her African sorcery.

The black rooster disappeared and the hens stopped laying. Well, he'd shown her what happened to witches! He'd done that much before the sniveling young hypocrite showed up.

The Deacon watched the trembling grasses surrounding him; his eyes shifted back and forth. He'd hear the splash when they fell into his trap, and the horrid cries! He snickered to himself. At dusk he could relax. They would not attempt the bogs at night. Nobody was crazy enough to cross the quaking bogs at night. One misstep and you fell in the grasses covering you from the world, the greedy sand sucking you down under the water. Why, he wasn't about to stir from his own safe spot, and he knew the bogs!

A few days here, then he'd sneak back and make Zillah help him get away. Miss High and Mighty, and her only a slave. She'd be afraid of him now. A grim smile split the cracked pink lips. He would force Zillah to come with him. She could fetch, carry and cook for him, like a slave should. She'd set the pig on him; that accursed beast followed her around like a dog. Miss High and Mighty Zillah—if she didn't obey him quick he'd whip the black skin off her.

He sighed aloud and rose from his hiding place. The sun was down—time to catch his supper. The Deacon skewered three fish over a small fire. He kept his ears open as he hunkered down to eat but the only sound was a chorus of spring peepers. The night was warm, moist with salt air. He relished the cloak of night; he was safe now.

The Deacon removed his black coat, folding it carefully and setting it upon fresh green shoots of bog grass. He lay down beside it and closed his eyes. Spring peepers throbbed their lusty ardor into the black night. The muffled roar of the breakers hitting the sands of Pulling Point sounded like a drum, echoing the eager chorus of frogs. He sniffed the sultry night air for rain. If a storm came there'd be even less chance of anyone venturing into the bogs. He dozed off, content.

Deacon Lamb woke to a black, still night. The distant surf pounded in steady rhythm, pulsating in an endless undercurrent of waves. He raised his head. Big breakers—must be a storm. The frogs were silent—animals knew. Sometimes the woods became unnaturally silent before a bad storm. Tiny yellow lights danced in the bog grass. "Swamp rot," he spoke aloud. Some people thought they were ghosts, but they never hurt anybody, so long as you didn't follow them into the swamp.

The Deacon slid his hand carefully across to his coat, feeling for the capacious pocket and the knife hidden inside. He had the knife and a stout wooden limb he'd found. He stretched out his legs. There was a heavy smell of spice to the bogs. The night air was so humid he was sweating. A cooling rain would be refreshing, although he had no cover and would probably catch quinsy. No matter, he'd make Zillah tend him. She was good at curing ills. He'd keep an eye on her so she didn't cause him ills, that's all.

A faint crackling of dry grass caused him to rise up on one elbow and peer into the dark. Something was out there; he was not alone on the bog. The hairs on his neck prickled. He reached for his cane and poked it into the embers of the fire, sparking a tiny flame. Slowly he raised himself a little higher, throwing a handful of dry grass into the embers. He'd a pile of sticks ready; with care he added one to feed the tender flame. He slid another on top, and a third. Fire would keep the animals at bay. He got to one knee and crouched there.

Two fiery coals glowed at him across the grasses. A large feral cat stared at him with red, glaring eyes. He could see the twitch of the snake-like tail, back and forth, like a barn cat waiting for a mouse. The Deacon froze. A panther here in the swamp? He'd never seen a live one before but he'd heard tales of this beast; horrifying stories of the creature howling and scratching like a demon from Hell at the door of an isolated farmhouse; of calves dragged from the barn, leaving a bloody trail into the woods. This one was big; bigger than any he'd heard tell. Fear hung like a lump of black lead in his belly.

Why did the creature torment him? Half its tawny hide was hidden in the dark, yet he could see its long tail twitching in mocking anticipation. The creature bared its fangs in a hideous grin. How many bounds would it take to leap upon him and shred him with its steely claws? He knew he must will his fingers to grab the shaft of the knife but he could not make them move. Waves of blood coursed through his skull like the pounding of the surf.

A light splash in the water and the cat faded into the night. The Deacon turned his head to see a great, strange bird standing on one stork leg, its orange beak long and sharp as a rapier. Two obsidian bird eyes glittered with cold malevolence. The beak flashed bronze in a menacing arc. The Deacon thought of blue herons and how they speared their prey. This creature poised to strike at him—at him! Its sword-like beak would penetrate his skull and slice through his brain like butter. Soon it would be within striking distance. The long snake neck of the crane arched, beak drawn up and ready to strike, coal eyes glittering evil.

The throbbing in his head spread down the back of his neck; his ears felt about to explode from pounding and pain. He attempted to gather his thoughts, to fight his fear, to rationalize what he saw. Two rare creatures of the swamp, nothing more! If only the drumming in his head would stop he could think properly. The Deacon gasped for air like a beached fish.

Two wild creature—creatures of Hell! Satan's demons come to torment him! He tried to pray—prayer would protect him. The words would not come. The Deacon heard a menacing hiss and he knew the sound: witchery! He was a victim of witchery! Zillah's curse.

The hiss came from the bog itself, rising up against him with glittering yellow lights, unlike any creature he'd ever seen. A creature of the swamps that shook and shimmered as it advanced upon him; long strands of marsh grass waving in a mound of bog come to life. Witchery! The bog come to claim him. A shriek as unearthly as a panther's wild sob swelled from his agonized throat. The instinct to flee, to escape the awful apparition, released him from his paralysis. The Deacon leaped up, running for his life.

They found his body three days later, a mass of bloated flesh floating in the swamp. The coroner was hard put to decide whether the Deacon suffered the heart attack *before* he fell into the swamp or because he fell into the swamp.

Chapter Twenty-four

Creasy spoke a few words over the old woman's grave; a poor sober mound huddled beneath the heart-shaped leaves of a lilac bush. Lacy purple buds swelled in clusters, filling the air with a cloying perfume. A grove of apple trees added their sweet smell. All in all, a pleasant resting-place, he thought

There were only three people to mourn; the minister, the daughter and the Rumney Marsh jailer who'd felt guilt because he'd been locked in his own jail when the mob dragged out the old woman. The son was missing. No one had seen him since that day.

The breeze billowed Deborah's gray wool cloak around her slender, drooping figure. She pulled the cloak tight with black gloves of kid leather.

Creasy took one of the gloved hands, pressing it lightly. "Is there anything I can do for you? Anything?" He worried about her calm demeanor, her eyes deep as black pools.

"Thank you, no," she said.

"What will you do? Will you return to Roxbury?"

"Yes, in time," she said. "When I've seen to things here."

He thought it would be best for her to get away from the source of her painful memories. Creasy could have beaten the Deacon for causing her so much misery, but the old man's body had been found floating in the marsh, bloated and corrupt, as was his soul. And that was a just end. Arriving in such a waterlogged condition, the wicked old man would steam in the searing flames of Hell!

Deborah did not invite him into the house for funeral cakes.
He would have liked to stay with her for awhile, and a swallow of
that fine brandy would not come amiss.

"I don't like to leave you alone," he said.

"Oh, I shan't be alone for long. Tom's about."

"Are you sure?" Creasy frowned. "I wouldn't be surprised if
he was half way to Quebec by now. I wouldn't blame him."

"No, he'll turn up." She spoke with quiet assurance.

With no encouragement to remain, Creasy repeated his offer
of services and took his leave. He jammed his fists into his coat
pockets as he strode to his horse. He'd see her again; even it
meant a daily ride from Boston to Rumney Marsh.

The task remained for him to console the widow of the late
Deacon Lamb. His limbs felt as heavy as lead. What could he
say to her? That her husband deserved his bloated end? That he
had caused grievous harm not only to the old Gammar but to her
daughter, as well? That the hand of God had plucked the poor
insect from his lair and squashed him like the foul spider he
was? How could he console Rachel Lamb with these words? He'd
have to think of something; it was his duty.

A friendly whuff from the mare's muzzle broke Creasy's
concentration. He raised his head at a joyous squeal of greeting.
Priscilla the Pig trotted out from a grove of saplings. She carried
a bone in her mouth, which she deposited at the hooves of the
mare, as an offering of good will. Priscilla lifted her piggy head
for approval.

"Oho," Creasy cried, "what mischief have you been up to
now, Miss Priscilla? Is this the jawbone of an ass for me to smite
the Philistines?"

The intelligent animal pushed the bone forward with her pink
snout.

"What is it, Girl?" he cooed. This was the animal that had
saved him from drowning.

The mare shied backwards from the object near its hooves.

"What do you have there, Priscilla?" He peered across the
mare's brown mane and squinted at the bone. It was a strange

sort of bone; it seemed to be wrapped in scraps of cloth. Creasy felt a queasy stir in his bowels. What if it was a human bone? He dismounted, patting the large sandy head.

"You did right to bring this to me, Priscilla," he praised. "Good girl!" He stooped to retrieve the dirt-covered object. It was about ten inches in length. He chuckled.

"A child's poppet? You found a child's poppet?" He tweaked the pig's sandy ear.

Priscilla grinned up at him, batting her red-gold lashes.

Here was the beloved manikin of some little girl or boy, who must be grieved for the loss of the plaything. Perhaps he could return it to its small owner. Creasy brushed off clumps of dirt. The poppet emerged in a manful little coat of flannel, tiny flannel breeches and painted stockings beneath painted black shoes. He spit on a corner of his handkerchief and wiped off the mud from the molded head. The head was cleverly fashioned from clay and wax. There was the little face, with blue dots for eyes and painted pink cheeks and a shock of dirty white hair . . . real hair, whether horse, goat or human. He nearly dropped the doll; his fingers trembled.

"Where did you find this, Priscilla?" His voice felt raw, although he had recovered from his injuries except for a sore spot upon his head. "Show me, Girl. Show me!" He held the poppet out to her snout.

Priscilla sniffed the poppet with a dainty care. She raised her ears, a gleam in her narrow eyes that seemed to answer his command. Priscilla turned her vast bulk and trotted into the grove of saplings.

Creasy followed on foot, striding to keep her in sight. They followed a deer trail through the woods, the pig leading the way in a brisk trot. Creasy splashed through a brook, confident that the pig knew where she was going. Priscilla never veered; she squeezed underneath fallen tree trunks, through thick underbrush and dodged around trees. Creasy panted with exertion, fearing he might lose sight of the pig. Her pale hide gleamed through the brush like a rotund ghost. Creasy ducked and dodged branches, suffering whippings across his face and hands. He must keep her in sight.

Priscilla wove through a grove of slender trees with the skill of an Indian warrior. Creasy stumbled after her. He burst into a mossy clearing, stopped short and nearly pitched forward over his own boots.

Priscilla rooted at the foot of a tall oak, snorting and snuffling and poking her broad snout into the mossy ground. Creasy tiptoed over to see what she dug up. The pig raised her head at his approach. A clump of damp sod clung to one pink nostril and a small black feather stuck out of the clump. It looked as if the pig wore a pagan nose ornament.

Black feathers were scattered and trampled over the ground. There were pieces of wood. Creasy picked up a stick and poked around in the moss. He uncovered the claw of a large bird; a crow, he thought. With the tip of the stick he raised a clod of soil and found a black candle laying there underneath. He could see that the wick was black from burning. He turned and found a saucer of red clay at the foot of the tree. He picked up the saucer, turning it around in his hands. There was a white ring that marked a liquid content. Creasy sniffed; there was no scent. He thought the white ring might be the residue of milk, a saucer of milk. For a cat? Small animals were associated with witches, but a cat this far into the woods?

In his childhood, Creasy had once set out a saucer of milk for the barn cats; he'd set it outside the barn door. When he returned, he found a plate filled with slithering garter snakes; he'd not liked snakes since that day.

He stood shivering, not from his fear of snakes but for what the empty dish represented, for what the black bird represented what the poppet represented. He had stumbled upon a summoning of Satan! Witchcraft—a site for witchcraft!

His heart beat in his ears. He stooped to pick up shards of a small wooden box that Priscilla's rootings had uncovered. These were thin slabs of wood, polished on one side; natural on the other. Creasy pulled the manikin from his coat pocket; it fitted in length. The ground seemed to spin beneath him.

Maleficium! Deny the evidence of his own eyes he could not! Murder by witchcraft, the most foul of crimes because it imperiled the very soul! The poppet in his hands bore the artfully crafted features of the late Deacon Lamb.

He could not bear the sight of the unseeing blue-painted eyes. Creasy wrapped the poppet in his handkerchief and stuffed the image deep into his coat pocket. He glanced around the secluded glade What if the witch came back? What if she found him here? His arms jerked involuntarily.

Priscilla whoofed in reassurance, regarding him with friendly pig eyes. No one should hurt him while she was by, she seemed to say.

Creasy squared his shoulders. Who was the witch? This was not the work of old Gammar Pisspot, safe at last from the miseries of this world. His chest felt as heavy as if an anvil lay there. Hetty Henry—who else could it be? He would have to confront her, to pray with her . . . to redeem her. And he'd have to do it before the Rumney Marshians found this site. Current thinking held that witchcraft ran in families. If one's mother was thought a witch . . . they would accuse Deborah, of course! He shuddered, his whole frame shaking. She must be removed to safety. Deborah was no more a witch than he.

Hetty, a quick-tempered woman of action, hated the old man and she was Priscilla's owner.

He nudged clumps of sod and wood back into the hole, stomping the earth down over feathers, claws, candle and all but the saucer, which he replaced at the foot of the tree. He took a branch and brushed it over the spot obliterating traces of the pig's foraging and his own boot prints. The pig would have inspected his work, snuffling about the spot, but a curt command brought her to attention.

"Forget this place. Don't show it to anyone else," he ordered. "There's a good pig. It's difficult to hide a thing like this, Priscilla, but I must have the chance to pray for the poor deluded woman who did this! We have to protect the innocent and redeem the guilty—that's our task." He bent to pat her great snout. The pig gazed up at him with intelligent eyes.

She followed him back to the tethered mare. Creasy remounted and Priscilla lumbered off. Their paths lay in separate directions. Creasy's path must return him at once to the old Pisspot shanty.

His knock was answered immediately, as if she were waiting for him. He stepped inside, brushing past Deborah without ceremony as she stood in the doorway.

"Pack what you need for a short stay in Boston, Deborah, I'm taking you to my cousin's house. It's not safe for you here."

"I'm not afraid," she said, closing the door behind him.

'Yes, well I am, for you. I have to find a witch—someone who foolishly practices witchcraft, that is. Worrying about you being attacked by a mob won't make my task any easier. I'll explain on the way. Just do as I ask, please." He folded his arms and stood before her like a statue. If he had to, he was prepared to carry her off by force

Deborah examined his face. Without a word she nodded and left him.

'An intelligent woman,' he thought. He sighed in relief.

Deborah clung to his waist as they rode past the village green. To divert her attention from the scene of her mother's tragic attack Creasy began to tell her of his findings in the forest. He did not mention Priscilla's role.

"Why did you fill the hole in? Why did you conceal the evidence?" she asked.

"I don't trust your good neighbors, that's why. That mob of vipers . . . ." he growled.

"You've removed me from my mother's house. Do you think I am a witch?"

He turned his head and frowned at her.

"I had reason to hate the old man." Her eyes were veiled behind a black hood.

"So did others." His back stiffened under her arms.

"The Deacon stands before Judgment, weighted by the death of your poor mother. I think he also bears the burden for the murders of the two ministers, as well. Perhaps he thought I was close to finding out and that's why he tried to drown me. He tried to pin the murder of Naboth Chieves upon your mother, that we know."

Creasy had been brooding about the Deacon for two days now. The old man knew both ministers; he had inherited the estate of one of his victims. He'd been quick to blame the old Gammar, and he'd been equally quick to blame Tom Pisspot. With that great lout hanging from a tree, no one would bother to look elsewhere for the murderer. It had been folly to underestimate the old man, just because he was aged.

"Wickedness knows no barriers," he said aloud.

Deborah's arms tightened about his waist but she made no reply.

Creasy knew she had once been engaged to one of the victims. "I will discover the truth," he vowed. "Their deaths shall be met with justice here on the earth, as Divine Justice shall punish the wicked old man with the flames of Hell. I'm just afraid those lumpkins from the village will go out looking for a witch to blame if they find that site," he added.

"That is why you are protecting me," she said, her voice low.

"And others," he said, "and others, as well. He would not name anyone else, even to Deborah. Priscilla the pig led him to the site of witchcraft and witches had their familiars, but . . . . Priscilla had saved his life and Hetty had hidden him from the soldiers. He owed them both his silence. He would have to pray with her, harangue her into Repentance, rescue her from her misguided course. Her folly need never be made public if only she Repented.

Creasy, conscious of the two arms around his waist, addressed himself to Deborah. "You'll like my cousin's wife, I know." He felt himself cheered at the thought of Abigail's flower-like face. "The two of you shall be sisters," he declared. "Abigail—that's

Mistress Mather—has had her hands full of late. Cousin Cotton Mather suffers from *melancholia* . . . well, he's a man of great imagination. I'm sure Abigail will welcome the relief of feminine companionship."

"I don't wish to intrude upon them," Deborah said.

"Oh, don't even think it. Everyone is welcome in the Mather house, I'll say that for my cousin. Everyone is welcome who comes through his door." With Deborah safe in the Mather household, that was one less worry for him. Neither sheriff nor mob nor tyrant could storm the impregnable Mather position. Just ask Royal Governor Edmund Andros!

Chapter Twenty-five

I was hardly in the mood for visitors when he burst in—I'd skillets to scrub, dishes to wash, baking to do and planting to oversee. We were shorthanded as it was. Zillah remained with Rachel Lamb, who had no more idea of inventory than the man in the moon. Not only did Rachel have to contend with the Lott estate but now she must render an accounting of her late husband's possessions. Well, what could I do but give in when she reminded me I'd offered her Zillah's services?

Meanwhile I had my own fields to plow, crops to sow, new fruit trees to set out, animals to pasture, workers to feed and murders to solve. The farm chores would not wait for revolution or funerals, as I told Increase Cotton when he accused me with his long face and solemn eyes.

"There were few mourners at her funeral."

"Well, I'm sorry I did not get to the old Gammar's burial, but I paid my respects and carried over a basket of food. I invited Deborah to come stay with me, but she would not. Nor would I, in her place," I said. "She has her own affairs to attend. And I've had my hands full with Rachel Lamb. I notice you haven't been in any hurry to console her!" The remark was rather waspish of me, I knew, and it hit home.

Creasy drew himself to his full height, looking more like a gaunt scarecrow than ever. "I was on my way there. You need not fear I would neglect my duty to the widow, even though her late husband tried to kill me."

I waved my hand at a wooden bench. "I don't fear that, Sir.

Sit down. You must be tired." I gave him a closer scrutiny. In all the turmoil of the past several days I'd forgotten his injury. "How's your head?"

"Of no consequence." He remained standing.

Now I'd offended him. Well, so be it. I was tired myself. I sank into a stiff-backed chair. "Just as well you've come here first. I've something to tell you." It would come hard to the young man that Deacon Lamb had evidently not murdered Naboth Chieves—too many people had seen him working in the fields that afternoon. I'd checked upon my return from Rachel's home.

"I know," he said.

"I would have told you sooner but I had to see the magistrates. Everything happened so fast, and now the Deacon is dead," I explained.

"But not by your doing."

Creasy bent from the waist, peering at me with stern eyes.

Oh well, if he wished to take credit for the search I did not care. I shrugged off his claim as male vanity.

"It was by God's will that the Deacon met his death," Creasy shouted.

I turned my head away. How rude! "There's no need to raise your voice! I'm not deaf!"

"Nor repentant. Oh unregenerate sinner . . . only in repentance shall the soul find redemption!"

"I very much doubt there is any repentance for the Deacon's like," I noted. The Deacon wasn't the type of man to admit his wrongdoings.

"Oh, but we must repent—we can be saved by repentance—we can!"

Creasy knelt, knees creaking, next to my chair. He took my hand in his large paw. "Only in true repentance can we find Eternal Salvation!"

"I don't argue the point, Sir." He looked so earnest and beseeching. Perhaps he felt some guilt for failing to save the Deacon's soul?

"It was not your fault." I spoke in as kindly a tone as I could muster. "How could you have known? We must bear the responsibilities of our own actions." The Deacon's loss was only justice, after all. He had attacked Creasy and I was certain he'd had a hand in the murder of the two ministers if he had not actually done the deed himself.

"It is a heavy burden," he intoned, "to make a charge of such magnitude, even in confidence."

"The charge should be murder," I snorted, "but you have no proof." I pulled my hand from his hold.

"Ah, but I have the proof, that is why I came."

I jumped up, nearly knocking the man over in my excitement. "You have proof? Show me at once!" Why, here he teased me with evidence to link the Deacon to murder! "When did this happen? Where did you find it?" I'd heard no word since the discovery of the Deacon's body in the swamp.

"Calm yourself." Creasy stood in haste. "I've shown it to no one. Told no one. It has been a leaden weight upon me—I thought of nothing but of speaking to you."

Very commendable of him to think of consulting me, but I was anxious to see the evidence. "Show me—show me!" I begged, grabbing his sleeve and tugging on it. Nobody wanted to prove the Deacon guilty of murder more than I. The magistrates would have none of my accusations. I had proof of his inciting the mob and of his attack upon Creasy, so that was the charge they warranted.

"Have no fear," he cried, removing my fingers from his sleeve, "I shall be as secret as the grave. I have never betrayed a confidence."

"I don't doubt your integrity, Creasy, nor shall I say a word without your leave," I promised. "Show me your evidence—come, don't torment me!"

"Torment? Oh unhappy woman, I have prayed for such a sign of repentance! I knew it was not hopeless. Come, kneel with me and we shall pray together. In prayer shall redemption bring glorious release."

"Sir, if you mean to teach me patience I fear your lesson falls upon deaf ears—not that I don't need the lesson, the timing is all. First show me the proof, then I promise to pray on my knees all night long, if you wish."

I watched as a long hand fumbled in a coat pocket. He pulled out a linen-wrapped object, cylindrical in shape. Silent, with pursed lips of disapproval, he unrolled the bundle, handing me a dirty doll.

"A child's plaything?" I frowned, twisting the thing in my hands. It was similar to the fashion dolls we women used to stay abreast of London styles, but this was male with a shock of white hair. I'd yet to see a grandfather doll, but the thing was artfully fashioned with black small clothes and coat. The eyes were painted blue.

"Can you deny the evidence of your own eyes?" Creasy searched my face.

I handed the thing back to him. "Probably some little boy lost it."

"Poor deluded soul! Think—think of how the Deacon died!"

I stared at the man with amazement as his eyes filled with tears. The man must be suffering from a bout of nerves. He'd gone through too much lately! Perhaps the blow to his head . . . . Still, I would try to be patient with the man.

"What on earth does a doll have to do with the Deacon?"

"Nothing! That's what I've been trying to tell you!"

The man must be mad. A firm hand was needed, I could see that. "Creasy, you must be tired. Perhaps you should lie down." I gestured to the stairs behind us. "I'll see you are not disturbed."

"I want to pray with you. I came to pray with you."

Even for a minister, the man was obsessed with prayer. Thinking to humor him, I took his hand in mine and led him to the stairs. "I will pray upon my knees. Perhaps you would care to recline upon the bed while you hear my prayers?"

Creasy, however, was not to be coaxed. His hangdog air was beginning to get on my nerves.

"Poor, weak, deluded woman." He shook his head. "He was a wicked old man—a murderer—not worth the loss of your soul! Let me help you. Pray with me."

"I thought we were helping each other, and calling me names won't help us find the murderer of Naboth Chieves."

"Nor will this." He held out the doll.

"A doll—a doll? What has a doll to do with it?"

"Nothing!"

Now I was really exasperated. How do you reason with a man who's lost his senses?

"Cease your stubborn defiance, Hetty, I beg of you. I can help you."

He gripped my shoulder, fingers digging in like a hawk's claw.

"With prayer we can banish this hellish vice into which you have sunk."

"Oh?" I could feel my hands clench. "What hellish vice is that, Sir?" I would not give him the satisfaction of flinching under his hand.

"No one need ever know, I promise you. With repentance you shall find redemption. Confess your ungodly practices and pray for forgiveness with me!"

"Ungodly practices? If you mean meddling in men's business just because I have ascertained that the Deacon could not have murdered Naboth Chieves—at least directly—why, I think your jealous nature is to be deplored. Women are just as capable as men at ferreting out the truth, indeed, perhaps we are even more capable. We do not let our vanity get in the way. And I think you are the weak and deluded fool." With a quick chop of my fist beneath his elbow I freed my shoulder from his grasp. He stepped back, not I.

"Oh, Woman, Woman . . . ." He rubbed his elbow. "You may question the sons of man 'til Doomsday comes, for all I care. It is your conversations with Satan of which I speak. You endanger your soul . . . ."

"Conversations with Satan?" I interrupted him, but I could not continue. Surely the man was mad! I shook my head in amazement.

"Denial is futile," he persisted. "I found the site."

He waited for my response but I had none to give.

"In the forest." He watched me with grave eyes. "Priscilla led me to it." Watching. "I met her with this . . . thing . . . in her mouth."

I did not know what to say; I did not know what he meant.

"I found the evidence—a coffin for this poppet, a black candle, black feathers—a site for devil worship." He shuddered.

My brain seemed to be smothered in wool. What was the man talking about?

"*Maleficium.*" He held forth the doll in gloomy triumph.

And I knew now the doll's likeness. Deacon Lamb! The back of my head throbbed. The man was accusing me of witchcraft!

I could not speak to defend myself. I kicked him hard in the shin.

He hopped up and down, yowling like a singed cat.

The sight broke my mute spell and released a torrent of abuse from my tongue. I'd picked up many a salty curse from my first husband: *Scurvy knave* and *false rogue* were two of the mild sort.

"Wait! Wait!" He thrust out one long arm to ward off my advance as he hopped about on his good leg. "It may be that I have wronged you!"

"May be—*may* be, is it?" I eyed the other bony shin, estimating how best to land my next crippling blow.

"I have! I have wronged you!" He hopped beyond my reach. "Forgive me! Please forgive me!"

Forgive the man for his baseless, wicked thoughts? Accuse me of witchcraft, would he? *Witchcraft!*

"Go!" I shouted, flexing my arm and pointing. "Out of my home!"

Creasy fled by the kitchen door out into the ell. I dropped into a chair. Witchcraft—summoning Satan—was a hanging offense. With the turmoil aroused by the old Deacon in this community, I'd be lucky to get a trial! Look at what they'd done to the old Gammar and her son! I could not help feeling ill; my stomach churned. If Creasy let one word of this out I'd be in real danger. How could he be so absurd? My anger ebbed, replaced by sadness. How could he think such a thing of me? I knew nothing of the black arts!

Did he believe me? I'd not made any cogent arguments except to attack the man, anger blinding me to reasoning. *Reasoning*; I clung to the word What were the facts here? Set aside my feelings and examine what he'd told me. A site for practice of the black arts, and Priscilla led him there. I repressed the anger threatening to arise; just because of Priscilla he'd blamed me! Priscilla roamed about freely; she knew everyone in Rumney Marsh. Perhaps she'd followed someone there or perhaps she'd found it on her own. She was a curious and intelligent creature; I'd no doubt she was capable of anything except conducting black rites.

Who would practice such rites? The taste of bile soured my mouth. I did not mean to make the same mistake as Creasy. I'd not make assumptions. I would speak to my candidate first. My limbs felt tied to rocks. I did not want to move from my chair, but I had a duty here. Before anyone else could be confronted or accused of this accursed crime I had to make a trip to Ipswich, to the home of the late Absalom Lott.

I forced myself out of the chair, packed a nightrobe, a clean apron and some coins in a satchel, pulled my black cape from its peg and wrote a letter of instruction for Elijah. I called a boy to run to the fields with the letter. Pulling my hood close to my face, I hurried down the path to the ferry.

Bob Stubb lifted my satchel into his little craft, leaving me to climb aboard on my own. Neither he nor I were quite prepared for the sudden splash and rocking of the boat. Instinct made me grab the railing. Bob Stubb spun around with a scowl for the invader.

There he sprawled, half in and half out of the craft. He pulled one long leg over, his boot wet and muddy. "Mister Stubb," he cried, gasping for breath, "I must have passage."

I'd half a mind to order Stubb to throw the man overboard but I thought better to wait, perhaps 'til we reached the ocean swells . . . . The picture this presented to my mind gave me comfort.

Creasy seated himself a distance from me. I turned my head, ignoring him for much of the journey. The usual exhilaration I felt from sun, sea spray and riding the waves was missing on this journey. Only when I heard the retching noises did my spirits pluck up. Creasy's face was green as the mold on cheese. Stubb and I exchanged glances, Stubb managing not to smile.

By the time the coastline appeared on the horizon I felt much improved. I even shifted my seat nearer the sufferer. When he lifted his head from the railing and moaned "Forgive me," with such pitiful glazed eyes, I acquired enough charity to speak to him.

Chapter Twenty-six

Hetty spent the whole trip glaring at him while the little craft bobbed up and down in the swells like a cork. Creasy's guts sloshed around like the smelly green water that filled the bottom of the boat. They nearly reached the harbor when Foxy Gabriel rowed past them in a dory, cutting them off and screaming threats and imprecations directed at him. Well, what could he do but pull himself together and answer the Quaker's taunts with some barbs of his own?

The Quaker shook his fist at Creasy. "*Preacher, thou swallowest false prophecies greedy as a dog that eats the crumbs from his Master's* table," the Quaker ranted.

"*A living dog is better than a dead lion! Ecclesiastics IX*" Creasy shouted back.

"*Second Peter: The dog* is *turned* to his *own vomit again.*" the Quaker sneered.

Creasy, angered, shouted out: "Oh, yes? Well, *Tobit* V: 16!"

"That's Apocryphal!"

"And so are you!"

The cantankerous Quaker pulled beyond ear shout. Then Hetty released a stream of invectives at him, which she kept up as they docked, and all the way to the late minister's door.

Creasy thanked the Lord for the civility of Zillah, who took their coats and cloaks and seated them in separate places in the kitchen. The servant produced two mugs of foaming beer for them, handing her mistress a list of the inventory with her drink.

'Good,' Creasy thought, 'that will keep her occupied.' He

looked around at the trunks and boxes that were neatly stacked at one end of the kitchen. Zillah was very efficient at her work, he could see. Now she was building up the hearth fire and producing kettles and skillets. In a short while the two were called to the table.

Creasy dug into a smooth molasses pudding with buttery johnnycake as a side. He accepted with gratitude a plate of fish rolled in corn meal, a dish of stewed apples and more of the excellent beer. Silently he blessed the woman with every bite. Zillah was a true gem; Creasy hoped Hetty recognized the worth of her servant and did not berate her the way she berated him. His ears still burned at her language!

Pushing back his chair from the table, Creasy groaned in satisfaction. Hetty still pecked at her food. Zillah took his plate and mug, carried them away, and returned to stand at his elbow.

"Sir, would you care to see the minister's study? There are his papers which need to be sorted."

"Hetty?" He glanced over at Hetty, asking for her permission with the inflection of his voice.

"Someone has to do it," she growled, waving her hand to dismiss him.

Creasy was glad to follow Zillah to Absalom Lott's study. He preferred his own company this evening. The servant left him to sort through boxes of paper; of old sermons and correspondence. His fingers sorted through the sheets with rapid concentration. There was nothing here of a recent date. He moved on to the desk and lifted the lid. A profusion of papers filled each cubby; he pulled up a stool and perched upon it.

Zillah entered in her silent grace and handed him a mug filled with a steaming brew.

"An infusion of borage and clotbur, Sir, to relieve the fatigue of travel," she said in her soft voice.

The hot liquid warmed his throat and revived his brain; Hetty had a gem in this servant, he thought once more. Creasy knew what he wanted from the Ipswich minister's study; the last sermon Absalom Lott wrote, no doubt sitting at this very desk. It was a suggestion from Cousin Cotton; find the last sermon, which would most likely yield a clue to the minister's thoughts. It was the fashion to preach upon current happenings. Most of Creasy's sermons for the past year had alluded to tyrants.

Lott wrote in a crabbed hand; perhaps he sought to save paper. Creasy rubbed his eyes and sipped at the infusion as he sorted through the cubbies. No sermon was to be found but in the top right-hand corner he pulled out a single sheet of paper and turned it over, Here was a crabbed sheet of notes for Lott's last sermon, the one he never preached. The lines were crossed and recrossed with citings of scripture. Smudges and smears made it difficult to decipher. Too bad the man hadn't the chance to write out his sermon in full, but scripture was important in determining the topic. What were the minister's concerns before he died? Would these notes reveal something of his murderer?

At first reading there seemed to be two themes; the first on judgment and a second on love. Here were several citings from the *Song* of *Solomon*, but the main text was clearly *Romans II, 1: Wherein thou judgest another, thou condemnest thyself.* This text was twice underlined at the top of the page.

Now what did that mean? Creasy stretched, throwing his long arms out and opening his mouth in a gaping yawn. It had been a tiring day, what with the old Gammar's grave, the ride to Boston and back, and then an unexpected trip to Ipswich. Ah, how weary in body and mind he felt. Bless Zillah for bringing him this clotbur tea! It helped ease his aches.

Perhaps these scrawls would make more sense to him if he rewrote them on a clean sheet. He borrowed a nibbed quill and dipped the tip into a jar of ink. He started with the theme, which was underlined thus: *Wherein thou judgest another, thou condemnest thyself.* Now, that could certainly be a warning to the congregation of Rumney Marsh, however Lott preached in Ipswich. He found no references to witchcraft scriptures.

Here were the references on love and desire from *Song*; here *Proverbs* on false witness; *Kings* on evil and *Ezra* on punishment, but what evil? Which evil, murder or witchery?

The answer looked to be in *Deuteronomy XXII*, but how did this fit in with the murder of Lott? And who was the fearful hypocrite of *Isiah*?

Creasy rubbed his hand across his forehead, leaving a streak of black ink over one brow. What were these scriptures all about? What was their purpose? There seemed to be a woman in the story. He was not at all surprised at this, and what woman more troublesome than Hetty Henry? He had the feeling that Hetty was a little too bossy to be this particular female.

How about the Deacon's wife? Now there was a flirtatious baggage. What if Rachel Lamb was in love with Naboth Chieves? By all accounts the minister was something of a charming dog. How did Absalom Lott fit into this? Was Absalom Lott in love with Rachel Lamb? Was she in love with him? Did she make it a point to seduce any unattached minister who came her way?

He considered other possible women. To be fair, there was Deborah who had been engaged to Naboth Chieves, but he doubted she knew Absalom Lott. And it was difficult to imagine old toothless Gammar Pisspot as anyone's heart's desire. So who was the unknown fair one in Absalom Lott's notes? As he studied the page his eye fell upon the cited *Song of Solomon: I,5.* He took another sip of tea and reflected. The answer was almost standing in front of him.

"Come," he spoke aloud to himself in his growing excitement. "If you rearrange these citings thus . . ." He drew a series of circles and arrows and studied the results:

> Romans II, I (underlined;) Solomon VIII, 6 ; Proverbs XIV, 5; Solomon I, 5; and VII, 10; Kings XIII, 2; Deuteronomy XXII, *25; Ezra VII*, 26; *Genesis IV*, 8; *Romans II*, 1 (repeated;)
>
> *Romans VIII, 19; Psalms XXV, 18; Isiah XXXIII*, 14; *Jeremiah XV, 21.*

"Ah, yes," he said, pleased. He pushed his stool back. He

knew the sermon as surely as if Moses himself had come down from the mountain, handing him a piece of smoking slate.

"Hetty! Hetty Henry! Come here!"

I paused on my way to my chamber, which was actually the bedchamber of Absalom Lott. Creasy waved a sheet of paper at me as I stood in the doorway, his face a beacon to match the candles that lit the room.

I entered against my will, which urged sleep, but his obvious excitement roused my curiosity.

"Look at this!"

He thrust the paper in my face. I saw inkblots, circles and curlicues; all very unintelligible.

"Look, look," he persisted. "It's all here. The key is in *Genesis*, which I misread as *Jeremiah*—a natural mistake, you see, because that prophet is also cited: *And I will deliver thee out of the hand of the wicked, and I will redeem thee out of the hand of the terrible.* Don't you see?"

"No," I said. "I can't make head nor tail out of your scribblings."

"Nor could I, at first, of Lott's." He waved the paper in the air. "But then I wrote his citings out—forgive my handwriting—and put them in this order and it all made sense!"

"Not to me, it doesn't. What are you saying?"

"I know, Hetty. I know whose wicked hand Lott sought deliverance from and for what. I know who killed Naboth Chieves and who murdered Absalom Lott and who led Deacon Lamb to the slaughter!"

He threw his hands above his head, which was bobbing like an apple in a bucket as he spoke. I felt quite dizzy watching him.

"Whoa, Dobbin, slow down. You mean you found this in his sermon notes?"

"Didn't I tell you I wanted to go over his recent sermons? I thought they might tell me his concerns, and I was right. The last three were scathing denunciations of Andros' government. oh, the Governor would not have liked them one bit!"

"Are you saying it was as we first thought? That the Royal Governor or his henchman, Secretary Ruckenmaul, ordered the man murdered?" I could hear my own voice rise in my excitement.

"No, I am not saying that at all. Listen, please, and try not to interrupt." Creasy scowled at me.

"I did not find his last sermon, the one he would have preached had he lived—perhaps he'd no chance to write it out. I found the notes for it—a list of scriptures, with one underlined which I knew must be his topic. See—here is the sheet."

Creasy picked up a small piece of paper covered in what appeared to be chicken scratchings. He set it back down upon the desk.

"Then I wrote them all down, the scriptures, and rearranged them thus. Wait . . . let me show you."

I bent over the desk beside him and watched and listened as a long finger pointed to each scripture in turn. He rocked gently on his feet as he spoke, his voice low but expressive.

"I knew a woman was involved from the *Song of Solomon* references . . . ." He held up one finger to silence any comment from me. "I knew the identity of this woman when I read *First Solomon: I am black, but comely, O ye daughters of Jerusalem, as the tents of Kedar, as the curtains of Solomon.*"

He glanced at me to see if I understood its import; I nodded.

"They tell a story, you see, the scriptures. The theme was the judgment of *Romans II*, namely that the minister had condemned himself for judging someone in haste and out of jealousy. Again *Solomon: For love is strong as death; jealousy is cruel as the grave.*"

I said nothing although I was bursting with judgments of my own.

"Then enters the false witness of *Proverbs: false witness will utter lies.* That false witness was Deacon Lamb, who told poor Lott that the woman he loved had been forced—ahem—against her will to illicit intercourse with Naboth Chieves. This is cited in Kings and *XXII Deuteronomy. But if a man find a betrothed damsel in the field, and the man force her, and lie with her, then the man that lay with her shall die.*"

"It is a lie!" I could not longer keep silent, so furious was I. "Naboth Chieves tried to seduce her in Lamb's barn but one of the farmhands heard her cry out and came to her rescue. Rachel Lamb told me all about it."

Creasy nodded. "I can understand Lott's response. No doubt I should have acted the same way, which was *by Ezra VII, 26: Let judgment be executed speedily upon him, whether it be unto death or to banishment.* It's the old story of Cain and Abel. *And it came to pass, when they were in the field, that Cain rose up against Abel his brother, and slew him.*" Creasy paused. "Naboth Chieves was Lott's brother in the ministry."

"Don't you think it's time we had a talk with Zillah?" I found I could not look too deeply into the man's eyes, which were soft with unshed tears and dark as charcoal. Murder was bad enough, but murder of one minister by another was unthinkable.

"Don't you want me to finish the story?"

"I think it best that Zillah hear what you have to say." I spoke in as kind a manner as I could. "After all, she is deeply involved in this tragedy. She must have her chance to explain.

Creasy nodded. We both dragged ourselves back to the kitchen, out feet as reluctant as our souls to have this confrontation. I took Creasy's arm to bolster my own spirits as much as his. I felt as if we were walking into a play by Master William Shakespeare, except this Desdemona was alive and ripe for vengeance.

Zillah waited for us, greeting us with mugs of steaming herbal infusion. "This will soothe you."

I looked at Creasy but he avoided my eyes. As for Zillah, she took a seat at the long table, folding her slim brown hands together. Her face was composed, her expression tranquil.

I sat across from her, accepting my mug and breathing in the fragrant fumes with gratitude. A sip of the hot liquid soothed my dry throat. Creasy seated himself beside me.

"I sat up to wait for you," Zillah explained. "I don't retire until everyone else is abed." She spoke to Creasy, as I knew her duties.

Creasy took time to sip his infusion. Finally he reached across the table and touched her upon her shoulder, a finger grazed her sleeve light as a butterfly. "Zillah, I must speak with you. There are things I would like you to confirm."

She returned his gaze with calm doe eyes.

"It was you, wasn't it? You were the lady whom Absalom Lott loved."

"Yes." Her voice was low and musical.

Creasy leaned back in his chair. "I knew it from the scriptures—the notes he left for his sermon. They tell a story, you see. They tell me that Deacon Lamb made a false accusation against Naboth Chieves . . . ."

"I told Mister Cotton it was all a lie," I interrupted.

"Mistress Lamb told me what happened."

Creasy went on, as if I had never interrupted him. "Absalom Lott sought out Mister Chieves, to punish him. They had a fight and Chieves was killed."

"It was an accident." Zillah's eyes were dark as a night pond Her smooth brow was unfurrowed.

I marveled at her composure.

"Deacon Lamb was a spiteful old man. He told Absalom that I had been ravished by Mister Chieves. He gave Absalom a stone adze, one of the field hands saw the exchange. Absalom took it, I don't know why. Perhaps he did not know what he was doing. Mister Chieves carried a cudgel when he traveled, but my Absalom would not have been afraid of that." Zillah's voice held a note of scorn.

"Where is the adze now?" Creasy asked.

"It's here, in the barn. I found it under a pile of hay."

"I'll look at it tomorrow. Go on—why do you say it was an accident? Who told you?"

"I met him, Absalom, late that afternoon. I knew something was wrong. He was supposed to walk past Mistress Henry's house to see me that noontime but he did not come. He told me what happened. The old woman saw it all—it was as Absalom said."

"You spoke to the old woman? She would not speak to me or to my cousin Mather," Creasy frowned.

"You are a stranger to her. She knows me." Zillah's gaze was steady.

I thought to myself how much alike were the old crone and the beautiful young woman before me—for Zillah was beautiful with her doe eyes, her high cheekbones, her sculptured mouth. Both were outcasts; one a slave, one little better; both led hard lives; both were foreign to New England shores; both were witches, or thought to be.

Much as I'd pitied the old Gammar I felt more sorrow for Zillah's plight. She'd lost the man who loved her. Such a loss is not easy to bear. And she'd had to hide her feelings, could not make public display of her grief—or of her love, which must be hidden from the world. People would not take kindly to a slave acting above her station. Hiding her love, oh that must have been the cruelest cut of all!

"Be that as it may," Creasy went on, "what happened between the two ministers?"

"You must understand that Absalom was near mad with anger."

Zillah leaned forward slightly, the only sign of anxiety witnessed in her. "He did not mean to kill that man—just give him a beating."

"Which he deserved," I muttered. No one paid any attention.

"My Absalom met with that man on the road. Instead of telling the truth, that man told Absalom that I had lain with him willingly and many times. He laughed at Absalom. So my Absalom pulled that man off his horse and they fought. That man hit Absalom with a whip. Absalom swung the adze without thinking. He did not know that man was dead—he just walked away. He wanted to see me, to see if I had been harmed. He did not believe that man's lies." Zillah lifted her head; she looked at each of us in turn.

Neither of us challenged her claim. I could well imagine Absalom Lott's feelings for this woman. I thought of my first husband, Jack, and the difficulties we'd faced in our young courtship. I wished the two lovers had trusted me enough to confide in me.

"Then what happened?" Creasy asked.

"We met—he told me about the fight. I told him I was unharmed, that it was all lies. My Absalom was upset that the old man lied to him. We did not have much time, you understand, so we kissed and he left me. I did not see him again." Her voice was low.

I strained to hear every word, so intent was I upon her story, even though my eyelids were beginning to droop. There was a question I had to ask.

"Why did Deacon Lamb tell such a lie about you? Did he know about Absalom Lott's affection for you?"

"Oh yes, Mistress, he knew. My Absalom was not a coward— he was not ashamed of me. It was I who forbade him to tell others—until such time as I gained my freedom. He asked Mistress Lamb to free me, but the Deacon would not hear of it. Absalom offered to buy me, then. Mistress Lamb might have sold me to him, I think, but the Deacon opposed that as well."

"I am so sorry" I reached over and placed my hand over her folded fingers. Zillah held her head high, but her hands were clenched tight beneath mine. Further questions could wait, I decided. I turned to Creasy, catching him in a wide yawn. "May we finish this conversation tomorrow?"

Creasy snapped shut his jaws. "There is just one matter we must discuss. I know we are all tired, but I cannot leave this." Creasy rose and draped himself over the chair, facing Zillah. "I found the site of black magic in the woods. I found a poppet in the image of Deacon Lamb."

Zillah shrugged. "Deacon Lamb murdered my Absalom. I knew this but who would believe me, a black woman, a slave? There must be revenge upon him. The blood of my ancestors called for it. I made a poppet in his image and buried it with the proper ceremony."

Murder, Mather and Mayhem | 203

"But Zillah," Creasy cried, his face twisted in consternation, "you are a Christian woman! To call upon Satan as your ally . . . surely you knew the wrong in that!"

"Oh, Mister Cotton, I did not call upon Satan! I swear I did not! There are other means, taught to me by my mother. I called upon the spirits of my people—to them I sacrificed; to Ogun and to Shango and to Obatala. I did not call upon Satan. I know that would be wrong."

"These are other names for the forces of darkness, Zillah." His stern voice was tempered by a yawn. "However, we may speak of these things tomorrow and pray on them tonight. You must pray for forgiveness." Creasy straightened, releasing his hold upon the chair. "It was the wrong thing to do, Zillah, to try foreign sorcery. Fortunately no harm was done. The Deacon drowned in the bog, so you see that the Lord took vengeance upon him, just as it says in the Bible."

"Yes. The old man drowned in the swamp," Zillah agreed.

He nodded and rose from the table.

"Take that candle." I pointed to a handled wooden dish. "There's a cot made up for you in the hall behind the chimney. You'll be warm there. I hope that's comfortable for you?"

I dared him to object. He did not. "Good. I'll be up in just a minute." I had a few words of comfort for Zillah before I retired.

Chapter Twenty-seven

"Zillah! Zillah!"

I held my ears as he stomped into the room. His hair was neatly brushed and bound with a thin black ribbon, his face freshly shaven.

I am not of a cheerful disposition in the morning. I realized my hair hung in clumps from my cap; my eyes were red-rimmed; nevertheless I resented his greeting.

"You look a sight. What's the matter? Where's Zillah?" He looked around the kitchen. The hearth was black and cold. He turned back to me. "No offense. You look as if you've slept poorly, that's all. Me, I slept like a log. Shall I start the fire? For breakfast?"

"Why bother? There's nothing to eat anyway." I was in a sour mood.

"But . . . . Won't Zillah find something? She did last night. The woman's a miracle—like the loaves and fishes of last night's meal."

"Zillah won't be performing miracles today. She's gone."

"Gone? Where? When will she get back?"

"She won't be back."

He ignored my glare. "What do you mean, she won't be back? Where is she? I have to talk to her. We have much business together this morning. She's your servant—where have you sent her?"

"I don't know where she is, so it's no use pestering me. And she is not my servant any longer," I informed him.

"What do you mean, not your servant?"

"Zillah is a free woman. I gave her her freedom. She can go wherever she likes, and she has."

"You did what?"

I covered my ears at his shout. I had a throbbing headache as it was.

"You let her go? Without consulting me?" His voice rose two octaves.

"Consult with you? I must consult with you over my own servant?" The man was treading on dangerous ground.

"Have you forgotten there's a little matter of murder and witchcraft here? Have you forgotten that I represent the magistrates as well as the Reformed church of New England?"

"Take deep breaths," I advised, noting the fiery flush that crept from his neck to his cheeks. "Recall *Proverbs XV: He that is slow to anger . . . .*"

"Don't you quote scripture to me," he said, drawing himself to his full height. "I must speak to the woman. Where did she go?"

"I don't know where she went. She did not confide in me. She left during the night. I was asleep."

"Do you have any idea where she might have gone?"

"No. I told you, I don't know where she is or where she's going."

Creasy opened his mouth but snapped it shut just as quickly. "We won't get anywhere in this mood. Get your cloak," he ordered. "Let's go to Sprague's and get some breakfast. I need food in my belly before I can think what to do."

As I could not disagree with this sentiment, I complied.

We dined on warm beans and bacon, a thick white sauce frothing over the slabs of fried pork; on pickled eggs and large chunks of yellow johnnycake, washed down with mugs of cider. The pangs of hunger eased, he began to converse in a more agreeable tone.

"I am sorry Zillah ran away. I only wanted to pray with her, for her own good."

"I know."

"I should have thought of her in connection to the witchcraft practice."

"Why, because she was a slave?"

"No, because that doll was well carved. I think of the sticks and rags the old Gammar called her poppets—so primitive. An intelligent, creative mind made that doll."

"Yes, and that's why you accused me!"

"Yes . . . ." He hesitated. "That and the fact that you are Priscilla's owner. I should have recognized the rites as being African in origin."

"Zillah was born in the West Indies," I said, "but her mother came from Africa She was a great healer, so Zillah told me. She taught her daughter those arts as well. We must remember that."

"Did she speak to you last night?"

"A little." I took another bite of johnnycake and brushed tiny yellow crumbs from my bodice. I considered how much of last night's conversation was told to me in confidence or whether it was of such import that I should repeat what Zillah had told me. I'd have to decide question by question. I knew the questions were unavoidable.

"What did she tell you?"

"She said that the Deacon killed Absalom Lott, that they quarreled over the confession Lott was about to make."

Creasy nodded. "His intention is clear from the scriptures he chose."

"You were going to finish explaining them to me . . . ."

"I think the man felt great remorse for his crime. Here, I have the paper with me." Creasy withdrew a folded sheet from his coat pocket. He spread it on the table facing me. "He was brought to mind *of Romans VIII, 19: Vengeance is mine, I will repay, saith the Lord.* He asked forgiveness for his sins in *Psalms XXV. Look upon mine afflictions and my pain, and forgive all my sins.*" Creasy's long finger traced each scripture on the page.

"If I know Deacon Lamb, he probably told Absalom Lott to let the old woman hang, that no one would ever know." My trust in the old Deacon had long since vanished.

"I think he meant to blackmail Lott. But he saw his hold slipping away. That's recorded in *Isiah XXXIII*. *The sinners in Zion are afraid; fearfulness hath surprised the hypocrites.* A public confession would deliver Absalom Lott from his guilt and from his father-in-law. Thus we have *Jeremiah XV: "And I will deliver thee out of the hand of the wicked, and I will redeem thee out of the hand of the terrible."* Creasy glanced up from the paper, as if eager for my agreement.

I did agree. "Absalom Lott was not the kind of man to let an old woman hang in his place."

"That's when the Deacon killed him."

"With the adze," I interjected.

"Stunned him with a blow," Creasy corrected, "and then hung him to make it look a suicide . . . the foul old villain!" Creasy's face turned red with indignation. "Oh, that such wickedness should walk the face of this earth!"

I reached over and laid my hand upon his sleeve. "He walks no longer," I said, attempting to console him. "The Lord had rendered His judgment."

"He has," Creasy nodded. The color receded from his face. He lifted his mug and took a long draught of cider. The mug clanked on the table as he set it down. "Imagine the foolish girl thinking she could conjure up her African devils to punish the old villain. All she did was to put her soul in danger. Why, she might have put the entire community in danger with her ignorant superstitions!"

I was tempted to remind him how quick he had been to accuse me but I refrained, wanting to distract him from the direction I feared the conversation was taking. "Creasy, I feel the need for fresh air. Will you walk with me?" I rose from my seat.

He lifted himself from the table with a groan of pleasure.

"I have eaten too much. A walk will be welcome. Perhaps it will clear my head."

We strolled past the dock, down along the shore. The steady lap-lap of the waves was soothing to my nerves. A sweet breeze stirred my cloak. Squabbling gulls wheeled above our heads in a sky of bright blue. I was content to let Creasy begin in his own time. Perhaps his senses were as lulled as mine, for we left many footprints on the damp sand before he spoke, and then it was with a gentle sigh.

"What a pity I hadn't the chance to pray with Zillah for redemption!"

I took Creasy's arm, sliding my hand beneath and around "Do you recall Mister Wigglesworth's poem, "The Day of Doom?"

Creasy smiled, nodding. "Indeed, who does not know of that great epic?"

"I've always had a sneaking sympathy for the newborn babes—," I said. "They are assigned the easiest place in Hell as their punishment for Original Sin."

My companion looked down upon me, his black brows raised, questioning the connection.

"Isn't Zillah like a newborn babe in her innocence and ignorance of the demands of the Reformed Church?" I questioned. "Surely the Lord will understand her grievances and her lapse into pagan ritual."

"I mean Zillah no harm, rest assured." He spoke quietly.

"Will the magistrates go after her, do you think?" That was my worry—I did not wish to see her hunted and harried, like a doe in the forest "After all," I continued "it was not her fault if the two ministers fought over her. Had she known, she would have prevented that fight. So she said, and so I believed her. She is no wanton, Creasy—she did not encourage the attentions of that man, Chieves, I mean. He forced himself on her whenever the mistress wasn't looking. As for Absalom Lott, well, I can only say I believe he truly loved her, and she could not help but love him back. He was a most extraordinary man. You'll not win any friends in this town if you accuse him of murder, you know," I added.

Creasy sighed. "I know it," he muttered.

"As for her use of the black arts . . . . Well, she had reason to hate Deacon Lamb, although the pagan rituals she used for her revenge must be condemned, and so she understands."

"I had hoped to keep that a private matter, between her and me," Creasy frowned. "The woman is in need of spiritual counseling—her minister betrayed her in that, which is more a sin to me than his lust for her. I see no reason why her name should come into my report."

I gave his arm a grateful squeeze. Really, he was proving to be a man of sense!

"If Priscilla won't tell where she found the Deacon's poppet, no more shall I," he said.

I positively hugged his arm.

"No," he paused, "that is not a problem for me. I'm more concerned with proving my interpretation of Lott's sermon notes, with Zillah gone. It is, after all, my own interpretation. The magistrates may place a different interpretation upon what I believe to be the scriptural message.

"What other interpretation can there be?" I asked.

"A political one, given Lott's open quarrel with Governor Andros and Edward Ruckenmaul. It may seem expedient to blame the Royal Governor and his henchman, seeing as how we've jailed them anyhow!" Creasy unwound my hand from his arm so that he could wave both arms over his head in frustration. "I don't know how the magistrates are going to react. I don't know how I'm going to report this!"

"You have the Deacon's adze in the barn; he attacked you; he tried to hang Tom Pisspot; he ran away and hid in the swamp. You have proof enough to convince the magistrates, believe me."

"Confound that old man!" Creasy grumbled. "There is the wife to consider. She is innocent of the depredations of the Deacon, but how will this town treat her when he is exposed?"

I snorted; most unladylike, but I could not help it. "Don't worry about Rachel Lamb. And the people of this town are no worse than any other—if no better."

"Then there's the reputation of the minister of Ipswich to consider . . . He was duped into murder!" Creasy shuddered. "All this pain, caused by the malicious lies of the Deacon! They don't teach you how to deal with these things at Harvard, you know." He stopped and dug the toe of his boot into the sand.

I hugged my cloak about me. "What are you going to do?"

"I don't know," he admitted.

Creasy was silent. We walked on.

"When you first came to Rumney Marsh, Zillah said you drew lightening in your wake like a tall tree in a meadow." I smiled up at him. "Who knew what chaos would ensue? You looked so young and—inexperienced."

He rubbed his sore head with one hand. "My lack of experience nearly cost me my life!"

"The Deacon must have grown frantic with your meddling. He led you to Tom Pisspot—no doubt he hoped that great lout would crack your skull."

"He nearly did me in, and it wasn't a fair match. Tom had a club and I wasn't even armed!" Creasy claimed, aggrieved.

"Well, you've a hard head," I noted. "Then Gammar Pisspot, poor old woman . . . I shall never forgive him for that. Before she died she told Zillah what she'd seen."

"Told her? That's what I wanted to ask Zillah. I thought Gammar couldn't speak English? Does Zillah speak Gaelic?" He rubbed his head again.

"Ah . . . I don't know. Perhaps Gammar was a bit of a witch? I only know I believe what Zillah told me. The old woman told Zillah about the fight, that Naboth taunted Absalom. Creasy, are you listening to me?" I pulled at his sleeve.

Creasy frowned. "I'm still trying to figure out how Zillah communicated with a dying old woman."

"You don't want to know," I said, waving a hand. "Anyway it would be just like Naboth Chieves. He couldn't resist making sport of another man. Unfortunately it led to his own undoing. I'm sorry, Creasy, but I really can't find it in my heart to blame Zillah for making that image of the Deacon!"

"Ah, yes, the poppet. You did recognize it when I showed it to you, didn't you?"

"Yes, but not at first. Zillah made me a fashion-baby after I'd seen one in a Boston shop. You know what that is, the kind of poppet that is dressed in the latest court fashions?"

At his nod I continued. "It's a beautiful little fashion-baby, the one Zillah made. We use it to try out different patterns—she's a skilled seamstress, you know. She has elegance to her work that I can't achieve, but there it is. Anyhow, when you told me the circumstances, how the poppet was found, and for what purpose . . . . Well, I had to go to her and warn her. How could I let her be treated the way they'd treated Gammar Pisspot?"

"Why do you think I hid the evidence?" Creasy interrupted. "I wish you'd confided in me."

"How could I confide in you? You were so insistent upon accusing me and saving me against my will . . . ." I stopped speaking at his groan.

"I wronged you. I admit it!"

"You wronged me more than once." I could not resist reminding him.

"You don't know half the times," he confessed. "I'll make it up to you."

My glance must have shown my skepticism.

"Oh yes, I will." He stooped over to pick up a large, white-shelled conch from a ribbon of taffeta seaweed. He turned it in his hands, this way and that, admiring the pearly orange interior. Then he handed it to me.

I dropped it. "There's something alive inside it!"

Creasy chuckled.

"Throw it back." I pointed to the water. "It will die if we leave it out in the sun."

He retrieved it from the sand and tossed the conch far out into the waters. "There, a reprieve for the poor creature. Shall you grant me one?"

"I'll have to consider it," I said, and thought for a few moments. "There is one thing you can do for me."

"Name it. I'm at your service."

"In your report, place the blame for the death of Naboth Chieves where it belongs—on Deacon Lamb." I held up my hand to silence his protestations. "Why destroy the reputation of a good man? That death was an accident, and it was caused by a malicious old man who did not want to see his daughter's place usurped by a black woman—a slave. Absalom Lott would have freed her, you know, one way or another. Indeed, he proposed to marry her in the church. Can you wonder she lost her heart to him?"

"Indeed? To marry her?" Creasy's brows rose.

"Yes, he did. I believe that of him. And I could do no less than to grant her her freedom, which I did last night."

"And gave her money, no doubt?" The corner of his lips twitched.

"A few coins, yes."

"I slipped a few coins into her apron pocket last night, before I retired. It was hanging on a peg near the door."

A wave of relief swept over me. I had expected an assault of verbal indignation. "I thought you'd blame me for interfering. You've blamed me for everything else," I laughed.

Creasy stopped by my side. He grabbed me by my shoulders.

"Blame you? I don't blame you for this!" His voice was low, his dark eyes glittered.

I was about to speak when he bent his head and kissed me on the mouth. His lips were warm and dry covering mine. I was surprised. And pleased. We stood on the sand for a long while, me leaning into him for support. His hand slipped beneath my cloak and conquered my bosom. It had been a long time and I was a lusty woman. "Shall we go back to the house?" I whispered into a handsomely shaped ear.

We ran, hand in hand. I felt light as the gulls wheeling overhead.

We thrashed around the late minister's bed in a tangle of arms, legs and flying garments of small clothes, shirt, stockings both green and white, petticoats and gowns, under and over the blankets.

"Wait," I yelled, "you're too close to the edge!"

"Don't talk," he growled, making a grab for me.

I rolled away from the edge of the bed and he grabbed air instead, hitting the floor with a loud thump.

I sat up. "Are you all right?"

He sat on the floor, rubbing his knee, a sheepish grin on his face.

I could not keep back bursts of laughter.

Creasy, his face scarlet, forced a chuckle. "You pushed me!"

"I did not!" I giggled helplessly, tears spilling from my eyes. "You fell out of bed! I haven't fallen out of bed since I was two years old!"

"You pushed me!" My hysteria must have affected him; shouts of laughter doubled him over; he held his sides.

I saw one long arm sweep under the bed and come up with a cloth-wrapped bundle.

"What is it? I peered over the edge.

Creasy hauled himself up and sat on the bed beside me. He unwrapped swaths of linen from an oblong wooden crate. He dropped the box onto the bed and looked at me, eyes wide, mouth twisted into a grimace. He appeared to be paralyzed.

I reached over, lifting the wooden lid with two fingers.

"Oh!" Creasy let out a whoosh of air. His eyes grew round like china saucers.

On a bed of white silk lay a handsome male doll, complete from tiny periwig, linen shirt, waistcoat, small clothes and miniature leather boots. Three straight pins stood like tiny shafts planted in the heart of the poppet.

I felt the hairs on my neck prickle. Creasy looked as if he'd seen a ghost. "Who is it?" As soon as I asked the question the answer came to me. I felt cold all over.

"The poppet is meant to represent Absalom Lott." Creasy spoke in a voice as wooden as the box; his complexion matched the silk of the little bed. He made a deliberate effort to block the doll from my sight.

I dug my fingers into the bare flesh of his shoulder and peered over. He did not seem to feel my nails.

"What can this mean? Why did she make an image of him?"

I could not take my eyes from the doll. "There are other uses . . . . This poppet was made from love, not hate. She did love Absalom Lott, and there were many obstacles in her way. Poor fool"

Creasy placed an arm around me, as much, I thought, for his own comfort as for mine. His touch did comfort me, as a wave of sadness swamped me. When a woman loses her heart to a man, she will go to any lengths to keep his affection. We lose our minds as well as our hearts.

"Poor, poor fool!" I dashed at my watery eyes with the back of my hand.

"Why would she do this?" Creasy was utterly bewildered. I brushed back wisps of black hair from his face. If he did not look nearly so neat in his appearance as he had, he was infinitely more endearing.

"Why would she do this? Poor Zillah! Surely it was not this poppet that made Absalom Lott love her?"

"No, of course not," I agreed. "He loved her because she is Zillah." I didn't like to look at the doll, all the same. "Well, what shall we do with it?" I suddenly became practical, as is my wont. It was only a kind of fashion-baby, after all.

"Put it back under the bed," Creasy suggested, relief bringing color back to his cheeks.

"Cover it up, then."

"You do it. You opened it."

"No, Sir!" I slapped him hard on the shoulder. "I didn't know what it was."

"Well, it won't hurt you. It's only a poppet . . . ."

"Then you cover it up." I gave him a little push.

"Oh, all right," he grumbled. He clamped the lid on the box.

I had to admit the stare of the blue-painted eyes was unnerving; I was glad to see the box closed.

"Some sort of love-tribute, that's all it was, you baby." Creasy teased me with a tug at my hair.

"I'm a baby? Who fell out of bed?"

"I didn't fall, you kicked me out."

I caught up a blanket and threw it over his head. In the ensuing tussle the wooden box was kicked aside, tumbling unheeded to the floor.

Chapter Twenty-eight

The return ferry to Rumney Marsh was certainly a different journey from the original. We giggled, we whispered, we sighed and occasionally we held hands. Whatever Bob Stubb thought, I could count on his discretion. Bob puffed away on his green stone pipe, minding his business, which was navigating his little craft through the choppy waters off Marblehead.

To forestall my companion's playing the gallant fool and asking for my hand, I talked to him about my marriages; the first for love, the second that grew into love. I'd been left with mercantile ventures to run and a civic position to uphold. Both gave me great responsibilities and independence.

"I like my life as it is, you see, and have no wish to change it," I concluded. And so we remained in charity with one another for the voyage.

We stopped for a brief respite in Rumney Marsh, me to freshen and change clothes, Creasy to carry out a visit of condolence to the Deacon's widow. I could tell he was nervous about that, but he squared his shoulders, set his mouth in a grim line and trotted off on his mare. We planned to speak to the Selectmen at the meetinghouse by the Rumney Marsh green. I sent a boy out with the message to meet in an hour's time.

I did not press him upon his report to the Selectmen—that must be his decision, his conscience. My own conscience was clear on the point I'd expressed to him. The Deacon should take the blame for what he'd done.

I just wanted to be there when he confronted Cotton Mather with our findings.

A woe-begone little face greeted us at the Mather door. Telltale smudges beneath her eyes hinted at tears dried upon Abigail Mather's pale skin.

"Cousin Hetty! Creasy! Oh, how I've longed for your return!"

"Why, Abigail—what's the matter?" I asked, a sudden spurt of fear piercing my gut. Was Cotton ill again? Had Uncle Increase been arrested in London?

Creasy brushed past me into the hallway; he peered around. "Is she all right? Has anything happened to Deborah?"

"Oh, that woman!" Abigail wailed.

Creasy spun around. "What's the matter? Where is she?" He grabbed Abigail none too gently by the shoulders. "Stop sniveling and tell me what's wrong! Is she hurt?"

I sniffed. I gathered I did not have to warn my cousin about preserving appearances anymore. Men are so fickle!

"She?" Abigail drawled out the word. "Oh no, she's in fine health. She is a fine figure of womanhood, that's what my husband believes. She's got him preening like a peacock. All he does is talk about her—what a fine wit, what an understanding, what a paragon is Mistress Piscopot! Oh Creasy, why did you ever bring that woman into my home?"

"I see." Creasy released her. "So Deborah has succumbed to the famous Mather charm."

There was a storm in his eyes. While I had suspected his attachment to Mistress Piscopot I did not think it deep. The cruel blade of jealousy sliced through my innards.

"Where are they?" he demanded.

Abigail lips hung in an unaccustomed pout. "He's taken her with him on his round of good works. I think they are visiting imprisoned debtors today."

"And Deborah . . . how has she received his praises?"

"She is modest and reserved, the sly boots!" A flash of anger overcame Abigail's tears. "That is just the thing to charm him! A man as good as Mister Mather cannot abide a forward female."

I winced inwardly.

"He wants to undertake her religious conversion," Abigail addressed Creasy with great indignation. "Can you believe it?"

"Oh, I'll just wager he does!" Creasy's mouth hardened into a straight line; his brows drew together. "Abigail, do you know the long hours they will spend together? The time spent in reading aloud favorite scriptures? Kneeling side by side in prayer? The endless discussion on the state of her salvation?"

"I know!" Abigail wailed. She held a square of white linen to her eyes, dabbing at the welling mists.

"That is just like Cotton—using his silver tongue to convert the poor female to redemption! What a rotten trick!" Creasy balled up his fist.

Matters were worse than I thought. I could see that I must intervene.

"What will you do?" Abigail looked up at Creasy in breathless anticipation.

"Will it be such a dire folly if he undertakes her personal salvation?" I asked.

"Yes!" Both yelled as one.

"*Yes,* it would be a folly," Abigail turned to me. "He'd spare no amount of time to save her, and that would lessen the time for his good works and his congregation's care. You know he's solely responsible for the church, with Father Increase away."

"Well, we wouldn't want him to neglect his church duties."

I patted her arm and drew her down the hallway. "What would Uncle Increase say to that? You must point that out to your husband, Abigail. Tell him his father wouldn't like it—that will do the trick. Come, Abigail, you'll offer us some refreshment? We've had a long journey."

Brought to mind of her duties as hostess, Abigail conducted us to the best parlour. We sipped at tumblers of Canary while she was quick to provide us with light, gingery cakes. Abigail drank negus and waited for someone to speak. Neither Creasy nor I had any pronouncements to make. Creasy's face resembled an approaching thunderstorm

"You'll take her away, then, Creasy?" Abigail broke the silence. "What good will that do, Abby? He'll only trot over to Roxbury and pray with her there."

"But she can't stay here," Abigail wailed. "I don't mean to be inhospitable, but really . . . . She can't stay here! I am not feeling quite the thing, what with Mister Mather's nerves and the Revolution and the extra household work . . . ."

"She is free to leave, at any rate," Creasy scowled. "We've cleared up that business in Rumney Marsh."

"Good." Abigail was emphatic.

"I daresay she wants to leave, Abigail," I suggested. "It can't be agreeable to be in another woman's house with another woman's husband pouring his attentions upon you." I knew I shouldn't like it, and I was sure Deborah must be very uncomfortable with the situation.

"Perhaps . . . ." Abigail seemed dubious.

I studied Abigail Mather. She was dressed in her usual neat style, but her face looked tired and peaked. I had an idea. "Come, Abigail—if our companion will excuse us, I feel the need to freshen up a bit." I rose and practically dragged her from her seat. Creasy?" I made a small gesture of dismissal.

He half-rose from his seat. "Your servant," he mumbled.

So let him stew in his gloomy thoughts, I decided. Gentle Abigail was in real distress and I supposed I'd have to straighten everything out.

Abigail obediently climbed the stairs beside me. I pulled her into her bedroom.

"Shall I send Kate for hot water?" she asked, motioning to a nightstand with a pretty flowered basin on it.

"We're not here for me, Dear Cousin, but to take care of your problem." I spun her around, considering.

Hmmm, Abigail . . . . You've a nice figure. Can't you show it off a little more? Lower that whisk a little—show off your bosom." I tucked lace beneath her bodice as I spoke. "There, that's better."

She blushed with modesty.

"It's fashionable," I explained. "There now—you've color in your cheeks. I have a lotion to keep that bloom. Oh, I don't mean paint," I went on, digging into my pocket. "I know you too well for that, nor should I want you to paint your pretty face, which needs no adornment." I withdrew a small bottle and patted at her cheeks with some rose water. "A gay ribbon, perhaps, to liven your gown, neat though it is . . . ." I sought through the pocket which hung from my waist and pulled out a cherry ribbon which I threaded through the bodice of her gown.

"Do you really think I've a pretty face?" Abigail touched her cheek with one finger.

"You've a very pretty face. Your husband thinks so, too. You must allow your natural beauty to shine through, Abigail. After all, it is a gift from God." I pulled curls from beneath her lace cap so that they hung fetchingly around her face.

"But . . . but . . . he always speaks of modesty in a woman."

"Bosh! He's a man, Abigail. Cotton is as susceptible to a handsome woman as any other. Just as his cousin is susceptible to Deborah Piscopot."

Abigail leaned towards me. "Creasy feels affection for that woman?"

Her voice rose in astonishment.

I nodded. It was true, and I must face it. I faced it better than Abigail Mather, however.

She fell back into a chair. "I knew it! Now I've lost my dear Cousin Creasy—my best friend in this world!" Her lower lip trembled.

"Better that than your husband's attentions, my girl." I was less than sympathetic. Hadn't I warned her? "Besides, you have me. I'll come when you need me. Who knows better than I what a chore it is for you to wait upon Cousin Cotton?"

"Chore?" She sat up, perplexed. "It's no chore to wait upon my husband—the dear soul makes little demands upon me. Why, even when he was so ill, he begged me a thousand times not to wear out my health for his sake! Indeed, every time he sent me for a tray or for his medicine or to fetch the doctor or for a soft down pillow, he would apologize with a most affecting tear in his dear eye. Oh, to lose the affections of such a man—I could not bear it, Hetty! Indeed, I could not!"

"Now, now, Abby—you are in no danger of that. Trust me. Calm yourself or you'll make yourself ill."

"I think I have," she sobbed into her square of linen. "My stomach is so queasy I cannot eat my breakfast. It's the strain, I suppose. Send her away, Hetty. Let Creasy take her away from here, I don't care!

"Courage, Abigail—just listen to me." An inspiration popped into my head. "Don't let tears mar that rosy complexion."

Abigail stopped dabbing at her eyes. She raised them to me. "That's right," I urged. "You must greet your husband with a cheerful face. That lace whisk enhances your bosom.—You've a handsome bosom, Abigail, by God's grace. A husband likes to see his wife in fashion." I pinched and poked at her dress and stood back to examine my work.

"Now Cousin, let me move you to that chair by the window, I think. The light is better there." Abigail let me lead her to the chair in question; the light softened her figure. I draped her skirts artfully around the seat. "Here," I said, "read your Bible." I grabbed the Book from the bed stand and thrust it into her hands. What a pretty picture of piety—her husband would not be able to resist.

"You rest yourself and read the scriptures, Abby. I will send Mister Mather to you as soon as he returns."

She made no objection and I removed myself from the room.

I found Creasy pacing the floor of the parlour, a book in his hands. He was ignoring Sanguerdius' *Philosophis Naturalis* as I came close to examine the title.

"Abigail is upstairs, resting." I smiled at him.

"Oh." He stopped pacing. "Is she ill?" He spoke with real concern.

"No, just a little tired, that's all. She needs some time alone with her husband. If we could find a way to remove Mistress Piscopot from this house it would remove some of the strain she has felt."

Creasy's face brightened. "I'll be glad to escort the woman to her home."

"Oh, that is kind of you." The sarcasm in my voice escaped him. "You can ask the lady for yourself . . . . I'll take care of Cousin Cotton Mather for you."

We both turned to the door, warned by a draft of air and the sound of a preening male voice.

"Where are you, Dear Heart?" Cotton Mather's periwigged head peeked into the parlour. Spying the visitors he drew his entire person into the room. "Creasy! And Cousin Hetty! Back so soon? Where is our dear hostess? Does she know you're here? I do apologize for her neglect, Cousins. It's most unlike my fair consort to leave her visitors unattended."

"Oh, we're very well as we are," I volunteered, stepping forward.

Creasy peered over my shoulder at a dark-cloaked figure in the hallway. I ignored him.

"Abigail has seen to our comfort with her usual grace and thoughtfulness. I sent her upstairs to rest."

"Indeed? I wondered why my lovely consort did not come to greet me, as is her custom."

"Your wife is a paragon among women," I praised. "She must be no less, as the wife of Cotton Mather."

Cotton simpered.

Creasy's eyes remained upon the figure in the hallway.

Deborah Piscopot spoke to Cotton Mather, excusing herself. "I must put away my things."

Cotton Mather made a gallant bow. He turned a beaming countenance upon Creasy "Mistress Piscopot possesses a most wonderful understanding of my work, Cousin. I've been her guide to the many duties of ministering to a large congregation."

"Indeed?" Creasy's eyes were hard as a cat's. "But I've come with the conclusion of that business in Rumney Marsh. It is my sad duty to report we are now certain that Deacon Lamb caused the deaths of the two young ministers."

Well, that was true, I thought, breathing a sigh of relief. I had not wanted to press Creasy on the matter.

"His was an argumentative and jealous nature. We have testimony that the Deacon resented the natural courtesies and gallantries shown to his wife by Naboth Chieves—and he was the beneficiary of Absalom Lott's estate." Creasy paused to seat himself, slouching in the chair with his long legs stretched out.

"Mistress Henry will bear me out on this, I'm certain," he continued as Cotton drew up a chair. I followed his example. "We have a stone adze belonging to the Deacon as the weapon used in both killings . . . used in unpremeditated argument, we believe. What with the old man's attempt upon my life and his flight into the marsh, Mistress Henry and I came to that conclusion." He looked over at me. I nodded.

"We spoke to the selectmen of Rumney Marsh and they have agreed with our findings."

What Creasy did not relate was how we recognized two of the men who had taken part in the mob-attack upon Gammar Pisspot and her son. We properly cowed the selectmen into accepting our hints as gospel.

Cotton opened his mouth to ask a question but Creasy spoke first. "You were right to suggest that I examine Lott's sermons for his concerns, Cousin. I found his sermon notes. They were an immense help in exposing the venom the old man held against his son-in-law."

"Well, well . . . if my little skills have assisted in unmasking the wretch, I am glad to be of service. I see the hand of God in the Deacon's undoing—a Memorable Providence, as these vices bring judgment down upon the entire community if allowed to go untrammeled." Mather's voice rose in righteous indignation

"A Memorable Providence indeed, that the Deacon met a watery end," Creasy agreed.

Vengeance is mine, I will repay," I quoted with solemnity.

"Cousin," Creasy went on, turning to me, "we must give thanks to Mistress Henry for her assistance. 'Twas she who first convinced the magistrates of the Deacon's perfidy. Indeed, I owe her my life. Had she not found me and secured aid for me, I might not be here today. She is a woman of sense and of courage."

Creasy rose from his seat; he bent his body in a formal bow. I felt my face aflame.

"Well, well, Cousin Hetty! I see a modest glow in your countenance that becomes your womanly character. I am not one to withhold due praise, Cousin. That you are a woman of rare abilities I have ever granted—and of wit, a biting wit of which I have felt the sting upon more than one occasion, but we'll speak no more of that. Come, Cousin Hetty, I thank you heartily for your assistance to my cousin Increase, here, in what must have been puzzling and harrowing circumstances. I offer you my congratulations."

Cotton followed Creasy's example and made an even deeper bow.

Fulsome praise from this man was disconcerting to me; I'd never been the beneficiary of it before. While men would hear their praises sung to the sky, women, I think, would rather go about their daily chores secure in the knowledge that they had acted well. I would rather divert him from me to Abigail, who waited—dear, patient Abigail—upstairs for him. Still, I was gratified that Creasy thought to credit me.

So I said: "And let me congratulate you, Cousin. I wish you joy with all my heart."

"Joy? Unworthy of this precious emotion as I am, I do not quite take your meaning, Cousin." The great eyes lifted in innocent inquiry.

"Abigail . . . your wife, Sir." I leaned forward in confidence.

"Abigail—my helpmeet? "What of her?"

"Why, Abby's with child—didn't you know?" I kept the triumph from my voice with difficulty.

"Oh My Dear Heart!" Cotton Mather ran from the room.

"What was that about?" Creasy unfolded his long legs.

"Abigail is with child. It is usual for a husband to be excited by the news," I said.

"I know that. Why didn't she tell him?" He put out his hand but I would not reach over to take it.

"She doesn't know yet, that's why. But she is. Oh, it's in the back of her mind. Now she'll face it."

Creasy dropped his hand. "Well, I'm happy for them. Cotton will dote on the child."

"He'll dote on Abigail—that's the point." I rose as I spoke, smoothing out my skirts.

"You've managed things, once again.

"I'm good at managing things."

"Hetty . . . ." he hesitated. "I couldn't have managed without your help."

"Well, you'll have to manage on your own now. It's time I minded my own business." I expected him to reply in kind but he resisted, even though my look clearly challenged him.

"Thank you," I added, smiling. I felt lighthearted.

"Thank you," he said.

I nodded to Deborah Piscopot as I left the room.

The End